Gathe

Sto

The Salvation of Tempestria

Shifting Stars
Gathering Storm

Gathering Storm

The Salvation of Tempestria
Book 2

Gary Stringer

This is a work of fiction. Names, characters, places, and incidents either are the product of the author's imagination or are used fictitiously. Any resemblance to actual persons, living or dead, or locales is entirely coincidental.

First paperback edition May 2021

Cover Design by BespokeBookCovers.com

978-1-8382777-2-7 (paperback)
978-1-8382777-3-4 (eBook)

Published by Gary Stringer

Chapter 1

The Council of Wizards was in crisis: wizards were going missing.

There was no obvious pattern relating to faction, power, ability or involvement in Council affairs, so there was no way of knowing who might be next.

Exactly when this started, gentle reader, it was difficult to say. Missing people were an unfortunate fact of life, in ways both ordinary and extraordinary, such as demon attack. These disappearances were different, however. It wasn't always possible to determine precisely where they were when they disappeared, but where it was possible, investigations revealed an energy source of higher planar origins.

This was new: beings from the higher planes had never before shown any interest in taking mortals. They were often collateral damage, caught in the crossfire, but never deliberately attacked. If that had changed, and the shadow warriors were now kidnapping innocent Tempestrians for who-knew-what purposes, what could be done about it?

My mother, Catriona, already knew Aunt Dreya's views on the matter. She had shared her intention to kill Daelen StormTiger not long after Cat had moved in, and current events, more than two years later, as the Tempestrian chronometer flies, compelled Catriona to share something that had been puzzling her about it.

"Why Daelen, specifically?" Catriona asked her. "Why not Kullos, or that other one…the dark clone. The one that looks a bit like Daelen but isn't…has anybody heard that one's name, by the way?"

"Not that I know of," Dreya replied. "Anyway, what do you care which one I kill?"

"I don't, especially," Cat shrugged. "They're all about as dangerous as each other, as far as I can tell. They've got no business fighting their war here, and I'd be quite happy to be rid of the lot of them. Which is precisely why I ask the question: Why Daelen, specifically? Why do *you* care which one you kill?"

Dreya frowned. She'd never really questioned it. Daelen was a self-proclaimed Protector and seen as a hero to many, trying to save them from Kullos, who was generally viewed as the villain. Recently, though, there had been growing, popular support for the reverse sentiment. Dreya the Dark agreed with Catriona that there was little basis for either view, but that only further highlighted her question. Surely it wasn't a matter of killing Daelen because of his hero image or because he was famous. Those were not worthy motivations for Dreya the Dark. Yet, something was nagging in her brain, almost like a voice, her own voice, telling her he was the one she should go for. It was important.

'*Kill Daelen StormTiger,*' said the voice, '*and take his power.*'

The voice kept telling her to ignore the reasons why, but that wasn't how Dreya operated. She didn't do random violence. She didn't attack without cause.

"I don't know," she admitted, finally, "and I don't like that I don't know. If I didn't know better, I might suspect some kind of mental attack or a post-hypnotic suggestion, but my shields prevent any such thing."

Her shields were intact. From the day Dreya claimed the Tower, the only magical signature that had ever passed through her defences, apart from Catriona's, was her own. Still, the point was chiefly academic for the foreseeable future. Dreya knew she wasn't ready to take on a being from the higher planes. Not yet. Besides, she didn't even know how to find them if she wanted to. Nobody knew where the shadow warriors went, between battles. Dreya suspected the answer lay on some other world, but her best efforts to probe the cosmos with her magic had so far failed to prove their existence.

"Anyway, it's a moot point at the moment," Dreya told Cat, dismissing the issue. "After all, it's not as if Daelen StormTiger himself is going to come knocking on my door."

Cat laughed, "That's true."

And so, she let the subject drop.

Returning to their original topic of conversation, Dreya needed to share some news that she knew Catriona was not going to like.

"Cat," she began, "I just came from an emergency Council meeting."

"I know," Cat nodded, "you told me this morning, remember?"

"Yes, but I didn't tell you why it was called."

"About all those wizards disappearing, I presumed."

"Yes, but the situation's got even more serious for your faction in particular, though it affects everyone, really. Cat, I'm sorry to have to tell you this, but the latest wizard to vanish is Mistress Justaria."

For one of the Triumvirate to disappear was a severe blow to the whole magical community. If Daelen or one of his kind were proved to be behind it, that could be seen as nothing less than a declaration of war.

Catriona liked Mistress Justaria. The leader of the Red robes of Balance had been fair-minded at Catriona's Conclave, and the druidess had always taken to heart the conversation they'd shared afterwards. Justaria had been absolutely right that the college was entirely the wrong place for her, and in many ways, her encouragement to seek knowledge elsewhere was a key reason why she was now living and working in the Black Tower. More than that, she felt she owed an enormous debt of thanks to Justaria for her hand in events that had led to her close bond with Dreya the Dark. The chance to see the person behind the mask, the woman beneath the black velvet robes. The opportunity to come to know and understand Dreya in ways no-one else did.

Dreya had visited many of the known disappearance sites herself, but she understood Catriona well enough by now to be completely unsurprised when the druidess declared her intention to investigate this one personally.

*****

A red-banded falcon alighted in Justaria's garden. It wasn't large, but it was well maintained. Flowering plants were blooming in a wide border between the fence and the lawn on the right-hand side as she faced the white cottage at the end of the gently meandering path. Over to the left, the Red robe leader had gone for a different approach, with a blanket of buttercups and daisies encircling a sycamore tree.

Catriona reverted to her natural form and breathed deeply. She could immediately sense the signature of higher planar energy that had got everybody so worked up. But there was something else not quite right about this place. A spell of wizards had been all over Justaria's garden, probing with their magic and in their wizardly wisdom, turned up absolutely nothing.

"Wizards!" the druidess muttered to herself. "Can't see past their own spellbooks."

She sent a sympathic apology to Dreya, with whom she was linked.

'*Not wrong,*' came her reply.

Barring a few footprints where wizards had trodden carelessly, the garden was beautiful, but not immaculate. It didn't look like a professional job to Cat. More of a constant labour of love. Clearly, Justaria spent a lot of her free time planting, pottering and pruning, tinkering and tidying her garden. So why were the daisies bent over? If they had just been stepped on, why was it just the daisies and not the buttercups? And why all in one direction, towards the tree? Cat stepped lightly around to the far side of the tree where the trunk was in shadow. On the ground was a trowel with a sharp metal point, which had obviously been used to carve words into the bark:

RHYNAS

DESERT

The druidess wasn't sure where that was, apart from being somewhere overseas, but by concentrating hard, she was able to project an image of the words to Dreya, sympathically. In return, Dreya sent '*Meeting*' and '*Map,*' which Cat took to mean she would meet up with her and show her on a map.

Looking around Justaria's garden once more, there was no other evidence that Catriona could detect. It was a wonder the sorceress had found time to do as much as she did. She could almost picture the scene: whoever had come for Justaria, she had found out where they were taking her and delayed them long enough to leave clues.

At her Conclave, Cat had seen Justaria use delicate magic to make a pen inscribe words on a page with barely a glance. In principle, using a floating trowel to scratch words into a tree was no different. As for the daisies, they were just more evidence of Justaria's deft touch with magic. Still, it would have taken time, which told Cat something else: unless Justaria's case was different from all the others, wizards were not being kidnapped as everyone assumed. If it were a simple grab and teleport job, there was no way Justaria could have done what she did. She must have kept them talking, and if they were talking, it wasn't kidnapping, it was persuasion. Recruitment. That said, given the lack of reports of wizards saying 'no' to this recruitment, it was likely the sales pitch boiled down to 'join or die,' but still, recruitment for what?

As she was puzzling over that one, someone arrived who had the answer.

The wind suddenly picked up, and Cat was instantly alert. Storms didn't just start like that. Not natural ones, anyway. There was a flash of equally unnatural lightning, creating an outline of a member of the big cat family: a tiger.

Cat shifted to her tawny owl form, quieter through the air than the falcon, approaching the new arrival stealthily from behind. She changed in midair and stood on one of her Windy Steps.

"Daelen StormTiger," she said, scowling indignantly, arms folded. "What the hell are you doing here?"

Chapter 2

It all began on another world.

Daelen StormTiger woke, suddenly, coming face to face with an unexpected visitor.

Actually, gentle reader, though I say, 'face to face,' he couldn't actually see her face. Overall, she seemed to defy analysis, protected from even his powers of detection, save for a vague impression of a female figure with a white aura. This was Aunt Mandalee in her role as White Guardian of Time and Magic, conducting a completely legal and necessary Time Intervention to correct an anomaly. In terms of her personal Timestream, this was several months before she made herself complicit in my illegal plan to bring Daelen to me here.

"Oh, you're up, at last, I see," his visitor observed, then when Daelen got out of bed, failing to catch the bedsheets in time, she quickly turned away with a small scream, adding, "And now I've seen far more of you than I ever wanted to. Put some clothes on, for pity's sake!"

"Who are you, and what are you doing in my home?" Daelen demanded, though he did comply with her clothing request.

"Can't tell you that, not the first part, anyway," Mandalee answered, apologetically. "You haven't even met me yet. It would probably blow a hole in the cosmos the size of the Black Tower, which might not seem that big in comparison to the size of the cosmos, but it would be big enough to let some pretty important stuff fall out. Well, the Black Tower, for a start, I suppose. That would cause all kinds of anomalies. Look, are you dressed yet?"

"Yes," Daelen assured her.

She turned around, although Daelen wasn't sure how he could tell that, given that she seemed to shimmer in much the same way, whichever direction she was facing.

"Thank gods for that. Sorry, rambling there, trying to distract myself from what I just saw. Of course, that means I've seen both of you naked now, so my brain's going to be coming up with all kinds of weird stuff. Dear gods, I need a drink!" At last, she paused for breath.

"Finished?" Daelen asked.

"Haven't even started yet," the figure replied. Taking a deep breath, Mandalee began again. "You've overslept, Daelen."

"And since when were you my Timekeeper?"

"I'm not, although you're pretty close with the title. Anyway, it's not your fault – someone's been messing with your head and interfering with events that really ought not to be tampered with any more than they already have been. Which means now someone's got to tamper some more to get things back on track."

"Are you going to start making sense anytime soon?" Daelen asked.

"I ask myself that question all the time, so probably not, which means you're just going to have to pay more attention. Listen, you need to get yourself over to Tempestria right now. Events are moving there, and you're out of the loop."

Daelen shook his head. "I get an alert whenever there's higher planar activity, and right now everything's quiet," he disputed.

"That's because this time the activity is quiet. At least for now. I can show you telepathically better than I can tell you, if you'll let me," the visitor offered.

Although Daelen could sense his visitor had powers perhaps to rival his own, he was convinced she was no threat, so he agreed to give her limited access to his mind.

"Very well, shroud your powers. Absolute minimum level and follow me. We're going on a little astral trip."

The shadow warrior's consciousness left his body and followed his visitor where she led. They swept across the face of Tempestria so fast, even his senses couldn't make out more than a blur. Eventually, the image slowed and zoomed in. It appeared to be one of Tempestria's deserts, but things are not always as they seem. There was a wall of energy there that was a commonplace sight on the higher plane he once called home. It had no place here. The wall was curved, forming a vast dome. Slipping through the barrier, Mandalee showed him the interior. There, arrayed before him, concealed within the dome, was an army of demons from the planes of hell. Mortal wizards, warriors and clerics were there alongside them. More recruits arrived as he watched, but what really drew his attention was a fortress in the middle of the camp. It fairly resonated with power – a power with which he was all too familiar.

"We must go carefully now, Daelen," the visitor warned him. "We don't want to alert him to our presence. That would be very…awkward."

Daelen didn't need to ask, "him who?" for the answer was obvious. She was right to be cautious, because there was always a chance, albeit slim – that he could detect them even when they were only a projection and not really there. He was a dark, shadowy figure, sitting on a throne on a dais, in the centre of a chamber, in the heart of the fortress, in the middle of the camp, like an enormous spider in a city-sized web. He was Kullos.

"How is this possible?" Daelen whispered. "Kullos has never done anything like this, before. Why would he suddenly start building an army?"

"Because he thinks you are."

"What?" the shadow warrior demanded. "Why would he think that?"

"Because someone's been messing with his head, too," she explained. "Be very still and watch."

Daelen took her advice and remained absolutely still. The shadow warrior thought he could sense something. He wasn't sure what, but he didn't dare unshroud his power, so he simply waited. He didn't have to wait long before a new figure materialised, standing beside Kullos. Daelen had seen this being only once before, and then only briefly. This was the being Michael had described as a 'void-creature.' All he knew about it was that it had nearly killed Michael permanently and devastated an entire Quarthonian Faery community before some other unknown beings chased it away. Daelen could feel its power and malevolence, and it scared him. He, a mighty shadow warrior, was afraid of what this unknown creature was and what it might be able to do.

"Seen enough?" Mandalee asked. She sensed him nod.

Slowly, carefully, she pulled them back outside the fortress. They passed through the dome shield and then accelerated until they were back in their bodies where they had been standing all along.

"I've seen that void-creature before!" Daelen breathed. "It—"

To his astonishment, his visitor seemed to put her fingers in her ears and sing, "La la la! Can't hear you! Please stop talking!"

He complied, and Mandalee relaxed. "Whew!" she breathed. "That was nearly an even bigger hole in the cosmos. Daelen, there's a lot of Time manipulation going around at the moment. Most of it has already been accounted for, but this is new. I don't know anything about this void-creature, as you call it, and learning about it from you could create all kinds of trouble."

*****

She was right, gentle reader. Gaining information from someone in the past in this way is hazardous.

Imagine Scenario 1: Nobody else in her time knew about the void-creature, either. That could indicate that Daelen never told anyone.

Scenario 2: Daelen *did* tell someone, that information w*as* available in Mandalee's time, and it was just that Mandalee *herself* didn't know. In that case, Mandalee could simply tap into the years of research on the subject that was just sitting there waiting for her to find. But if Daelen told Mandalee directly at that moment, he might then decide he shouldn't share it with anyone from his own time, in the interests of preserving the Timeline. All of a sudden, we've switched back to Scenario 1. Now, when Mandalee returned to her present, the research that would have been done in Scenario 2 never happened. Such are the hazards of Time Intervention.

This is another reason the other Guardians are against my actions, but to me, the key point is that we *should* have known about this void-creature the instant it appeared in our time. The fact that we didn't is, in my opinion, reason enough to seek that information from the past.

*****

"Dealing with that creature will have to wait," Mandalee insisted. "I'm just here to fix the Time damage. That creature is a future problem, and you need to focus on Kullos. It's too soon for anyone to be messing around with you. Except me. I have to mess around with you but having too many people messing around with you at the same time is bad. Dear gods, now that I've seen you naked, I just want to go back up my own Timeline and rephrase all of that."

"I see, so you're some kind of Time fixer," Daelen suggested.

"Oh yeah," Mandalee agreed, her voice dripping with sarcasm, "that's a great title. I'll propose the change as soon as I get back."

"Well, whatever you call yourself, you travel in Time. I recognise the signs; I've done it myself."

"Don't I know it!"

While Mandalee continued to grumble about the trouble he caused through blundering about in Time, the shadow warrior wasted not a moment, scribbling a quick note which he left by his beside. He prepared to open a Prismatic Sphere portal to Tempestria, but his exasperated visitor yelled at him to stop.

"Daelen! Just wait a minute, will you? Dear gods. And they call *me* reckless. You're rushing to face down an army, and you don't even know where it is!"

Daelen shot her a confused look. "I assumed you'd tell me when we got to Tempestria."

"So many problems with that. One, I'm not coming with you – as I say, you haven't even met me yet. Two, I'm not just going to tell you everything, because it's too soon for you to know – I've told you only as much as you would have figured out yourself by now if you hadn't been tampered with. And I really need to find a better way of saying that. Three, you don't even know if what I showed you was the truth. I might be an enemy lying to you."

"I don't think you're an enemy. You have a very trustworthy aura."

"That's all part of my cunning plan to gain your trust and then betray you, or at least it could be. As it is, I'm not here to help you as such, just get your Timeline back on track. Fortunately, this Time meddler is obviously new at this because he's left me with a straightforward Intervention."

"Oh, so you're not a Time fixer, you're a Time intervener. Time interventionist?"

"Seriously, Daelen, one more crack like that and I'm going to come over there and knock you into the middle of next week and to hell with your Timeline! Look, this is what you need to know: wizards are going missing."

"Why should I c—"

"—Care about that?" Mandalee finished for him. "Isn't that a lovely sentiment from our so-called Protector? I've shown you why. Kullos is building an army."

"What's an army of mere mortals and demons to me?" Daelen asked, dismissively.

The arrogance of the shadow warrior was really challenging Mandalee's self-control, now. Her fighter's instinct was pushing her to show him what even one 'mere mortal' could do to him. But she maintained her composure, refusing to let him goad her into a mistake.

"If you want to find Kullos, you have to find his army," she explained with exaggerated patience. "To find his army, you need to find out where the wizards are going. To learn the answer to that, there's someone you need to meet. Now, I'm guessing you're not up with current Wizards' Council politics."

"Hardly!" Daelen scoffed.

"Tell me you at least know where the Council building is."

Daelen nodded, so Mandalee continued.

"Then go there, find a wizard – any wizard – and ask directions to the home of Justaria. Tell them you're investigating her disappearance. You might want to assure them that you didn't do it, while you're there, but that's up to you."

"Wait, you want me to just roll up to a wizard who might think I'm there to kidnap him, and ask directions?" Daelen was incredulous.

"That's right," Mandalee replied, acidly. "Daelen StormTiger is going to have to have a difficult conversation with a mere mortal for the first time in centuries. How will you ever cope? Well, you'll just have to. Find Justaria's place, Daelen, and find it quickly. Your adventure starts there."

Without another word, Daelen's visitor vanished.

The shadow warrior could only wonder at who she could have been, as he quickly stepped through a portal and headed for the Council of Wizards in Walminster, Elvaria's capital city and seat of power.

Once there, he managed to get directions, and now he was here, where some mortal girl seemed to be trying to wind him up.

Chapter 3

Daelen, unsurprised, didn't bother turning around. It took more than that to sneak up on a shadow warrior. Still, there weren't many mortals who would try. The typical reactions were either awe or terror. After the one he'd spoken to, earlier, this was two unusual mortal reactions in one day. Perhaps there were signs of change in this world, after all.

"If it helps," he offered, "I promise I didn't abduct Justaria."

"Well, obviously you didn't," Cat agreed.

"What makes you so sure I'm telling the truth?" Daelen wondered.

"Three reasons: First, she may have left under duress or threat, but she wasn't abducted at all. Not as such."

"And how do you know that?"

"Ah, you see, I have a special ability. It's called paying attention. Speaking of which, what are the chances of you turning around and paying attention to me? You really shouldn't keep your back to me like this. I'm running out of rude faces to pull at you."

Daelen smiled and at last did turn around to see the mortal girl, not levitating or flying like him, but casually standing on thin air as if it were solid ground.

She smiled and waved. "Hi, I'm Catriona Redfletching. My friends call me…yes, well, let's just leave it as Catriona for now, shall we?"

"Catriona," Daelen acknowledged. "What happened to pulling rude faces?"

Cat shrugged. "I ran out."

When it became clear she wasn't planning on saying anything else, he reminded her, "You said there were three reasons. What's the second?"

Cat shook her head. "Nope. Not like that. I'm an information trader. You don't get anything more from me until I get something from you. Like I said: what the hell are you doing here?"

Now that he was facing her and not looking at the garden, she had a quiet word with nature to subtly erase all trace of Justaria's message. She had a suspicion she already knew the answer to her question and intended to use her knowledge as leverage. After all, she didn't have the power of a shadow warrior, but information was a different kind of power. It could be a weapon or a shield, depending on what she needed. Thanks to their shared sympathic link, Dreya could pursue things her way, alerting the Council and using her form of power. That left Cat free to pursue her own independent line of enquiry.

Daelen confirmed her suspicion. "I need to find out where the wizards are being taken."

"Why do you care?"

"Hang on," he protested, "is it not my turn now?"

Cat gave a facial shrug, conceding the point. "Can't blame a girl for trying. OK, second reason: you just said you need to find them. If you were involved, you'd already know."

"But you couldn't have known that when you said there were three reasons. I hadn't told you, yet."

"So I guessed," Cat admitted. "The point is I guessed right. My turn: why do you care?"

"You won't believe me," he warned. "You'll think I'm crazy."

With a dismissive gesture, Cat replied, "All kinds of people don't believe me about things I've seen and accuse me of being crazy. I'm not so quick to judge."

"Alright," Daelen accepted. "A woman from the future woke me up, told me there was some kind of interference in Time and showed me what's going on."

"And what exactly *is* going on?"

"You're trying to have two turns again," Daelen admonished her.

"Whoops, so I am. Sorry. Your question?"

Daelen was surprised how much he was enjoying this. Who knew mortals could be so entertaining?

"You're not as innocent as you make out, are you?"

"No, I'm not," Cat concurred, "but just to show you how nice I can be, rather than count that as your next question, I'm going to volunteer my third reason." She could let him have this one because his reaction would tell her much. "The third and main reason why I know you had nothing to do with Justaria's disappearance – and by inference all the others – is that the signature of the higher planar energy that still lingers around her home is completely different.

It's not that dark clone of yours, either. Presumably, his signature is either the same or an inverse of yours. This signature is neither. Therefore, unless there's a new player in town, my conclusion is that Kullos took them, and I'm guessing that I'm not going to like the reason."

Oh yes, *that* got Daelen's attention. His eyes grew wide, along with his mouth. He had not expected any mortal to have such knowledge.

"How do you know how to read our energy signatures?"

"As I said: I pay attention," she replied, flippantly, "and that's the only answer you're getting until you stop trying to cheat the game. I gave you one freebie; you don't get another. My question – why exactly is Kullos taking them?"

"He's building an army," Daelen answered, still reeling from the mortal girl's last answer.

"Why?" Cat asked, taking full advantage, sneaking in a follow-up question.

"Because he thinks I'm doing the same and probably because he wants to tie up Michael."

Cat remembered well the Day of the Angel. Daelen had drawn Kullos away while Michael tried to save her village. In the same way, a decent-sized Tempestrian army could certainly keep Michael busy, leaving Daelen and Kullos to fight it out between them. What she couldn't immediately figure out was how that would help Kullos. In all previous battles that she knew of, Daelen plus Michael always won against Kullos. Subtract Michael, and it would be a stalemate. That meant a much longer battle and much more collateral damage until Kullos finally backed down. That was why Daelen needed Michael in the first place. So, how was Kullos expecting to win? Unless…

"He's got more power from somewhere, hasn't he?"

"You are one extraordinary mortal."

Cat didn't know whether to feel flattered or patronised. His intentions were the former, but she didn't like someone patting her on the head just because she could add up. For now, she chose to ignore it.

"As I keep saying, I just pay attention, although to be honest, I've completely lost track of our game. Which is fine, because I think you've told me all I need to know for now, so I win but thanks for playing."

"But you haven't told me where the army is, yet," Daelen protested. "You know, don't you?"

Cat nodded. "And don't bother looking for clues – I erased them all."

"I think you're forgetting who you're talking to," the shadow warrior warned her. "I don't like invading minds without consent, but I can and will do it if it means I stop Kullos from destroying your world."

"Yes, I've heard you lot can do that. Go on then. Just this once, I give you my permission to try it, and see what it gets you."

Daelen assumed Catriona was basing her confidence on defences she had developed against the mental attacks of mortal wizards. She could have no idea what she was dealing with now, but when he tried to enter her mind, it felt like getting his head stuck in a steel trap. He yelled in pain.

"Permission withdrawn," Catriona announced, releasing him, "and don't ever try that again."

Daelen shook his head to clear it. He could scarcely believe what had just happened.

"How?" he demanded.

"I have friends in high places," Cat replied, cryptically, "or rather *from* high places."

As if on cue, a small, green reptilian head appeared from one of her pockets. After tasting the air for a moment, fixing Daelen with her unreadable eyes, the snake disappeared again but continued to hiss for a moment before she was still once more. Except Daelen could tell she wasn't really a snake.

"This is Pyrah. I believe her people are from a plane just below yours. Apparently, not all your people have your…restraint…when it comes to entering minds and violating consent. So her people have developed defences against you. We share a sympathic link, so I'm protected, too, as is anyone else I choose to link with."

Just then, Pyrah hissed again, and Cat laughed lightly.

"Pyrah, please! Such language. To be fair, I did give him permission this once." Turning back to Daelen, she apologised, "Sorry about her. She doesn't like being in the sky, but then she isn't terribly impressed by you, either." With a well-timed blush, she added, "Never mind, I'm sure she'll change her mind about at least one of those things before long." Her smile grew to a grin, and she addressed Pyrah once more. "I won't let you fall, I promise!"

"Well tell her that if she's so uptight and so afraid of falling, then…"

Determined to regain control of the situation, before girl or snake knew what had happened, he teleported them down to the ground.

"OK, that was flashy," Cat conceded. Slightly disorientated, she sat down on the grass in Justaria's garden. "Bit rude, but flashy."

Daelen tried hard to be patient. "Look, Catriona, I really need you to tell me where Kullos' army is."

"I know you do," the druidess nodded. "So negotiate for the information. Forget the question-for-a-question game. Just tell me straight. Community opinions are divided on you, Daelen. Some want your head. Others think you're a hero."

"I'm no hero," Daelen insisted, joining her on the grass.

"And yet you claim to be our Protector while spending so little time here. Why is that?"

Daelen was hesitant. He wasn't used to this.

"I protect your world and can barely stand to be a part of it for the same reason," he admitted, finally. "Because I'm partly responsible for the danger it's in."

"Explain that," Cat ordered him. "Consider me to be a representative of the people of this world. Imagine I'm linked with someone connected to the highest authority in this land."

Of course, gentle reader, she really did have such a connection. Through their sympathic link, Dreya could get the essence of the conversation, if not the actual words. As Black Secondmage on the Council – and since she had the leader, Laethyn, in her pocket – she could take the information to the Council leadership and encourage them to take whatever action she felt was appropriate. Plus, she had Cat's exact location, so she could teleport in, grab her, and teleport back again in the blink of an eye, should Cat be in more danger than she could handle.

"We've heard all kinds of rumours," Cat told him, "but I want to hear the story from you. Justify yourself to the people of

Tempestria. Explain to us why we should trust you and help you, because right now, honestly…I don't know whether giving you my information is the right thing or not."

There was something about this druid girl that fascinated Daelen, so he decided to try opening up, try to make her see why it was so important that she give him the information.

Chapter 4

Before I relay my father's story, gentle reader, I feel I should explain how Temporal magic works. Without getting too bogged down with the intricacies of Time and dimensional harmonics, the best way I can think of to do that, is to fall back on another of my famous facetious analogies from my college days.

Temporal Magic is like Looking for your Keys.

(Once again, I was marked down for my 'irreverent treatment of the subject.' I'm sure you're sensing a pattern.)

Have you ever misplaced your keys? You know they must be in your house somewhere, but that knowledge does nothing to save you from wasting a chunk of your day turning your house upside down and inside out. Now, suppose you didn't know for sure they were in your house, but they're definitely somewhere in your street, or your town, or your country… Imagine having to search your entire world to find your keys. (How did you lose your keys that badly, you may ask? Well, it seems to me you can either (a) blame a Trickster, or (b) accept that this is an analogy and just go with it.)

Now imagine you have access to time travel. You might think that makes things easier – just go back to the moment you lost them and sort of *un*-lose them. Sadly, it doesn't work like that. It's like when a friend asks you, "Where did you last see your keys?" If you knew that, they wouldn't be lost. Asking "*When* did you last see them?" is equally unhelpful. Because now you have time travel, so maybe you last had them sometime in the last year or ten years or a hundred years… Time travel doesn't solve the problem, it just makes it worse.

Even if you lived outside of Time, even if you were immortal, you wouldn't have all the time in the world, because that's impossible: space and time are infinite. In fact, this only compounds the problem even further, because you now have to search for your keys in an endless amount of time in an infinite number of places. Plus, how many times have you eventually found your keys behind a cushion on your sofa, when you *know* you already looked there three hours ago? So now you have to search an infinity of time and space TWICE. Even if you could do that, even if you were Timeless, even if you were immortal, would *you* want to spend your entire life searching for your keys?

For the Guardians, looking for specific events in Tempestrian history is just like looking for your keys – the problem is knowing where to look. That requires co-ordinates.

When I say co-ordinates, I don't just mean a set of numbers or symbols. It doesn't work like that. Just as teleporting requires an image of where you want to go, temporal co-ordinates provide a vital sympathic impression of the destination.

This also explains why it is impossible to travel independently into one's own personal future: It's impossible to know for sure exactly where and when you're going to lose your keys. After all, you don't *plan* on losing them, do you? If you'd tried to predict exactly where your keys would be tomorrow, on the day before you lost them, you'd have been wrong, wouldn't you? In the same way, I can simulate *possible* futures, but if I were to try to travel to those imaginary co-ordinates, where would I be? The answer is, nobody knows.

I might go nowhere. On the other hand, in theory, I might *literally* go nowhere. Some vast, endless no-place where there is nothing. Even if I could survive that, with a starting point outside of all reality, could I get back, or would I be stuck there forever? Would forever be a thousand centuries, or a split second? In this no-place, where nothing existed, how could I tell the difference?

So perhaps now, you can appreciate some of the difficulties and dangers of what the Guardians and I do. In short, we must know precisely where and when we are going at all times. In terms of my analogy, what you need is for your friend to tell you that *they've* found your keys for you. They were behind the cushion on the sofa in their room. You left them there when they fell out of your pocket when you were playing that game last night before you went home. Fortunately for the Guardians, they have friends like that: they're called historians.

One of the great misconceptions about Time travel is that it makes history books redundant, when in fact those books are some of the most valuable tools any Time traveller could have: they tell you where and when to look.

*****

Our history books have helped me turn my gaze to the times and places in which the Original Three Guardians lived their early lives, and tell their stories independently of the way they may have recounted those stories in retrospect. In short, it's a first-hand account.

The reason I mention this, gentle reader, is that my father is different. He is not from this mortal realm, he's a higher planar being. So, when I come to try and detail his personal past, in addition to a universe of time and space, I have whole other planes of reality to consider. An Infinity of Great Cosmic Sandwiches. Once we get to the era when Daelen met Cat, Mandalee and Dreya, history books once again come to my rescue, but Daelen StormTiger has been around for a long time, so some of the most significant parts of his story happen in places and times beyond any books.

That's one of the reasons Mandalee has gone to fetch him: we need more information if we're going to fight the Monster that now threatens us.

My decision to remove Daelen from that particular point in his own Timestream was not arbitrary. The 'right moment' had to satisfy three conditions. He must have met Mandalee and Catriona, so he'd be inclined to help. He must be at the peak of his powers, so he'd be *able* to help. And he must be alone, yet in a precisely known location, so we would know exactly where and when to look for our key. Our key to survival that is.

The last condition was the hardest because it seems like a contradiction. If somebody knew precisely where he was, how could he be alone? If he was alone, how could anybody know for certain precisely where he was? The answer to that conundrum I will keep to myself for now. (I may have promised you an accurate account, gentle reader, but I still reserve the right to delay the reveal of specific details for dramatic reasons.) Suffice to say, Mandalee and I wanted to bend the rules, and the other two Guardians were having none of it, so we locked them in my room and did it anyway.

If all goes well, we will return my father to his Timestream a moment after we took him, but by doing this, for that short period, to all intents and purposes, Daelen StormTiger will not exist. If I'm right, the cosmos will be able to survive without his presence for that short time, and he will help us save the world. If I'm wrong, and the cosmos *can't* survive without him, then everything we know will collapse into the void, and worse still: his ego will be completely insufferable.

My point is, when history books fail us, we must fall back on legend. The Legend of Daelen StormTiger. Or to put it another way, gentle reader, I believe it is time, at last, to take us all the way back to the beginning…

*****

…Long ago, before any known history books were written, Daelen StormTiger gazed upon the world below him like a tiny, shining bauble. A precious, delicate thing to be handled with care. He was its Protector now. He had to be because, the way he saw it, he was partly responsible for the danger it was facing.

Daelen's people were at war – war beyond the imaginations of the mortals Daelen watched below him. It was not known how long this war had been raging, or even how to relate the passage of time in the higher realms, to what mortals experience on Tempestria. Suffice to say, a very, very long time. Daelen was a frequent visitor to our mortal world, treating it as a refuge from the war at home.

It was a simple matter for entities of his kind to Descend to the lower planes. To make the transition, he needed to shed those parts of his essence that couldn't fit within the confines of this realm. He would leave those parts of himself behind, ready for him to reclaim when he returned, like so much left luggage. The hard part was returning. That required a dimensional control device to form a connection between the two parts of his essence and bridge the void between the planes. These devices were endlessly customisable, taking on almost any shape, design and colour. To many of his kind, they were as much a fashion accessory as a practical device. As a young boy (or at least his species' equivalent) Daelen had often enjoyed dropping down a few levels to wind up those who called themselves 'gods' of Tempestria, though they were no such thing. In fact, Daelen knew one person who firmly believed that mortals could one day surpass their so-called gods. Perhaps even the shadow warriors – Daelen scoffed at the idea

Kullos had long been a friend to Daelen's family, ever since Daelen's father had been killed in the war. In fact, having no family of his own, Kullos was soon accepted as part of theirs. As a shadow warrior Champion, Kullos was at the forefront of their war, and as Daelen grew up, they became close. Daelen worked hard and quickly grew in power until he became a shadow warrior, too, and Kullos' most trusted Lieutenant. His right hand man.

However, it is often said that war can change people, and the change in Kullos epitomised this. He became increasingly agitated, nervous and paranoid, finding neither sleep nor rest. Daelen saw the shift happen almost overnight, but no-one knew exactly what had happened to initiate such a transformation. Whatever the cause, Kullos began to see enemies in the shadows and in the light. He saw danger where there was none, except that which he created himself, though he could never accept that. He began to lash out at his allies, his friends and ultimately his family. At first, it was verbal, and Daelen was able to pull him back from the edge of the abyss. He frequently opposed taking action against Kullos, firmly believing he could get through to him if only he kept trying. Despite his efforts, however, things continued to get worse, until one day, Daelen came home to find his mother, Farrella, severely injured and unconscious. He immediately summoned healers and rushed to her side.

The healers arrived, and as they began to stabilise her for transport to a healing facility, Farrella came around and whispered Daelen's name.

"What happened?" Daelen asked. "Who did this?

"Ku—Kullos," she croaked.

Daelen was stunned. He hadn't wanted to believe Kullos would go that far, but clearly, he had.

Sharing her thoughts telepathically, Daelen saw it had finally happened: Kullos had turned on Daelen's mother in a ferocious attack, accusing her of plotting against him. He had raved that she was in league with his 'real enemy,' another shadow warrior, who was planning to kill him.

Consumed by rage, Daelen growled, "Well he's right about that. Another shadow warrior *is* planning to kill him: me!"

Farrella had fought Kullos as best she could, but she was really only alive because Kullos had suddenly rushed off, deciding he had a 'better idea' of how to find his 'real enemy.' Farrella had slipped into unconsciousness then, so she didn't know where Kullos had gone.

The healers interrupted to say they really needed to take Farrella to a healing facility for proper treatment and she allowed herself to be transported away.

If Kullos' shadow warrior instinct was untempered by thought or reason, if he truly believed some imagined 'real enemy' was plotting to kill him, there was no telling what he might do. Daelen had not a moment to lose. He had to find Kullos before he did any more damage.

Forcing down his fear and panic, Daelen admonished himself to calm down and think, he remembered that Kullos kept a personal energy record – a kind of diary – and rushed to find it. He broke into it, feeling they were way beyond issues of privacy and quickly scanned his most recent entries.

No-one knows precisely what Daelen read at that moment, gentle reader. All he would ever say was that he felt himself go cold.

"Of course," he berated himself. "I should have known!"

Kullos had long been against Daelen's penchant for visiting the mortal realm and one world in particular. It was the world upon which Daelen now cast his protective gaze. The world we now know as Tempestria, but according to the legends, in those days it had another, more ancient name. Some say that knowing the world's original name would reveal Daelen StormTiger's true motives for his self-imposed status as this world's Protector. Others believe that the revelation of this name would spell the end of the world. Daelen always refused to confirm or deny any of this.

More than once, Kullos had forbidden Daelen to ever again take corporeal form. He considered it, "an obscene, filthy, disgusting state," but Farrella disagreed and always overruled him. Daelen realised this is where Kullos had gone.

Presumably, in his delusional state, Kullos was convinced his `real enemy` was hiding here and plotting against him. If he was here to kill that enemy, then he would tear our world apart without a second thought to do it.

Daelen had no choice. He Descended quickly – too quickly. Setting up his control device would take time. Time our world didn't have. He had to stop Kullos and protect our world before it was too late. But if Daelen Descended without a control device, there would be no way to access what he left behind. Maybe his people would be able to help him, but he didn't know for sure. As far as he knew, Descending through the planes without a control device had never been done. This action could very well mean there was no way home. But he couldn't stand by and let Kullos destroy this world, so he discarded his excess self and Descended.

Chapter 5

Daelen took the form of a tall, muscular man with shoulder-length dark hair and grey eyes. He flew across the world, seeking, searching. Remembering why he loved this place, this world, this reality. He recalled his very first visit: He had never seen a world like this before.

That is, he had never seen *anything* like this before.

Forgive me, gentle reader, but that's still not quite what I'm trying to say. Let me put it like this: He had never seen anything *in this way* before – light and colour; form, texture and shadow; unfiltered, unenhanced. It was pure and precious and beautiful. Then there were sounds and smells, taste and feeling. To have only five senses, to be capable of only a superficial perception of reality was stunning. An electrical storm gathered around him as he flew. He had never felt the rain on his skin before. That is, he had never before had skin that could generate such sensations. The clouds blew away and the heat of the sun and the cold of the altitude combined to create such incredible, unfamiliar sensations.

He snapped his thoughts back to the present. He didn't have time for reminiscence.

At last, he spotted her. Someone he knew well. An ally and friend. Someone he knew would be on his side. She looked very different in her human form – she had many others – but her aura was unmistakable. She had hazel eyes and brown hair bound into a long, thick braid. She wore a short dress of brown leather in the style favoured by huntresses of this age, with tall boots to match.

This individual is known to us as Blessed Alycia, Mother of Nature. No-one knows what kind of entity she was, or even if she was ever truly more than a myth. The way Daelen told this story, it was always open to interpretation. Still, whether she was a real person or a metaphor, according to this legend, Alycia was particularly fond of a group of mortals who had always shown her much kindness and friendship. They seemed especially receptive to her form of power, expressing it as nature magic, making them the very first druids. While this nature magic was an aspect of her own self, it was a form of expression unlike anything she had encountered before. It was gentle and serene, but also intense and violent. It was a power that favoured balance and harmony and yet strived for constant change and progress. It seemed to her that it was at once the most creative and the most destructive power this world had to offer. Alycia looked up at Daelen and gave him a dazzling smile and a wave. For a moment, he was relieved. He had found her…but so had Kullos.

It all happened in slow motion. Daelen saw Alycia's expression change from surprise and shock, to fear and terror as Kullos lashed out with the power of their native realm. Alycia hastily tried to shield herself, but some of his power got through and slammed into her mortal body, which collapsed to the ground, barely moving.

Daelen flew down as fast as he could, placing himself between them, praying to the gods he had once taunted to use their limited powers to keep her alive and help him. He prepared to defend himself and the fallen Alycia, but it seemed Kullos wasn't going to attack him. In fact, he seemed to think Daelen was on his side.

"Daelen!" he called out. "You came to help me. I knew I could count on you. You know, don't you? You can see it, can't you? Just like me. No-one else can see it, Daelen. Or no-one wants to. Only you and me. We're the only ones who see the evil all around us. They're all against me, Daelen. All of them. All except you."

He was ranting and raving, paranoia in total command, all rational thought gone, but still, Daelen hesitated. He didn't know what to do – attack Kullos or try to help Alycia. If he did the latter, he knew Kullos would take that as a sign that he, too, was against him and his reaction was predictable. Daelen didn't know if he had the power to defend them both. But if he spent his time and energy on attacking Kullos, he might not have enough of either to save Alycia. He felt frozen, paralysed. He was a trained fighter, powerful and deadly when he needed to be, but he was totally unprepared for the magnitude of this choice: save Alycia or save the world.

Kullos continued his raging. "Your mother is working for the enemy. Plotting against us, against me! I had to stop her, you know that, don't you? She made me do it. I tried just hurting her a bit, to get her to admit her betrayal, but she wouldn't. She kept claiming innocence, thinking me a fool that would believe her lies. She just kept on defying me. I would have destroyed her, but I realised: It's not just your mother – it's everyone! They've all gone over to the enemy. She was just distracting me, keeping me busy while others completed the weapon."

"Weapon?" Daelen wondered.

"Yes!" Kullos cried. "They tried to hide it in this disgusting world of flesh and matter – the one place they believed I'd never go. Well, it won't do them any good. No! I'm going to make sure they can't use it. You can help me Daelen. Help me destroy this foul, stinking place and take the weapon with it!"

"I cannot allow that," came a new voice.

The voice belonged to a man – a man of almost impossible size. More than seven feet tall with a colossal barrel chest and limbs like those of a tree. His dry skin stretched thin as parchment over a bony frame, the horns on his head poking through holes in his wide-brimmed wizard's hat. This being was a demigod, granted the powers of all of the gods, equally, in a rare moment of agreement between them.

"Daelen!" he called out, "I am Ossian Miach Kaidool, and your prayers have been answered. The gods have seen your plight and sent me to stand at your side at your times of greatest need. We have made a pact with Alycia. She has become a friend to this world, and I will defend her. You deal with Kullos."

Kullos was enraged, turning on Daelen.

"So even you betray me. You seek to use the so-called gods of this contemptible world to destroy me, but it won't work. All of Creation is against me, but you shall not have your satisfaction!"

There ensued a terrible battle as Kullos sought to destroy Daelen. The younger shadow warrior bought the demigod the time he needed to kneel beside Alycia and use his powers to slowly, carefully revive her. Leaving Alycia to recover, the demigod moved to fight by Daelen's side. Daelen and Kullos were too evenly matched. They could probably battle for hours without ever breaking the stalemate, but the demigod's presence was enough to tip the balance of power in the younger shadow warrior's favour. Kullos was beaten back until he was forced to retreat and Ascend. To aid his escape, he ripped energy from Ossian Miach Kaidool whose mortal body was slain by Kullos' might. Daelen was saddened by his loss, but he knew that death was not the end, not for a demigod. Indeed, the gods sent Daelen the knowledge that this was Fated to be at the end of every Final Battle. Daelen wondered how many of those there would be.

He set aside the upper chamber of the temple he had built so long ago, where his friend and comrade would sleep, protected until needed once more. He knew that day would come, for Kullos was bound to return.

Over time, Daelen became increasingly aloof, setting himself above and apart from this world. Where it had once been an escape, now it was a prison, albeit one of his own making. He was a prisoner of conscience, but a prisoner, nonetheless. Despite Alycia's efforts, one day Daelen chose to leave the world entirely. While he could not Ascend, he could use his power to move 'sideways' to another mortal world. He created a Prismatic Sphere, a portal to another world he had seen. A very different world, a world without magic. There to heal his scars and forge a life. It didn't last; he supposed it never could.

Daelen received a distress call from Alycia. Kullos was once more Descending to rain death on Alycia's world, and Daelen was honour-bound to answer the call to arms. He raised Ossian Miach Kaidool from his slumber and together they fought as they had before. For her part, Alycia would not fight but instead extended her powers to protect and shield the world she loved. Once more, Kullos was driven back, forced to retreat and Ascend, again killing the demigod in the process. Daelen returned his friend's body to the crypt and when it was sealed, he once more left this world behind.

This dance became familiar over the centuries. Each time Kullos was defeated, but never utterly defeated and each time Ossian Miach Kaidool was slain. The demigod was weary of this and wished only to be allowed to remain in peaceful oblivion forever, but he knew this was the purpose for which he had been placed in this world.

Just when they believed nothing would ever change, once – just once – they danced to a different tune and the world was ripped asunder.

Kullos had by now completely lost control and this time he Descended while retaining more of himself than ever before. More than this realm could handle. Ossian Miach Kaidool was raised, Daelen fought, Alycia protected and shielded, but the power that

Kullos commanded this time was unstable. He channelled the full force of his power at Daelen, ripping the shadow warrior's shields apart. It slammed into his body, not destroying it, but changing it. Daelen tried to absorb as much of the power as he could, trying to use it, assimilate it so that it would not destroy him, but the power was not what it should be. He didn't know why, but it seemed as if two incompatible powers had somehow been forced together. The two halves of the power were too different to assimilate. They were equal and opposite, containment of both was impossible, and the resulting reaction caused Daelen to split in two. Each a reverse copy of the other, light and dark clones, and as they separated, excess energy spilt out before they each managed to staunch the flow. They both fell unconscious.

Alycia had not Daelen's power and knew she couldn't fight Kullos the way he did, so instead, she tried to deflect it away to protect the mortal creatures of the world she loved. Trying to take advantage of this break in the pattern, Ossian Miach Kaidool implored her to rip away his power herself, rather than let Kullos do it. He would die the same as always, either way, but at least this way his death would do some good. So, with apologies, Alycia slew him and tried to use his power to force Kullos to Ascend. She didn't quite manage to get rid of all of him, but a good-sized portion was ripped away. Caught in the backwash of all this power in his already drained state, his mortal form was thrown out into the void, floating somewhere between this realm and that of the gods.

Under the stress of such immense, unstable power, the void threatened to collapse. The combined forces would rip the world apart if something drastic wasn't done to prevent it. In terror, agony and distress, Alycia could not, would not see her beloved world destroyed, robbing the mortals of their boundless potential, so she acted.

No-one knows precisely what happened next. Even Daelen never understood it. All we know is that, if this legend is to be believed, that was the day the void storms began, swirling and dancing in the sky. Alycia gave herself wholly to the protection of our world, but even as she lay there, exhausted, she looked around at this mortal, physical realm and smiled. It was saved, and it was beautiful. Her actions bound her to this world. It would forever be her prison. Unlike Daelen, she could never leave this world for another, but she could think of no greater justice than to accept this sentence as her penance. Her mortal friends, the ones who called themselves druids, flew to her side to help her if they could. She knew there was nothing they could do, but she appreciated their efforts. Even as she surrendered to her sleep, she vowed that her power would always be theirs, so that their druid magic might help heal the scars that the shadow warriors' battles left upon this world.

Alycia's actions shattered Kullos' control device, so he could no longer Ascend. Nor could any other shadow warriors Descend to the mortal realm to wreak further devastation, for she had placed a barrier in the void between the mortal realm and the plane of the gods, preventing such travel.

Alycia reflected on how often the druids spoke of the Mother of Nature as a mythical force that protected their world and needed their protection in return. In their eyes, she had become just that: Blessed Alycia, Mother of Nature. With that beautiful thought, she slipped into a blissful sleep.

And, gentle reader, she remains in that state to this day, even my day, if one is to believe the legend. As I have said, I do not know for sure how much of this is true, or what to make of it if it is. Only one thing is certain: Daelen was not the man he was and he had not his former power. Fortunately, neither did Kullos.

But they were still extraordinarily powerful and dangerous by mortal standards, and it wasn't long before the dance began again. Only now it was a three-way struggle between Kullos, Daelen and his dark clone.

*****

When he finished his tale, Daelen implored Catriona to believe that he would give anything to stop Kullos harming Tempestria any further, to stop him permanently or at least take the battle back to the higher planes.

"But I don't know how to do that," he told her. "None of us can penetrate Alycia's Barrier. My dark clone and I have no control device and Kullos' is destroyed, so all I can do is battle him forever and try to minimise the damage we do in the process."

Chapter 6

Daelen's story was enough to persuade Catriona to trust him at least to some extent. Still, she wasn't done negotiating. All of her experience as an information trader came to fruition with this meeting. She revealed that the place he was looking for was overseas but would say no more unless he agreed to take her with him.

"Why would you ask such a thing?" the shadow warrior demanded, incredulously. "I can't put you in danger like that!"

"I'm putting myself in danger," she countered. "You've got nothing to do with it. If you refuse, I'll simply find a way to go there by myself, but it makes more sense to go with you."

Daelen did not immediately get to answer, as a storm flared up around them. As before, Cat knew it wasn't natural. Daelen knew it, too, and both were on their feet instantly.

Out of a shimmering blue portal, flew Daelen's dark clone. Cat had never seen him before, but now that she had, she understood why he was called that.

Catriona had some experience with the relatively new medium of photography. Only a few days ago, she'd enjoyed a day out in Gaggleswick with Dreya and they'd stopped at the newly refurbished studio, where they'd had a few photos taken together. In comparison to the 'real' Daelen, if one could call him that, his dark clone looked like a three dimensional photographic negative.

The dark clone landed, ready to confront Daelen.

"Hello, you!" he greeted them, in a cheery voice that was at odds with his sneering expression. "What's this? Have you traded in Mr. Bony for a human pet? I can see why you would. She's way prettier."

"Actually, I'm half-Faery," Catriona shot back.

"Really?" the clone remarked, drawing out the word. "Shouldn't you have wings?"

Catriona wasn't sure how much of the bile she felt rise up inside her, in response to the casual racial slur, came from herself and how much was transmitted from Dreya, via their sympathic link.

At first, Daelen couldn't understand how his dark clone had managed to get the jump on him. Then the shadow warrior remembered his visitor from the future telling him about someone interfering in Time. It was why he'd been asleep in his other world when he should have been here. If this Time meddler had shut off the system that alerted him to Kullos' activity, it made sense that alerts for his dark clone would also be disabled. His visitor had said it wasn't Daelen's fault, but the way he saw it, he had really screwed up this time.

Ordinarily, the village surrounding Justaria's home was quiet, but already, the word was spreading about this confrontation and people were fleeing the scene.

Still, Catriona stood her ground. Dreya was in her head, offering to teleport her out of there, but Cat told her no. Having learned so much about Daelen, this was an opportunity to gather information about his dark clone. Then, just as Dreya returned to the background, another voice thundered into her mind.

'*Catriona,*' came the voice, '*it's me, Daelen. Sorry for barging through your defences. I promise I can't and won't read anything unless you project it to me, but I need your help. My clone loves the sound of his own voice – please keep him busy while I talk to you like this.*'

'*Alright,*' Cat agreed.

Catriona could tell this connection was painful for him, and choosing to trust his good intentions, asked Pyrah to ease off on her barriers, but not take them down. After all, if Daelen could get in her mind with effort, his dark clone could, too, and Pyrah didn't know if she could block both at the same time.

She gritted her teeth against the dark clone's words and used them.

"No wings on me, I'm afraid. Speaking of which, can you fly around like him?" she asked, indicating Daelen.

"Of course, little pet," he returned.

"Can I see? Please?" she begged. "I asked him, but he was all mean about it," she pouted.

"Aww!" the clone remarked in mock sympathy. "Is my brother being mean to our little pet Faery? Don't worry – I'm way nicer than him, and I'd be happy to show you how I fly."

With that, he flew all over the place, as if it were the most impressive thing in the world.

'*Excellent, keep him busy,*' Daelen approved. '*Listen, this shouldn't have happened. This is all wrong. I'm always alerted before he appears so I can have Michael fighting at my side, but he's still locked in his tomb.*'

The dark clone got bored of flying, then, and landed once more. Catriona applauded with feigned enthusiasm as he took a bow.

"Any other requests, little pet?"

Cat was getting really sick of him calling her that, but kept a smile fixed on her face as she asked, "What's your name?"

"My name?" The clone seemed thrown by the unexpected question.

"Yes, of course. Well, I can't keep calling you 'dark clone' now, can I?"

"Little pet," he replied with exaggerated patience. "My brother obviously hasn't explained the word 'clone.' You see, we were split from the same being – Daelen. The original was Daelen, he's Daelen, and I'm Daelen."

'*If my clone and I fight all the way to Michael's Tomb,*' Daelen continued in Catriona's mind, '*we're going to leave a trail of devastation right across Elvaria.*'

'*Can't you teleport?*' Cat wondered.

'*Not with him here, we can block each other's powers,*' Daelen explained. '*That's why I need Michael in the first place.*'

Meanwhile, Cat kept up her performance for the clone, laughing self-deprecatingly.

"Oh, but that's just too confusing for my poor little mortal brain. Why don't I call you Nelead?"

"Nelead? What kind of a name is that?"

"It's an anagram," Cat clarified. "In fact, it's Daelen in reverse, and you're kind of the opposite of this Daelen, so I thought it kind of worked. Frankly, it's either Nelead or Fred."

"Call me Fred. No, wait, don't call me Fred. Actually, I'm warming to your anagram idea, but I don't like Nelead. Let me see, what could I use…"

He spent the next few minutes running through and rejecting various anagrams of Daelen, talking to himself and completely ignoring druidess and shadow warrior.

'*That should keep him busy.*' she told Daelen, mentally. '*Pyrah's willing to bite him if it will help.*'

'*It wouldn't stop him while he's at full power, and if anything happened to her, he could ravage your mind in a second.*'

'*So, you need me to get Michael for you? I have a friend who could teleport me there.*'

'*The defences won't let you pass without the right power signature,*' Daelen told her.

'*Actually, I have a sort of tool, a staff, that has higher planar energy inside it.*'

The shadow warrior didn't know how that was possible, but he didn't waste time arguing. '*Don't bring it out in front of my clone.*'

'*Wasn't planning to,*" she assured him, resisting the urge to roll her eyes. As if she'd casually wave her most precious possession around under the dark clone's nose. She just wanted to know one thing. '*Will it let me in?*'

'*Maybe,*' Daelen allowed.

'*Maybe? We don't have time for maybe. There must be a way to make sure I get in.*'

"I've got it!" the dark clone declared, suddenly. "Aden-El!"

'*Really?*' Cat remarked in her head. 'That's *what he's going with?*'

"Aden-El!" she enthused aloud. "That's perfect!"

"You know what's even perfecter?" Aden-El asked.

Cat shook her head.

"You can call me Aden for short."

"Aden," Catriona acknowledged. "I like that. Well, my name's Catriona, but you can call me Cat for short."

"Me-ow!" Aden quipped.

'*You never told* me *your nickname,*' Daelen complained, good-naturedly.

'*I just did,*' she shot back. '*Any bright ideas, yet?*'

'*There is one way, but there are risks to you. I can't allow it.*'

'*Not your call,*' she insisted. '*Be clear. Be concise. Get out of my head for thirty seconds. I decide.*'

*****

You will recall, gentle reader, how I told you shadow warriors Descended to the mortal plane by shedding those parts of themselves that couldn't fit and leaving them safely back on their home plane. In much the same way, it was possible for him to temporarily keep a part of himself, his essence, inside a mortal's body. If he did that with Catriona, the security surrounding Michael's tomb would recognise that part of him and grant her full access, including the authority to wake Ossian Miach Kaidool.

*****

He had done it only once before, Daelen explained, seemingly distracted by the memory. Long ago, when he had a relationship with a mortal woman called Rose. Catriona even reminded him of her in some ways, although Rose had been quite a lot older…

'*Don't care about your past girlfriends!*' Cat sniped, interrupting his reminiscence as she continued to engage Aden in a mixture of small talk and flattery. '*Just tell me the risks. Quickly.*'

Daelen snapped himself out of it. She was right, of course. He couldn't imagine why he'd distracted himself with such thoughts at a time like this.

'*If you're quick, it should be OK, but the longer you're exposed, the greater the chances of serious complications.*'

'*Like what?*'

He answered her as best he could, telling her everything it could mean for her. As he quickly listed the potential consequences, her eyes grew wider and wider. When he was finished, Catriona swallowed, nervously, but quickly composed herself.

'*Thirty seconds.*' she insisted. '*Out of my head. You promised.*'

The instant he left her mind, she reached out to Dreya. Some of these complications could affect her, too.

In the end, though, Dreya simply projected '*Support*,' telling Cat it was her choice, and she would back her either way. She could either agree to help Daelen or let Dreya teleport her away and leave the two shadow warriors to it.

"Are you alright…'Cat'?" Aden asked with feigned concern. "You seem to have turned quite pale," he continued, still with the most pleasant tone, sugar coating his poisonous words. "You're not coming down with some disgusting Faery disease, are you, little pet?"

Catriona told Daelen her decision.

'*Do it. I can't let anyone else's home and family be destroyed like mine was.*' Besides, the chance to learn about a shadow warrior's true nature was irresistible.

'*You're sure?*'

'*Completely. I know the risks, and I want to help. How do we do this?*'

'*Just follow my lead.*'

Speaking to his clone for the first time, Daelen told him, "I've had quite enough of you calling her that! She's not ill – you're upsetting her. Catriona is no-one's pet. She's my girlfriend!"

"Yeah," Catriona nodded, "it feels like I've known him forever."

'*Thank you, Cat,*' came Daelen's voice in her mind, '*and I'm sorry about this. It's the only way. This means nothing, it's just what we planned, OK? It's nothing more than that. I'm sorry. I swear, it means nothing.*'

'*Do it,*' she insisted.

With that, he kissed her full on the lips, and she kissed him back with equal passion. When he broke the kiss, she was reeling from the multitude of unfamiliar sensations. There was a piece of Daelen StormTiger inside her, and she could feel it.

'*You're sure that was nothing? It sure felt like something to me.*'

'*I'm sorry,*' he repeated.

'*It's OK,*' she assured him. '*My choice, remember?*'

Meanwhile, Aden looked ready to throw up.

"Yeurch!" He pulled a face at the sight. "That is truly disgusting. Snogging your pet? Kullos is right – it ought to be illegal, consorting with lower life forms. Thought you'd got it out of your system way back, but looks like you've had a relapse. Yeurch!"

Daelen powered up, apparently enraged. "How dare you speak about Cat like that! I'll tear you apart!"

'*Cat, get ready to fly.*'

Daelen pulled his beam cannon out of his pocket dimension and fired it at Aden, who shielded, quickly and powered up his own version, firing back.

'*Now! Go!*' Daelen shouted in Cat's mind, who immediately shifted to her falcon form and took to the sky.

However, she couldn't resist the urge to at least do something to Aden, after all she'd had to put up with.

Shifting back and standing on her Windy Steps, she fished a pebble out of a pouch and called out, "Hey, Aden!"

Glancing her way, he saw her repeatedly toss the stone in the air and catch it again.

"Let's see if you can catch this while you're flying! I'll be so impressed if you can!"

"You're going to throw a stone at me?" Aden scoffed. "What do you think that tiny thing's going to do?"

"You've lost perspective, Aden!" Cat shouted back, throwing the pebble and asking the wind to guide it straight and true. "Far away things may look small, but when they get closer…" the stone grew into a boulder about the same size as Aden himself, "…they're much, much bigger!"

She laughed as it slammed into him, but then, not being foolish enough to wait around for any retaliation, she retook her falcon form and flew away.

Daelen smiled. Her intervention distracted Aden – only for a moment, but it was enough for him to get on top in the fight. Hopefully, he would be able to keep his clone on the defensive and thereby minimise the damage to the local area.

"You see?" he grinned. "My new girlfriend's amazing!"

*****

Cat flew only a short distance to the *FaerWay Tavern*. The name and winged sign rankled her even more after Aden's remarks, but it was the nearest, best landmark for Dreya's teleportation. Otherwise, they might waste more time trying to find each other in some other, less specific location. Dreya materialised just as Cat shapeshifted. She took her hand and, thanks to that physical contact,

Dreya was able to teleport them both to a secluded spot, as close as possible to Michael's Tomb, without setting off any defences.

Once there, Dreya handed Cat a map, showing the Rhynas Desert, overseas, as Catriona had thought, on the continent of Northern Alloria.

When Cat thanked her, Dreya simply shrugged. "It's only a map."

"You know I don't mean just for the map. I mean for everything. For…you know."

"I know, but I am going to ask for something in return."

"Better be quick – Daelen needs Michael's help."

"It'll only take a moment," Dreya assured her. "I just want to propose something."

"Didn't our whole relationship start when I proposed to you?"

"It did," Dreya agreed, "Now I'm asking you."

"Propose away, then," Cat invited her.

"Keep me a secret. Let me be a rumour, a story, nothing more. I'll be the ace up your sleeve. I can strengthen our link so I can be at your side in a heartbeat wherever you are."

"You make that sound so altruistic, Dreya," Catriona remarked with a wry smile, "but I know you better than that."

Dreya returned the smile. "Better than anyone, and I'll keep nothing from you. You've convinced me to stay my hand for now, but I'm still not ruling it out."

Cat understood. "If it comes down to it, surprise could be key, and you know I won't stand in your way. Just please, give me as much time as you can to gather information."

"Have you ever known me to be reckless?"

Cat laughed and shook her head. "Never. That's more my thing. Alright, my answer to your proposal is 'yes.' I promise. From now on, until the time is right, you're my little secret. Actually," she considered with a mischievous grin, "I think I kind of like that."

"Shall we seal it with magic, then?" Dreya asked.

"Absolutely," Cat agreed.

The word had barely left her lips before Dreya stepped forward and kissed them. Catriona returned the kiss, tenderly at first, then with increasing passion.

Cat thought back to the first time they had done this. The night she lost Mandalee. She had been devastated, inconsolable. It was all her fault.

*****

Dreya was a revelation. Cat's feelings had already started to surface, and she'd begun to realise how Dreya felt, too. The way she expressed it was unconventional and not everyone would understand, but that didn't matter. That night, once Cat began to calm down and recover, they had shared something special, sharing not just their magic, but their bodies, too. That was the first time Catriona had seen the Faery woman beneath the robes, and a million things about her suddenly made sense.

There on her back, were a pair of tiny, vestigial wings.

Growing up with the Faery, Catriona knew that prejudice was not a uniquely human trait. Faery such as Dreya always took great pains to hide their wings – literally, because strapping them down was painful. Most modern Faery claimed to consider it barbaric, but still, if anyone ever found out, such individuals were often the object of scorn, bullying and discrimination. Therefore, they might well choose the pain of the strapping over the pain of rejection.

While Dreya never talked about her childhood, Cat could guess how it must have been. The stares, the comments, perhaps even violence. All of which the child Dreya had been powerless to stop. It was beyond her control. But the child had magic, and as the child grew up, she swore she would never be powerless again. She would be the Greatest Mage Who Ever Lived, and she would be in control of her life. Always.

"You are beautiful, Dreya," Cat had told her. "All of you, everything about you is absolutely beautiful."

"Flesh is fleeting," Dreya insisted, "magic is all."

"No, it's not," Cat disagreed. "Actually, I think a balance of the two is just about perfect."

"With you here, I think you might be right," Dreya accepted.

*****

That night was beyond anything either woman had ever experienced before. And after what they had agreed today, it would likely be some time before they experienced it again. This kiss would just have to sustain them both until then.

But this kiss wasn't just a kiss. It was a kiss that sealed the binding magic, ensuring the promise could not be broken, except with another kiss to release her from it. From this moment, Cat would find ways to hide any hint of their relationship. Until they could meet again.

After a moment, the magic subsided, and they broke the kiss.

"How was that for you?" Dreya inquired.

"Magical!"

"And how did mine compare to the other one?"

Cat made a dismissive noise. "Pfft! The other one? That was just an essence transfer. It meant nothing."

With one last, brief embrace, Cat took off towards Michael's Tomb, and Dreya teleported back to the Black Tower.

Chapter 7

The ancient crypt lay on a rocky outcrop of the northernmost tip of Elvaria. Below, the ocean swelled and churned, while above the winds swirled and howled. The whole place looked ready to fall into the water with the very next gust of wind, the next raindrop, the next breath, yet it had stood unmoving for many hundreds of years. Some even said thousands, but that was surely impossible.

From her memory of seeing Michael on the Day of the Angel, his tomb seemed the perfect match for the Champion of the Gods himself. Made as he was, from all skin and bone, seemingly devoid of flesh and muscle, one would think he would be a fragile creature, ready to collapse at any moment. Yet, he was an imposing figure. Next to the shadow warriors, he was the most powerful being in the world and had endured longer than any other on Tempestria.

Catriona walked up to the large iron gates that served as the entrance, saying, "I, Catriona Redfletching, have come to free you from the bonds of death. I come here to break the rune seal that binds you to your prison."

With a short wave of her hand, the gates and the mighty doors beyond them began to grind loudly open. Dust and debris flittered out from the now-gaping orifice. Silence rose to greet and envelop Catriona as she stepped inside.

She began to walk up the long staircase. Daelen had been very clear on this point: she must ignore the stairs leading downward to 'The Wishing Well' and instead climb upward, following the illuminated sign that read, 'The Tower of Dreams.'

"I wonder if he does," Cat murmured to herself. She'd never thought about it before.

Catriona did not dream. Not that she knew of, anyway. Her whole life, she had never once woken up with even the slightest impression of anything since she settled down to sleep. Cat didn't value dreams the way others seemed to, so she didn't feel she was missing anything. Still, if her life were like Michael's – waking only to help Daelen tip the scales in his favour, in his recurring battles, and Fated to die at the end – it would surely be a mercy to at least dream of a life.

Or would that be even more cruel, she reconsidered? To dream of a life one could never have. Surely, that would make his real life a waking nightmare.

She made a mental note to discuss none of this with Michael when he woke, because either way, she didn't think she could bear the answer.

The spiral staircase wound so high, the top was shrouded in darkness. Assuming it had a top.

"What if it's like a bottomless pit," Cat wondered, "only in reverse?"

She dismissed the idea. This wasn't the time for flights of fancy. Thinking of which, flying seemed a much preferable option to all those steps, so she shifted to Tawny owl form, the better for seeing in the dark, and flew up the stairwell.

As Catriona reached, at long last, the uppermost level – for it did have one, after all – the air grew increasingly stagnant, and that made flying difficult, so she alighted on the balcony and shifted back again. Despite the stillness of the atmosphere, impossibly, there was dust dancing in the non-existent winds. Torn tapestries clung to the walls, though the scenes depicted on them were long faded. Reaching a metal door, she paused, sniffing at the air, almost tasting the remnants of age-old magic still present there in that dusty crypt. Cat stopped for a moment and looked at the door, wondering what might lay beyond. Pushing a button at the side, as Daelen had told her, caused the metal door to open by itself. A moment later, she was stepping beyond to end the speculation and find out.

*****

What my mother saw in that chamber was beyond her ability to describe, and so, if you'll forgive me, gentle reader, I shall use my own words, rather than my mother's impressions.

One might expect a crypt or tomb to be dark and foreboding, with stone archways and thick pillars supporting high domed ceilings, filled with candles and cobwebs. And in many ways, so it was, but set against the walls were control panels with buttons and flashing lights. Bleeps sounded a very slow, rhythmic heartbeat, matching the progress of oscillating lines on screens. In short, gentle reader, it was high technology on a world where the word had not yet been used in that context. To my mother at the time, it was magic – just magic unlike any she had even imagined, much less experienced. She immediately had a million questions and probably a million more that she didn't have the words to frame into sentences.

*****

But Catriona didn't have time to stop and stare. Daelen needed her. Secretly, she found she rather liked that idea. A being from a realm far beyond the gods for whom, it was reasonable to assume, rooms such as this crypt were commonplace, *needing* the help of a simple half-Faery druid girl. Her overriding thought, however, even above that, was the firm belief that one day, the people of Tempestria would also have commonplace rooms like this. One day, the magic in this place might be contained in something no larger than her staff. Perhaps, even, one day, Tempestrian children would play with toys that were more sophisticated than this, and this Crypt would stand as a museum of knowledge and skills long since surpassed by newer and more wonderous invention.

On a dais in the centre of the room, was Ossian Miach Kaidool, Champion of the Gods, asleep in all of his bony glory…

In all of his bony *naked* glory, it turned out, as Catriona stepped closer.

Daelen had called this a 'Regeneration Casket' and told her that all she needed to do, was wave her hand over something called a 'hand sensor' on a 'control panel,' which would recognise that part of his essence that she now carried within her, awakening Michael from 'stasis.'

The words were strange, but looking at the bank of tiny dancing lights before her now, there was one area upon which there was inscribed the outline of a hand. It seemed to Catriona that whatever fancy language one might use, it was clearly saying, 'Place Hand Here.'

Doing so, she closed her eyes and prayed, "I call forth both heaven and hell, all that is holy and all that is demonic; I call forth the Powers of Magias, Blessed Alycia and the Great Maker that

Created all. I plead that you breathe life back into this great warrior's body. I know that I ask for both heaven and hell to be moved, but please Great Ancient Powers, do this, that he might help us save this precious world."

Catriona couldn't see or hear anything outside, but she imagined that the sky began to grow eerily black. The howling of a wolf could be heard over the growing howling of the winds. Surely, the whole world quaked as if to swallow its people down into its depths.

In reality, though, gentle reader, this was nothing more than my mother's overactive imagination at work. Indeed, the task had been completed before she even stopped speaking.

The ancient warrior sat up and quite startled Catriona, saying, "A simple 'Wake up, Michael' would have sufficed."

"Really?" Cat sounded disappointed. "Seemed a bit anti-climactic to me, although I do have a…friend…who always says I have a flair for the dramatic."

"Did you make up that whole speech on the spot?" Michael asked.

Cat nodded while trying desperately to keep her eyes firmly fixed on his face and not anywhere…lower down.

"Then your friend is right. It was very impressive."

"Thank you."

"The second thing that strikes me about you is that you are not Daelen StormTiger."

"It's the long hair, isn't it?" she joked. "That's what gave me away. It's happened before. Seriously, I'm Catriona Redfletching, you can call me Cat. I'm here on Daelen's behalf. He needs you to tip the fight in his favour."

"Just for a change," Michael nodded, wearily. Catriona turned her back as he rose and stepped free of his coffin-like bed. (Or bed-like coffin, if you prefer.) "Which one is it this time?"

"Both, really," Cat replied, "although Aden's the more immediate danger."

"Who?"

"Sorry, I mean the dark clone. That's what he calls himself now: Aden-El, Aden for short. My fault. I suggested anagrams."

"And he went with Aden-El?"

"I'm afraid so."

Cat could hear him getting dressed, so she continued to stare at the entryway.

"So why did Daelen send you and also, how?"

"Why? Short version: his alarm clock broke, someone changed the time, and he overslept. So now he doesn't know when either Kullos or 'Aden' are going to be around. How? Again, short version: he put a piece of his essence inside me so I could get past the security."

Michael touched her shoulder, gently but firmly, and spun her around to face him. Thankfully, he was fully dressed now. He looked angry, but not at her, it seemed.

"Did he explain what that could mean for you?"

"Yes, he did." Cat nodded, solemnly. "He had to make it brief, there wasn't much time, but yes, everything he did was with my fully informed consent. I had to make a choice quickly and I made it." She smiled, nervously, and Michael let her go. "Anyway," she added, trying to lighten the mood once more, "believe it or not, this isn't even the most ridiculous radical idea I've ever had in my life."

"I believe you," Michael replied. "Please excuse me, I need to charge up so we can join Daelen as soon as possible."

Cat decided not to ask what he meant by 'charge up,' and simply watch instead. He moved over to a bank of flashing lights in the East wall, pressed some buttons and placed his hand on another 'control panel hand sensor.' In response, an alcove sprang to life, buzzing with higher planar energy. Words and numbers scrolled down a screen like some kind of incantation, which meant nothing to Cat but clearly did to Michael who muttered to himself that 'it' (whatever 'it' was) was now safe.

"By the way," Cat remarked, "the magic in this place is fascinating."

Michael explained that it was actually technology. "But your mistake is understandable. How did Daelen put it? Ah, yes: Any sufficiently advanced form of technology would be indistinguishable from magic."

"Then how do you know it isn't?" Cat wondered, challenging the concept. "If it's indistinguishable, by definition, you can't tell the difference. So, if it was sufficiently advanced, even for you, even for Daelen StormTiger himself, how could you be sure it wasn't really magic, rather than technology?"

Michael considered that for a moment. "I suppose I couldn't," he admitted, at last.

"In that case, any sufficiently advanced form of magic would be indistinguishable from technology."

"I like you," Michael decided with a grin. "You're trouble."

"So I've been told," she agreed, grinning back.

Michael stepped into the alcove and seemed to absorb the energy within. Cat would have expected it to be painful, but if it was, Michael hid it well.

Cat decided to forgo any questions about what he was doing; it was unlikely she would understand the answers. Instead, she latched onto something else.

"This 'Regeneration Casket,'" she ventured. "Fancy name for healing device, yes?"

"It reverts my body back to its original default settings," he answered, "but keeps my mind as it is. I wouldn't be much use if I forgot everything every time."

"What if you wanted to change something about your body?"

"Why would I want to do that?"

"Not saying you would, but hypothetically, could you change your…" she stumbled over the unfamiliar words, "default settings?"

"In principle, yes," he answered, "but in practice, you would need a way to show it what you wanted, and if you already had the default body you wanted, you wouldn't need the machine to change it."

"You might if you only had it temporarily without the machine," Cat mused. Now the big question. "Would it work for a human?"

"Species wouldn't matter. It would use whatever default settings you programmed it with. Why are you asking all this?"

"Oh, just thinking out loud," Cat replied, dismissively. Years ago, she'd made a promise to a friend and though she knew she might never see her again, she continued to work on that promise. She'd let Mandalee down once; if ever she gave her a second chance, that would never happen again.

Changing tack, she went back to their earlier conversation.

“When I told you this wasn’t the most ridiculous radical idea I’ve ever had, you said, ‘I believe you.’ What did you mean by that?”

“I simply imagine that being touched by an Angel is likely to lead to a remarkable life, and a spirit that won’t be constrained by what others think is impossible.”

Chapter 8

It took Catriona a moment to process Michael's answer.

"Touched by an Angel?" she wondered. Then it hit her. "Wait, you recognise me? From all those years ago?"

She had never imagined he would. Frankly, she wasn't that conceited.

"I have a feeling I would always recognise you," he replied, cryptically.

Choosing to let that go, Cat asked what he remembered about that day. He told her how sorry he was that he had been unable to stop the void-creature, but promised he had done all he could.

"Void-creature?" Cat wondered. "Is that what that Monster was?"

Michael shrugged. "That's just my name for it. I have no idea what it really was."

He went on to tell her about the three figures who appeared and how they, too, tried to stop the void-creature before the Angel turned up.

Cat vaguely recalled something about that, although she'd been much more focused on the loss of her home and the death of her father at the time and then she'd been knocked unconscious by her mother just moments later. Finally, Michael told Cat how the Angel appeared and beat back the Monster before talking to him.

"After that, you know more than I do," he concluded. "What did the Angel say to you?"

Cat shifted, uncomfortably. As an information trader, she appreciated the value of what he'd given her and she wished she could offer something of equal value in return, but she couldn't.

"Sorry," she apologised, "but if my Angel wanted you and the gods kept out of it, I have to assume there was a good reason, so I probably shouldn't discuss it any further. Same goes for my staff. I'm planning to talk to Daelen about it, but it will have to be just him and me. Sorry."

The alcove powered down, and Michael stepped clear.

"Not at all, my dear," he assured her, kindly. "The gifts of Angels are precious, and only a select few may touch them."

"Maybe, but of course, my visitor wasn't an actual Angel," Cat pointed out.

"What makes you so sure?" Michael wondered. "They do exist, you know. Daelen has seen one, though from what he's told me, I doubt it's the same one. Anyway, speaking of Daelen, are you ready to go and save him?"

"Ready," she affirmed. "Teleportation, I presume."

He nodded.

"Which means you need a clear image, so you know where to go."

Again, he nodded.

"The image that's currently in my head, so you'll need to go in and have a look, yes?"

Another nod.

"I'm afraid so, yes. If you don't mind – pardon the pun, I don't mean to joke about it."

"A sympathic link won't be clear enough, I suppose?"

"Sorry, no. It has to be full telepathy."

"Thought so. These things will be a lot easier when photography takes off."

My mother was quite right about that, gentle reader. Broadly speaking, in those days, a sympathic image versus a telepathic one was like the difference between having a vague drawing of a pub and labelling it '*FaerWay Tavern*,' versus having a high-resolution photo of the place itself along with exact map co-ordinates.

"OK, I'll let you in. Why not? I'll throw down the welcome mat. I just hope you can find space. It's getting rather crowded up here, these days. I'm going to need a bigger head."

"I do hope not," Michael protested. "Your head is the perfect size, just the way it is."

Cat raised her eyebrows in amusement.

"Thank you. That may be the oddest compliment I've ever received, which, considering the company I keep, is quite an achievement, so congratulations on that. Just hold on a tick, I'll get Pyrah to lower her defences."

"Pyrah?" Michael wondered.

The green snake poked her head out of Catriona's pocket, and Michael immediately sank to his knees.

"Forgive me, Mistress Pyrah," he gasped. "I had no idea I was in the presence of one such as yourself."

"Erm, message from Pyrah: You may stand, and you have her permission, as well as my consent, to enter my mind for a moment," a puzzled Catriona responded. "Message from me: What the f—?"

"—I'm a creature of the gods," Michael replied, quickly, cutting her off. Though he was back on his feet, he was still clearly in awe of the little green snake, "But sometimes even the gods have gods, and Mistress Pyrah is one of the most revered of all Ysirians."

"Ysirians?"

"That's the name of her people. She's Ysirian. She has not told you this?"

"I know she's from one of the higher planes," Cat shrugged, "but I don't think she's ever mentioned the name of her race. To me, she's just my friend, Pyrah."

"Who exactly are you, Catriona Redfletching? Touched by an Angel, host to a shadow warrior and friend to a god of gods?"

Catriona flushed at his reverent tone. "I'm just Cat. Just a simple half-Faery druid girl. Nobody important."

Michael shook his head, his eyes wide. "I hate to contradict you, Cat, but I'm certain you are quite, quite wrong about that."

*****

Cat and Michael materialised in the middle of a pitched midair battle between Daelen and Aden. Both had already expended a great deal of energy. Cat could tell by the power readings that were considerably lower than they had been a few minutes ago. Not to mention the mass devastation all around them. She wondered what would have happened if she hadn't gone to fetch Michael. She knew 'Aden' generally gave up and ran away, but what if he didn't? Would they have kept fighting their futile battle to the point of mutual destruction? What could they possibly hope to achieve by that?

Still, she supposed that was why Daelen had Michael.

'*And now he's got me, too.*'

As the Champion of the Gods moved to fight at close quarters, Catriona kept her distance and worked her magic from afar. That would give her time to react, should anything nasty come flying her way.

She fought with wind and ice and water. Trees reached up to grab Aden, lightning strikes assailed his body. All the while, she kept on the move, on the ground, in the air, shifting to falcon form, shifting back and dancing on her Windy Steps. All of her training with Dreya paid off. Except, of course, this wasn't training, it was for real, and the energy beam that Aden fired towards her was not merely a beam of light. But she was ready, her hand in her bag of sand. The druidess threw it in the air, and it formed Nature's Mirror. Just as Dreya had explained, there wasn't time to do all this, given the speed of the energy beam, and yet the mirror formed precisely when she needed it to, reflecting the beam straight back, so it slammed into Aden's body and knocked him to the ground. All three combatants stopped for a moment, and stared at her, not believing what they had just seen.

To Aden, Catriona yelled, "That's from all the Faery to show you exactly what we think about all the slurs about wings!"

Aden got to his feet and conjured a Prismatic Sphere. Ignoring Catriona, he spoke to Daelen.

"Three against one? That's hardly sporting. Still, I've got to hand it to you, brother. These mortal pets are really useful things. Maybe I should get one of my own. Bye, y'all!"

With that, he stepped through his portal and disappeared.

"If I ever say something as inane as 'Bye, y'all,'" Daelen instructed Michael, "kill me immediately."

Michael rushed over to check if Catriona was alright, Daelen a step behind.

"Me?" she queried. "What about you? No offence, Michael, but aren't you supposed to die in every final battle?"

"That rule only applies to Kullos," he explained.

Daelen nodded, adding, "There could be no such rules about my clone. Michael was created more than two centuries before I was split."

"Although there is also my Curse," the demigod told her, "which says that I shall die permanently in the final war of the shadow warriors."

"I've promised to break that Curse," Daelen insisted.

Michael shook his head. "Can't be done."

This was clearly a very old argument, and Cat was keen to return their focus to the present.

"Well, either way, right now, since Aden's run away, we need to deal with Kullos."

"And the void-creature," Daelen put in, "for all that I've been told it's not my problem. If it's there when I attack, then it's my problem."

"Wait, the void-creature's back?" Cat demanded, forcing herself to catch her breath and slow her heartbeat.

She could not panic in front of these two and she told her mind she did not need any flashbacks to the Day of the Monster, thank you.

"You know about it?" Daelen wondered.

Cat was grateful when Michael stepped in and covered for her. "The monster that killed her parents, along with many of her friends and neighbours," he explained, gently.

If there was any possibility of Daelen talking her out of joining him on his mission before, this news removed that chance entirely.

Acting on a sympathic suggestion transmitted by Dreya, Cat volunteered, "I think we should try and limit knowledge of this void-creature. We particularly wouldn't want your clone finding out. He's already not happy about being outnumbered. If he knew of the power of the void-creature working with Kullos, he might decide to throw his lot in with Kullos, too."

"Then we'd be in even more trouble," Michael agreed.

"Well, I wouldn't expect Kullos to be willing to work with my clone," Daelen mused, "but then I wouldn't have thought he'd build an army to take on Michael, either."

"Exactly," Cat affirmed. "You can't go on like it's business as usual. Things have changed, and you need to do the same. Whether it really is Time manipulation or not, I don't know. But either way, I'd say it's time to throw the old rule book on the fire. The fight between the four of you isn't just about you anymore. That void-creature attacked my home and Kullos is dragging us mortals into his army. They have to be stopped. We might not be able to control much about this situation, but we can control the information."

"Catriona's right, Daelen." Michael backed her up. "You must place a block in my mind, so I don't remember the void-creature, and then send me away. I will rendezvous with you when you're ready to make the final push to Kullos' fortress, and I'll bring help."

Michael explained his reasoning. His was the only mind that was vulnerable to Aden's telepathy. Even if he tried not to think about the void-creature, that would be like telling someone not to think about elephants. Plus, he knew there was something else Cat wanted to discuss with Daelen that he could not be privy to.

"If we're doing this, though, we need to know where we're going," he reminded the druidess.

She nodded. "Daelen," she began, a determined look in her eyes, "swear to me, with Michael as a witness, that you will take me with you, and I promise I will give you both the location. There will be no more tricks from me, and if you want Tempestrians to believe you are in any way trustworthy, there will be none from you, either."

The shadow warrior was torn. He could see the value of Catriona, more so than any other mortal for centuries, but his instinct to protect was telling him to keep her safely out of it. To buy himself time to think, he formed the mental block in Michael's mind, as agreed.

"The way I see it, there are three reasons why I should be with you," Cat pressed.

"First reason is this: I do not underestimate your power, or that of your fellow shadow warriors, but have you ever wondered why the most powerful mages in history are so often defeated by those with less power? Power isn't everything. Power breeds confidence; great power breeds over-confidence. When a being of your power goes into battle, your first instinct is to hit your enemy with the most powerful weapon you possess. There's no subtlety, no finesse, just mindless brute force. Trouble is, that makes you predictable, and so your enemy can take steps to defend himself. You try and overpower your enemies. I out-think them."

"You can't out-think an energy beam," Daelen disputed.

"Really? I think Aden would say I just did. He was predictable, that's why I could deflect his weapon blast. I anticipated he would do it." She left out the part about her magic having a temporal element. “I’m concerned that your power may lead you to underestimate our enemy and in my experience that is fatal. Across this continent, there are bashed and broken towers, the bastions of wizards, some of whom are bashed and broken themselves. They underestimated me and look where it got them.

“We’ve said the rules have changed, Daelen, but I fear that you have not. You’re set in your ways, predictable. Your enemy has adapted. You must change, too, and I think I can help you with that. Lower power weapons, wielded with guile, ingenuity and creativity can usually win the day. In short, I believe in brain over brawn. With you and me together, we have both. That’s why I should be with you.

“Second, there’s my research. There’s somewhere en route to our destination that I’ve always wanted to visit but never had the means. You do. Joining with you is my best chance for success in my research, and as far as I'm concerned, that means my place is at your side. I'm your shadow now, Daelen, so you'd better get used to it.”

When it became apparent that Cat wasn't going to say any more, Daelen prompted, “What's the third reason? You said there were three.”

Of course, she had just been waiting for him to bite.

Flashing him a dazzling smile, and fluttering her eyelashes, she explained, “That's simple. Why go off alone when you can enjoy the sweet, charming and delightful company of yours truly?”

Michael rumbled with laughter. “I think you buried the headline there, Cat. Tell you what, my dear, why don’t you walk with me a bit while he reaches the only sensible conclusion he could come to. He can catch us up, you can tell us where we’re going, and then we’ll go our separate ways. Don’t forget, you need to get Daelen’s essence out of you, too.”

Cat took Michael’s arm and began walking with him.

“I won’t forget,” she assured him, although the druidess had no intention of giving it up until she’d determined whether it would help her understand her staff more and she couldn’t test that theory until Michael was far away.

“Tell me honestly,” Michael requested, smiling conspiratorially. “Are there really bashed and broken towers all across the continent, owned by bashed and broken wizards?”

Cat matched his smile with one of her own.

"OK, I may have exaggerated, slightly," she confessed. "I've demolished a total of three towers…and I rebuilt them all, afterwards and no-one got hurt apart from once when I lost concentration, and a brick landed on the wizard's foot. But I healed him right away."

Michael laughed. "Catriona Redfletching, you are a rebel."

"Well, a friend of mine has taught me that it's often good to have something of a reputation. It has a way of making people more co-operative."

"Couldn't agree more, my dear. Why do you think the gods made me look like this?"

"Oh, I don't know," Cat disputed, leaning close. "I think you're quite cuddly, really."

Chapter 9

Daelen caught up with the other two and agreed to Catriona's terms.

"Takes him a while, doesn't it, Michael?" Cat commented with a sly wink.

Michael snorted. "For him, that was fast."

"I'm glad I'm splitting you two up. You're a bad influence on him, Cat."

"Yes, I know, I'm trouble," Cat admitted. "But don't worry, you'll soon learn to love me."

Without any further ado, she took out the map Dreya had given her and unfurled it to show her two companions where they were going.

As one might expect, Daelen had explored most of Tempestria in his long life, and he remembered the area. On the southern edge of the Rhynas Desert, lay a forest called the Corolis Wood. Just as the foliage got noticeably thinner, there lay the ruins of an ancient temple. Michael knew it well and confirmed the map co-ordinates. That became the designated rendezvous. Using their powers to cross the ocean was best avoided as it was bound to be detected by Kullos. That meant a voyage of approximately ten to twelve days, but Daelen was keen to stop for a week part way there. He wouldn't immediately say where or why; only that it was necessary. Once on land, the journey would take another four or five days from the nearest harbour. That was three to three-and-a-half weeks until they could meet at the temple ruins.

As for what they would do about Kullos' army when they got there, well, they had a few weeks to think about that. Cat indicated that she had a few ideas but would say no more for now. She couldn't even if she wanted to because many of her ideas relied upon Dreya. Even allowing for any complications that might delay their journey, they should have time to scout around for a day or two before finalising their plans. They would begin the attack in exactly one moon cycle.

They were all clear on the plan as far as it went, so Michael bade them farewell and teleported away.

*****

Daelen wanted to remove his essence from Catriona's body as soon as possible, but Cat insisted on showing him something first, and retrieved her Crystal Mage Staff from her pocket dimension.

The shadow warrior admitted he had never seen a device quite like it before, "containing all those different powers together like that. Like a perfect merging of the technology of my realm with the magic of yours."

"Having seen Michael's tomb, I wondered if it was something like that. Any idea to what purpose?"

"None that I can think of," Daelen admitted. "Do you mind if I take a closer look?"

"Sure, go ahead," Catriona agreed and held it out to him.

The instant their hands touched on the staff, there was a mighty discharge of power, the blue crystal flared, and Daelen screamed in pain. Cat yanked the staff free of his grasp, but the damage was done, and Daelen collapsed to the ground, drained of energy, unable to move and barely conscious.

Cat immediately shoved her staff back into her pocket dimension out of harm's way, vowing that this was the last time she was letting anybody touch it. Cursing herself, she belatedly realised it was a clear pattern: Mandalee, Dreya and now Daelen – the more powerful they were, the bigger the reaction.

"Daelen!" she cried, rushing to his side. "I'm so sorry. That was stupid. How bad is it? Can I help?"

Most druid magic in the world was used for healing, of course, but Cat herself had minimal experience of it. Besides, her powers worked with nature, and Daelen's nature was quite literally alien. She wouldn't know where to start.

"I'll— I'll be OK. Just get me somewhere— somewhere warm and secure so I can recharge...sleep. I'm— I'm in your hands, Catriona Redfletching. Strangely, I'm not as worried about that as I should be."

Cat thought quickly. She considered breaking into Justaria's house – she was reasonably sure she'd understand and forgive under the circumstances. She dismissed the idea, though. She didn't have time and energy to waste, trying to penetrate her magical defences. Even more ludicrous was the notion of a sympathic communication to Dreya, to ask if she'd mind sheltering the being that she was still at least half convinced she should kill. No, Daelen presented too tempting a target in his present state. Fortunately, their sympathic link wasn't active at the moment, meaning Dreya was busy and not paying attention. As long as Cat didn't transmit a sympathic shout, she could keep her girlfriend out of this.

In the end, she knew of only one place nearby that would work. Warm, dry, comfortable, defensible and a public building, so no problems getting inside, though it would create quite the stir. She briefly cursed the cosmos that kept bringing her back to that place, like some awful, offensive joke, but it was still the right choice. It wasn't that far, but she couldn't carry Daelen there. Well, the druidess reconsidered, she could if she were to change into something large enough. Cat had been working on a grizzly bear form, but that might start a panic and make things worse.

Maybe there was merit in her first idea, after all, with just a slight alteration. Not breaking into Justaria's house, but her stable, instead. Any Tempestrian of Justaria's standing would have their own horse, and the stable would have less security than her home. Again, Catriona could have changed into a horse herself – she'd done it before – but Daelen couldn't get himself onto her back without help.

"Daelen," she began, "I'm going to get us a horse, but I'll need you to help me get you onto it, so save your strength, OK?" Daelen nodded, so Cat continued, "It'll only take a minute or two – for once I'm going to take your brute force approach."

Running over to Justaria's stable, which stood at the far side of her house, out of sight of where Daelen lay in her garden, Cat took one look at the wooden doors and immediately knew the fastest way of gaining access. Grabbing her little-used bow and arrows from her pocket dimension, she called upon even less-used wizard magic to light a small fire at the end. She fitted the flaming arrow and fired, using her druid powers to turn that flame into an explosion large enough to blow the doors off entirely. She would accept responsibility for the damage at a later date, once the crisis was over. Putting bow and arrows away, she ran inside the stable, projecting sympathic reassurance and calm to Justaria's horse. She threw on minimal tack and saddle as quickly as possible and walked the horse out.

As she led it around the front of the house, she was shocked to see someone dressed all in white, sprinting towards the fallen shadow warrior, with some kind of magical sword in their hand. Acting fast, Cat asked the grounds to please grab them, while she simultaneously threw a water bottle, to land, with the aid of the wind, between the would-be assassin and their target. The water spilt and grew into an ice wall, separating them. The assassin hacked free of the restraining vegetation and spun to face Cat.

They gasped when they saw they saw each other.

"Mandalee?"

"Catriona?"

Continuing to walk the horse up the garden path, Cat approached her old friend, warily, telling the garden to stand down for the moment. She collapsed the ice wall only when she was in a position to stand in between hunter and prey herself.

"Why are you trying to kill Daelen?" Cat asked. "He's not a demon!"

"I don't just hunt demons anymore," Mandalee replied, "I'm an assassin now. I hunt the wizards who summon demons in the first place."

"But Daelen isn't a wizard, and he doesn't summon demons."

"His kind cause a lot more damage than any demon," Mandalee insisted. "You've never had much love for them before, why are you defending him now?"

"Well, for one thing, it's my fault he's in the state he's in right now. Besides, I've talked to him, and I'm starting to see him in a different light."

"I've talked to him, too," Mandalee retorted. She glanced at her timepiece. "About two hours ago. He was rude, arrogant and condescending."

"Oh, I see, and those are capital crimes now, are they?" Cat shot back.

"No, but destroying the world is."

*****

That morning, the demon-hunter-turned-assassin opened her eyes and immediately regretted it, the brightness of the sun was too much for her today.

"Dear gods, what was I drinking last night?" she groaned and lay back in bed.

For a moment, Mandalee couldn't remember where she was. Then it came flooding back: Walminster. She hadn't expected to be back in this area after only two years – or ever, really – but this was where she had to be.

About a fortnight ago, she had accepted a most unusual contract. Strangely, she couldn't remember much about her meeting with her client. Female, she thought, although Mandalee of all people was wary of making snap judgements about such things. Still, she knew who her target was, that was the important thing. That knowledge and the rightness of this task burned in her mind.

The timing was critical, and she'd been on the wrong side of the continent. Five hundred miles to travel in fifteen days. Thankfully, it was summer, so it was doable. She'd thought about calling her giant albatross for a lift, but that would have meant leaving Shyleen behind. That she would not do.

Despite being assured that if she struck at the time and place that she'd been told about, her prey would be weakened sufficiently for her to take out, she was still going to need all the help she could get.

As it was, by changing horses regularly, she'd made it with a day to spare, so she'd taken the opportunity to check out the renowned city nightlife. Given the nature of her assignment, she thought it might very well be her last night on Tempestria, so she really let herself go. She found a bar that looked promising. Good music, great dancing and a whole lot of drinking. Mandalee even decided to forgo her mask, and the entire night went off almost without a hitch. Except for one particular bartender who decided to address Mandalee as 'sir' in a really pointed way. The first time she let it go. The second time, she gave him a warning look. The third time she told him that if he said it one more time, she would give him a reason to question his own gender identity by cutting off a particular part of his anatomy. After that, he wisely kept his comments to himself and Mandalee had thoroughly enjoyed herself.

A little too much, it seemed, because she suddenly realised it wasn't just the brightness of the sun that had bothered her, but also its position in the sky. She'd overslept.

She leapt up, gathered her things and mentally called for Shyleen.

"Well done, Mandalee," she berated herself. "Today the world ended because the person who was supposed to stop it went out partying all night. But hey, she had a great time, so it's not all bad."

She forced herself to calm down. The Council building was only five minutes down the road, and it was something of a transport hub with stagecoaches ranging out all over. It was vital that she make it in time. Fortunately, she knew the place quite well: Compton, just ten miles outside Walminster. The town where she'd first met Catriona in the form of a naked boy with nothing but a strategically placed staff. She couldn't help a small smile at the memory, but she stifled it instantly. That part of her life was in the past, while she needed to focus on the present. She could afford no more delays or mistakes. Everything was depending on her to get this right, for Mandalee's target wasn't a Trickster, a wizard, or even a Greater Demon. Her objective was something much, much worse.

She had to kill Daelen StormTiger because, her client had told her, if Mandalee didn't stop him…

…he was going to destroy the world.

*****

Mandalee had no sooner reached the Council building than a strange ball of blue light appeared in the sky, through which stepped Daelen StormTiger, accompanied by his usual signature freak storm, disrupting the natural weather patterns of the day.

Anticipating an attack of some kind, the wizards and other locals fled the scene. Mandalee just froze. She was supposed to kill him in less than two hours while he was 'weak and vulnerable.' Yet here he was, flying overhead apparently at full strength and power. Did he know? Was he here to kill her first? There was no point running. It wouldn't make any difference if he attacked her now.

'*Maybe he's here for some other reason,*' she sent to Shyleen. '*Maybe he won't even notice me.*'

"You there!" Daelen called out. Mandalee winced. "You! Dressed all in white with the cat!"

'*Not a word,*' the assassin warned her leopard before she could project a wise-crack into her head. So much for not noticing her. She consoled herself with the reminder that at least she'd had one fantastic party before she died.

"Can I, erm, sorry, can I help you?" she yelled up at him.

"Are you a wizard?" he asked.

Mandalee couldn't believe what she was hearing. A higher planar being stopping a passing human for a chat. If she hadn't been so terrified, she would have laughed.

"Not a wizard, sorry."

"It's OK if you really are a wizard," Daelen assured her. "You don't need to worry. I promise I didn't do it."

"Oh no, sorry, I'm sure you didn't," Mandalee called back, having no idea what he was talking about. "But honestly, I'm a cleric. So, if you've got an injury you want me to look at, I'm your gal!" She let out a nervous giggle. "Otherwise, sorry, I don't think I can help you. Sorry."

'*Why do you keep apologising?*' asked Shyleen in her head.

'*I don't know. I have no idea what I'm saying.*' Mandalee thought back.

'*That is obvious,*' Shyleen snarked in response.

Daelen laughed. "As if I would ever need healing from a mortal – no offence."

'*Quite a lot taken if you don't mind,*' she grumbled to Shyleen.

"I rarely even talk to you lot – you're just not interesting enough yet – but you still might be able to help me," the shadow warrior continued. "Where might I find the home of one called Justaria?"

"Well, as I say, I'm not a wizard," Mandalee repeated through gritted teeth, "so I'm not exactly familiar with…"

'*Stop!*' Shyleen cried out in her mind. '*You may not know where this Justaria lives, but you know where Daelen is supposed to be two hours from now. Why not send him there?*'

'*That's a ridiculous idea,*' Mandalee shot back. '*I love it.*'

"But wait!" she called out again before he could fly away. "I think I have heard that one, now that I think about it. Yes! I remember now. You need to fly to a town called Compton, roughly ten miles northeast. Can't be more specific, but failing anything else, just ask at the *FaerWay Tavern*."

"Good enough," Daelen accepted, and then flew off without so much as a 'thank you.'

"You're welcome!" she called out, anyway. "Don't mention it. Oh, that's right – you didn't."

'*I am so going to kill him.*'

'*If you get there in time,*' Shyleen sent back.

Mandalee looked at her timepiece and swore. Thanks to the shadow warrior's appearance, everyone had scattered – people and horses alike. If she could set off now, a horse and coach might just make it, but by the time things settled down enough, it was going to be too late.

'*I'm going to have to fly. Sorry, Shyleen, you'll have to make your own way there.*'

Shyleen sent a mental farewell and immediately ran off, while her friend used her magic to summon her flight.

"Rule one: don't let your prey see you coming," she berated herself as she waited impatiently. "It's rule one! But no, I've got a better idea: why not give your prey directions to the place you're going to kill them? Dear gods, I need a drink!"

Chapter 10

Outside Justaria's house, Daelen weakly protested at Mandalee's assertion, but Cat shushed him.

"This is a private conversation," she insisted, "it's nothing to do with you. Just get on the horse."

She helped him stand and mount up. He was still vulnerable and she needed to get him away, but she couldn't turn her back on Mandalee when she was in this mood.

"What are you talking about?" she demanded. "He's not planning to destroy the world."

"OK, let's say he isn't. Let's say it's something he does by accident. So what? When a wizard lets a demon loose, whether it's a plan or an accident makes no difference to those it kills. If the world ends, it doesn't matter whether it was intentional or not."

"But how could your client possibly know about Daelen destroying the world by accident before it happens?"

"I don't know, but she was right about him being weak and vulnerable if I attacked here and now."

Cat was stunned. "Your client told you that? When?"

"A couple of weeks ago, now."

"But it only happened a few minutes ago!"

"Exactly," Mandalee concurred. "So, if my client was right about that, maybe she was right about the rest."

Cat shook her head. She hadn't been convinced by Daelen's claim about a Time traveller before, and while evidence was starting to mount up, now, Cat continued to be sceptical. She certainly wasn't ready to surrender her free will or Daelen's life to some vague prophecy that may or may not be from the future.

"Who is this client of yours?" Cat wanted to know. "And don't give me any crap about confidentiality."

For the first time, Mandalee seemed to waver in her certainty. "Actually, confidentiality is kind of moot…I don't really remember much about her."

"How can you not remember?" Cat was incredulous.

"I don't know," Mandalee admitted. "It's all kind of vague. All I know is that it feels…right that I kill him."

Catriona latched onto that. "You mean, like a post-hypnotic suggestion?"

"Yes, now you mention it," the assassin agreed in surprise. "That's a brilliant description. How in the world did you come up with it?"

"I've…" Cat hesitated. She couldn't talk about Dreya. "…heard of similar things before. The point is, do you really think that's a good enough basis for killing Daelen? When you go after a wizard, do you kill him just because of some vague feeling, because somebody points a finger, or do you do your research?"

"I…do my research," Mandalee answered.

She hated to admit it, but her old friend made a good point. All of a sudden, this action didn't feel as right as it had before.

"Maybe your client is from the future, maybe not, I don't know. What makes you so sure she's telling the truth? OK, she was right about today – that doesn't mean she's right about tomorrow. Suppose someone told you it's going to rain today, and it does, are you going to automatically believe everything they say from then on?"

Mandalee gave a wry smile. "As I recall, you can use your magic to make it rain anytime you want."

"Precisely," the druidess agreed. "If your client really is from the future, who knows what powers they might have to influence what happened today?"

Mandalee groaned. "Why are things always so complicated with you around, Cat?"

"The world's a complicated place," she replied with a shrug. "I just embrace that. Right now, there's more going on than you realise. Tell me, have you heard any reports of wizards and clerics going missing? Or an increase in missing persons, generally?"

Mandalee confirmed that she had. She had assumed there had been an increase in demon activity.

"You're right, but not in the way you mean. Kullos is building an army of mortals and demons."

"He's what? Seriously?"

Catriona nodded. "Daelen and I, we have a plan – sort of – and I'm going with him."

"What?" Mandalee snorted. "You're going to save the world, now?"

Cat shook her head and chuckled, gently. "Nothing so grand. I'm just going to do what I always do: gather information, gain knowledge, find out how it all fits together and act on what I learn. My almost killing Daelen wasn't part of the plan, so I'm not going to let you finish the job."

"But what if you're wrong? There may be no other chance to stop him, like I was told."

"Wait – is *that* what your client said? Her exact words? 'Stop him'?"

"Yes, that was it, I remember now. She said, 'He's going to destroy the world. You must stop him.' What's your point?"

"That's for you to work out. Sorry, Mandalee, but I can't discuss it any longer." She mounted up behind Daelen and took the reins. "The bottom line is, Daelen and I are going now. I won't fight you, Mandalee. Never. But for the moment, Daelen is under my protection, so to kill him, you'll have to kill me, too. I don't believe you'll do that."

Without another word, Cat nudged the horse into a trot out of Justaria's garden, which now looked somewhat worse for wear, and out into the street.

As Mandalee watched them ride away, a familiar feline figure emerged from the shadows.

'*How long have you been there?*' Mandalee asked.

'*Long enough,*' Shyleen replied.

'*What do you think she meant?*'

'*That sometimes you are meant to kill and sometimes you are not.*'

'*But I'm an assassin and a demon hunter,*' Mandalee protested.

'*That is not* all *you are,*' the leopard countered.

Mandalee shook her head, emphatically.

'*I left all the other parts behind a long time ago.*'

'*You left them near here when I got hurt,*' Shyleen pointed out, philosophically, 'so *you are in the perfect place to pick them up again.*'

*****

When Daelen StormTiger came around, he found himself lying on a bed in one corner of what appeared to be an inn. It was quite the hive of activity.

Catriona Redfletching was standing over him, protectively, with her back to him, staff in one hand, while her other hand hovered near her belt from which all of her spell components hung. She was watching the crowd intently, ready to strike at the first wrong move. Pyrah was reared up on a barstool, hissing and showing her deadly fangs. The plants in the tavern had grown considerably, too, creating a natural barrier. Several blackened, smouldering marks suggested that the druidess had made her power and intent quite clear, and judging by the faces of those around, Daelen could tell they were convinced.

"Look, I'm really quite easy to get along with," Cat was saying, "but my friend needs undisturbed rest, and I do not know who I can trust. Therefore, I will not risk any of you coming near while he is vulnerable, or trying to leave, so word gets out to an assassin. I apologise for the inconvenience and the disruption to your day, but please just stay calm, enjoy your drinks, your games and your conversation like nothing special is happening. Then no-one will get hurt."

As an additional precaution, Daelen did not look like himself. He was using something he called a 'perception filter,' which worked even on minimal power. This meant that anyone who was not expecting to see Daelen would just see an average guy, with no particularly distinctive features. Most people wouldn't know higher planar energy if it was clearly labelled, so almost anyone who tried to get a power reading would think he was just some wizard. The latest in a line of wizard lovers that rumour insisted Catriona had enjoyed.

Just then, Pyrah looked around and saw Daelen was awake.

Daelen guessed she must have sent a sympathic message to her half-Faery friend, because Catriona remarked over her shoulder, "So, you're back with us then, eh? How are you feeling?"

"What happened?" he asked. "What's going on?" Then with a weak smile he added, "and while I'm going for the clichés, 'Where am I'?"

"You passed out on the way," Cat explained. "It was all I could do to keep you from falling off. As for where," she pointed to a twisted metal sign on the floor that depicted a Faery with wings hovering over a road, along with the words '*FaerWay Tavern.*'

"That's disgusting," Daelen spat.

"Well, I don't like vandalism, either," Cat replied defensively, "but I couldn't stand to look at it any longer."

Daelen shook his head and winced. "No, I mean, the *sign* is disgusting," he clarified, then in answer to Catriona's surprised look, saying, "A very long time ago, a…" he hesitated, "…friend once taught me a few things about Faery culture."

Rose. Her name was Rose. She had been with him for twenty years, all those centuries ago. Twenty years exactly from the day they met to the day she left. Seeing the way Catriona used magic was bringing forth old memories. Painful memories. Good memories.

Before he could try to speak further, she hushed him.

"Just relax, sleep…or I'll knock you out myself."

By the look in her eyes, Daelen was prepared to believe she might just carry out that threat, and he was in no position to argue. He couldn't remember the last time he felt so powerless. By contrast, Catriona looked so formidable. He realised it made her very attractive, but he dismissed the observation as a symptom of exhaustion.

"Yeah, I hate this place," Cat agreed, in response to his earlier point, "but it was the only practical option."

She went on to explain how a couple of helpful souls had 'volunteered' to fetch a bed from one of the rooms. There was no way she was letting them get trapped in one small room with only one way out.

"It's amazing how helpful people can become when they meet my sweet serpent," she reflected, stroking Pyrah's head for a moment. "Pyrah just seems to have that kind of positive effect. Once you were settled, though, I had to take a few…precautions to make sure you got the rest you needed."

Cat grabbed a drink from a nearby table and threw it a few feet in front of her. The glass smashed, the contents pooled on the floor, and she used that liquid to create a frozen shield of ice to further cut off the crowd.

Relaxing, she sat down on a stool and casually inspected her fingernails. "So, it's all been quite exciting, really."

Daelen couldn't help smiling at his companion's attitude, but there was one thing she seemed to have forgotten: there was still a piece of him inside her.

"It would be best if you gave me back to myself, now," he told her.

"Best for me or best for you?" the druidess asked, pointedly.

"Cat…" Daelen began, understanding but not wanting to answer.

Catriona was having none of it.

"Don't avoid the question. Would returning your essence to you now, as you are, in this state, be good for you or not? And don't even think about lying to me."

"No," Daelen answered reluctantly. "It would be better for you, but expending effort on reintegration would set back my recovery significantly."

"How long before you recharge?"

"Three, maybe four hours."

"Then thank you for your concern, but the subject is now closed for at least the next three hours. It's my fault we're in this mess and my responsibility to get us out of it. You say you're not a hero, so don't act like one. Don't worry about saving me, save yourself first. I can defend this position against just about anybody mortal, but if your clone decides to drop by again, I'll need you at full strength."

"I can see there's no use arguing with you."

"Good, you're learning. Now, those three hours don't start until you're asleep. There's nothing to worry about, so just close your eyes."

*****

But for my mother, there *was* something to worry about, gentle reader. She didn't plan on telling Daelen this, but after her confrontation with Mandalee, something strange had happened. Her staff fell out of her pocket dimension – that hadn't happened for years. She caught it, reflexively, almost letting Daelen fall off the horse in the process, and an otherworldly voice came to her:

White faction first attempt gone. Two attempts remain.

*****

"Go to sleep," Cat insisted, "or I'll start singing '*Angels Among Us*'."

"What's that?" Daelen wondered.

"Oh, just an old Faery lullaby. It was the first thing that popped into my head."

"Then sing it," he requested with a smile.

Cat flushed, clearly embarrassed. "What? You want me to sing a children's lullaby to a 'grown man' in front of all these people?" she whispered.

"Why not? You brought it up."

"I wasn't serious," she insisted. "What will they think?"

"They'll think it's cute."

"Exactly. I'm trying to act tough, not cute."

"Are you saying you can't do both at the same time?" Daelen asked, slyly.

Catriona couldn't believe it. Suggesting she couldn't do something was the surest way to make her determined to do it. She saw it as a challenge. But they'd only just met – how could he possibly know that?

"Oh, alright!" she surrendered. "But if the lullaby doesn't send you to sleep in five minutes, I'm knocking you out instead."

They spoke no more, then, as Catriona sang[1]:

Angels among us, stars in the night,
Watch o'er your sleep, shining so bright,
Safe in their light, as you close your eyes,
Love will surround you, 'til morning you rise.

Angels among us, shed you no tears,
Bright Angels guard you, quiet your fears,
Nature's embrace, is gentle and strong,
Love will surround you, all your life long.

*****

---

[1] Fits to the tune of Rockabye Baby

That lullaby brings back memories for me, gentle reader. It was sung to me many times when I was little. Hearing it like this, I can close my eyes and almost believe my mother is singing it to me, though of course she never could.

Chapter 11

Dreya the Dark was surprised by an alert. It was telling her there was someone in her grounds that her defences had identified as a threat. For a sorceress of Dreya's power and ability, there was very little in the world to which she would attach that designation. She peered out of a window, and her eyes widened at what they were showing her. She hurried downstairs, emerging from her front entrance, just as her visitor reached the base of the steps that led up to her porch.

Her visitor grinned, manically, and greeted her with, "Hello, you. Today's your lucky day. Of all the mortals in all the world, I've chosen you to be my new pet! Isn't that brilliant?"

Dreya had to remind herself not to use his new chosen name – she didn't want him to know about her link with Catriona. She could only refer to him – if she must address him at all – as Daelen's dark clone.

*****

Let me pause for a moment, gentle reader, to catalogue the power at Aunt Dreya's disposal, as she did then, mentally, trying to make an unbiased estimate of its effectiveness against this higher planar being.

She had her straightforward wizard magic, of course, which was by itself beyond what any other wizard could boast. Blood magic was available by pricking her finger. That was best facilitated via the red and white roses that had framed her door since Catriona first 'proposed.' Cat had worked on them since, and they were now intertwined with Ulvarius' black ones, as a symbol of the three factions of magic, working together to advance its potential. Or as Cat had succinctly put it: diversity is strength. It would be better to use the red or white ones, however, because they were blessed by a White cleric, Mandalee. They wouldn't hurt as much as the first time, thanks to the indirect sympathic link, via Catriona. The pain Dreya would feel she was willing to accept in exchange for adding an element of cleric magic to her attacks, along with Catriona's druid gifts. Add to that her power words:

compressed magic ready to fly at her enemy in an instant, plus her intense, high energy beam, modelled on what Daelen and the others fought with. Finally, through the study of Catriona's staff, she had a better understanding of how to combine the three flavours of magic with higher planar energy.

As I mentioned earlier, Dreya had been investigating the sites of wizard disappearances. Those sites that could be identified by the presence of higher planar energy that still lingered there. But if you thought she was doing that for purely altruistic reasons, gentle reader, then you really haven't been paying attention. Certainly, she did not like the erosion of magic that the loss of wizards would cause, but that would not be sufficient reason for her to investigate personally.

No, it wasn't so much the missing wizards that interested her; it was the residual higher planar energy.

*****

Even with all she now commanded, Dreya knew that if Aden-El had not been so depleted from his recent battle, she would have been in trouble. Then again, if Aden-El had not been so depleted, he would have had no need of her.

Casually pricking her finger on the thorn of a red rose, Dreya the Dark felt her powers combine within her body, allowing them to swell slowly, gradually.

"Is this the part where I'm supposed to be flattered that a being such as yourself considers me worthy of such an honoured position as your pet?"

"Not worthy, no, but you are the only mortal wizard whose power even registers."

Dreya knew that was nonsense. She could be of no possible use to him unless he honestly believed Aden plus Dreya would overpower Daelen plus Michael. Taking the equation further, since Daelen and Aden were equal in power, that meant he must consider Dreya to be more powerful than Michael. She wasn't sure if that was true, but if she played this right, it soon could be.

Not reacting to the insult, she simply asked, "I take it you want my assistance against Daelen StormTiger?"

"If you catch on that quickly, you might be more useful than I thought," he retorted.

"Well, that's a remarkable coincidence, because I've been interested in killing him for quite some time."

"Oh yes, coincidence is the word," Aden agreed, nodding. "It's not like I heard a rumour or anything. That would be ridiculous!"

Still refusing to rise to the bait, Dreya remained calm, her face impassive.

"But the thing is, you're his dark clone," she reasoned, "which, as I understand it, means, essentially, you *are* Daelen StormTiger."

"I am as he, and he is as me," Aden replied, obviously trying to sound clever, rather than just saying 'yes' like a normal person.

"In that case," she considered, "I don't see why I need to go hunting for Daelen…not when, to all intents and purposes, he's standing right in front of me."

Drawing her magic through her blood – her own wizard magic, plus a helping of druid magic from Cat and a hint of cleric magic from Mandalee, she teleported behind him, unfolded her power word, "PAIN," and Aden was in agony. While he was off-balance, not allowing him time to regroup, she hit him with wave after wave of wizard spells. Whenever he seemed to be on the verge of recovery, she brought to bear another of her power words: 'STUN' 'FREEZE' 'BURN' 'BREAK' 'SHATTER.' She knew 'DIE' wouldn't be effective. Not until she wore him down. As she fought, she was always on the move – something she had learned from Catriona.

She kept her grounds' defences powered down because they would be ineffective against him – after all, they had been useless against her when she took the Black Tower. Better to keep them intact for more mundane threats, rather than let Aden destroy them. She did, however, instruct her elite guards to stand ready in specific positions around the 'battlefield.' They would not interfere unless Dreya mentally ordered it. If things started to go wrong, they might prove enough of a distraction to let her execute an emergency teleport, but she was confident that would not be necessary.

Principally, they were there for another purpose. Not having a temporal element to her magic, unlike Catriona, Dreya needed time to weave her magical shields into the right form to absorb or deflect the energy of his beam cannon. Not just around herself, but around her guards, as well. Now they were all ready. So, taking another leaf out of her girlfriend's playbook, she decided it was time to set a trap with an easy escape, see if it would goad him into springing the real trap.

Instead of attacking him directly, as she had been, she 'trapped' him in a twenty-foot-tall cylinder of fierce, magical flames. This was the moment Dreya would find out if she'd got her calculations right, although if she hadn't, she didn't suppose she'd live long enough to regret it. Her four death knights stepped out onto the battlefield, coming to stand at four compass points around the column of fire. The three ghouls also emerged, floating ten feet off the ground, again forming a ring around the fire. Dreya levitated at the pinnacle of an irregular pyramid, relative to her guards.

Aden recovered quickly, flying up and out of the firetrap, pulling his powerful cannon out of his pocket dimension.

"Big mistake, little pet," he taunted. "Some of your pinpricks were actually starting to hurt. But as fun as this has been, it's time to have you put down."

As much as he was trying to hide it, in reality, he was in a lot of pain, and the humiliation of that pain being inflicted by a mere mortal helped morph that into rage. A rage that he channelled into his cannon blast as he streaked upwards towards Dreya, following in the wake of his own power. He expected the blast to kill the witch but instead, she absorbed what she could and reflected the rest, the beam splitting into three until they each hit one of her ghouls. Each ghoul absorbed as much as they could, channelling and equalising it in a ring between them, before passing it down to the death knights. They, in turn, created their circle of power, completing the circuit. Before Aden knew what was happening, he was hit by eight separate high energy beams. Trapped inside this pyramid of power, he couldn't escape. Since the attacks were coming from all directions, there was nowhere to go. He tried to teleport, but Dreya had already taken steps to prevent that. Finally, the beams stopped, and he fell all the way down to the ground, hitting with a hard impact.

Dreya floated gently down and disclosed, "I've been working on my own version of what you just did. Let me show you." A beam of magical energy shot out from her hand, backed up by the extra power she had gained from absorbing part of his attack. "I think I've got the technique down pretty well, but I'd appreciate any feedback you might have." She shot him a second time. "Well?" She shot him a third time. "Did I do it right, or do you have notes?"

Now that he was stunned, she began siphoning off his power, taking as much as she dared to absorb without risking her own safety. Once he was sufficiently drained, a power word backed up with blood magic should be enough to finish him.

"I suppose this is the part where I make some grand, gloating speech while talking about myself in the third person," she deadpanned as she checked the preparation of the power word – this was one she did not want to get wrong.

As she prepared, however, she felt that post-hypnotic suggestion kick-in again. The same voice that had been telling her to kill Daelen was now warning her it was too soon. For a moment, she thought she caught sight of a shadowy figure at the edge of her vision. Perhaps the source of the warning. Refusing to be dictated to, however, Dreya chose to ignore it.

"But in the interests of avoiding the clichés, all I'll say is—" she never got to the word 'DIE' because Aden pulled out a knife and threw it at her. Not expecting that kind of attack, she only partially deflected it, and it took a slice out of her right arm. It only took her a moment to recover, but it was long enough for Aden to open up a Prismatic Sphere and escape.

Dreya swore, cursing herself for her hesitation and letting him get way. She'd won the battle on points but missing out on the kill was annoying as hell. Still, there was nothing to be done about it now. Thanks to Aden, she was more powerful than ever – or she would be after she'd rested and healed. She'd just have to kill the dark clone another day. Kill him and drain his power. She couldn't take it all at once without harming herself, but between Dreya and her elite guards, it would be safe enough. Or maybe she'd go after Daelen next. She was happy for Cat to gain his knowledge – she was exceptionally good at that – but when the time was right, Dreya would have his power, too. After that, they wouldn't need Daelen to go after Kullos. She could just do it herself. Then the world would finally be rid of all three of them, and she would forever be the Greatest Mage Who Ever Lived.

*****

Miles away, in the *FaerWay Tavern*, the crystal on Catriona's staff glowed, and she heard the same ethereal voice that had spoken before:

Black faction first attempt gone. Two attempts remain.

*****

Daelen awoke after a little over three hours. Cat could see he was looking a lot better. His energy levels were back up again – not all the way but improving almost in front of her eyes.

Cat asked if it was now safe to give back that portion of his essence that she still held inside. It had definitely been useful, helping her to unlock more of the security protecting the core power of her staff. Now she wanted it gone.

"Yes," he assured her, "I promise you it's safe. The problem before was the extreme difference in energy levels between what I had when I entered you and what I was left with after the battle and the accident. Now the difference is not so great, it will not be such a shock to my system."

"OK, I take it that means we'll have to kiss again?" Cat inquired.

"I'm afraid so. If there were any other way…"

Cat shushed him. "It's just an essence transfer," she reassured him. "No need to make a fuss. As you said, it doesn't mean anything, right?"

"Right," Daelen affirmed as he rose from his bed and stood before her.

For a second, Catriona thought she saw a flicker of disappointment flash across his face, but she dismissed the idea as pure fantasy. Daelen offered to go somewhere private if it made her more comfortable, but Cat just pulled him close and kissed him passionately in front of the whole Tavern. They had no idea there was an essence transfer going on. They thought it was merely the relief of a young woman whose lover had just recovered from a terrible injury. Many of them even applauded.

Playing to the crowd, the druidess curtseyed, and removed all of her magically created barriers with a flourish and a reiterated heartfelt apology for keeping them captive for so long. Pyrah returned to her nest in Catriona's pocket, and the crowd left the Tavern.

To a stunned Daelen, she explained, "People talk, and news of this will spread. They don't know who you are, but many will recognise me in the stories they tell. This way, the narrative will be that Catriona has taken a new wizard lover and they're off on some whirlwind adventure together. If the stories spread to the ears of our enemies, they should have no reason to pay it any heed because they'll have no reason to connect it with you."

"Good plan," Daelen conceded.

"Thanks," Cat smiled. "It's all part of being an information trader. Control the information and you control the situation."

Now that Daelen was back on his feet again, it was time to get back on the road. Having 'borrowed' Justaria's horse, Cat felt responsible for him. The best thing they could do, she decided, was to keep him until they reached the port where Daelen's ship awaited them. The port maintained secure stables for the convenience of travellers. Daelen offered to pay. He insisted it was the least he could do.

"Speaking of trading information," Cat ventured, returning to their previous conversation, "as I mentioned before, there's somewhere I'd like you to take me on our whirlwind adventure. Don't worry, it's on the way – not even a day out of our way. It's on the island of Esca."

"I know it," Daelen agreed. "I'd planned to make a stop anyway, on another island near there, to take on fresh water and supplies."

Puzzled, Catriona dug out her map and unfurled it. "There aren't any other islands near Esca," she asserted.

Daelen just smiled, "Not one you can see, no," he acknowledged, mysteriously. He would say no more about it. She would just have to wait and see.

They engaged in small talk for a while as they rode for a few more hours until it began to grow dark, and Catriona, who had been up for nearly twenty hours straight, yawned repeatedly.

"Daelen, can we stop for the night, soon, please?" she asked sleepily.

"Of course," the shadow warrior agreed. "Do you want to try and find an inn?"

She shook her head. "No need for that. I'm happy to sleep under the stars. It's been a while. Let's just find a comfortable spot before I simply fall asleep right here and fall off the horse. Oh, and do you mind taking first watch?"

Daelen told her she should just sleep and not worry about a thing. Cat maintained that she was quite capable of keeping watch, but he reassured her that he didn't doubt her for a moment.

"The way I see it, you've done more than your share already, today. You guarded me for hours, carrying a part of my essence inside you for far longer than you should. I think it's my turn, now."

Cat decided he was right: she'd scored enough points for one day. Better to make sure she did equally well tomorrow rather than try and score any more tonight.

*****

When Catriona woke up, the first thing she noticed was the smell. Bubbling away over the campfire was a stew pot. Rabbit, if she wasn't mistaken. Daelen was sitting with his back against a tree, blades in his hands as if guarding her, but strangely unmoving. As her brain warmed up, she realised why: Daelen had fallen asleep.

"So much for keeping watch," she grumbled good-naturedly, wandering over to him. "It's a wonder you haven't boiled our breakfast dry."

The instant she touched him, however, he crumbled to dust. Catriona screamed in shock, which was only compounded further when Daelen rushed back to their campsite and ran to her side, asking what was wrong.

Cat poked him in the chest to try and re-establish her grip on reality. Thankfully, this one did not turn to dust.

“What the hell was that?” she demanded.

“Oh yeah,” he replied with a sheepish grin, “I guess I should have told you I can do that. I vanish, leaving a simple copy to make it appear to any onlookers as if I’m there when I’m not.” He explained further that it crumbled because he didn’t have the energy to make it more solid.

The druidess exhaled, deeply, allowing her heartbeat to slow. Torn between hugging him in relief and slapping him for scaring her, she ultimately did neither.

“It's a good thing I like surprises, shadow warrior,” Cat remarked, acidly. “There are plenty of them with you around.”

Daelen laughed, “You're not without a few surprises yourself, my dear druidess. I'm just trying to keep up.”

“Fair comment!” Cat admitted, grinning.

She was definitely wide awake, now, so she suggested he finish cooking breakfast while she had a quick dip in a nearby river.

Chapter 12

Travelling to the harbour at Kingsville Piers took most of what turned out to be a generally uneventful day, other than one slightly awkward conversation they had both been avoiding.

"Daelen," Cat broached at last, "I just wanted to thank you."

"For what?" he asked, knowing full well what she meant.

"For trusting me with part of your essence, part of who – what – you are. When you were inside me, I got a glimpse, no more than that, but enough to realise something I never understood before. Daelen, we throw around words like 'higher planar being' without any real concept of what we're saying. This body isn't really you, is it?"

The shadow warrior shook his head. "No, it's not. Same goes for Kullos and…'Aden.' This body is a shell, albeit one I've grown quite attached to."

"But why are you called *shadow* warriors? All I sensed was light, or at least, that's the closest word I know to describe it."

Daelen flushed as if this was embarrassing to talk about.

"That is because I am incomplete. What Kullos did to the original Daelen StormTiger all those centuries ago split me in two."

"What does that mean?" Cat asked, then when he hesitated, she offered to drop the whole thing.

"No, it's not that," he assured her. "It's just difficult for me to put it in terms you can understand, and I don't mean that to be insulting. The fault lies with my ability to explain rather than any lacking on your side."

"Just do your best," Cat encouraged him.

He considered for a moment, then smiled and stated, "We're light in a box."

"You're what?" Cat laughed.

"We're light in a box," he repeated.

"That's ridiculous."

"Most of the best explanations are," he asserted. "Just imagine it – light in a box."

"OK," Cat agreed.

"Now imagine someone coming along and tearing the box in two. What happens?"

"The light spills out," Cat answered. Then she grasped the implications. "So, what you're saying is, the true nature of your people contains the light, keeps it in shadow, hence the name. But Kullos ripped open your outer shell…" she trailed off, considering her next words, "…your skin?"

"Essentially," Daelen nodded.

Thinking more about the analogy, Cat was horrified.

"So, when you say Kullos ripped your original in two, you mean literally?"

Again, Daelen nodded.

"How are your insides not falling out?" Cat blurted out before she could stop herself.

"Well, physiologically, it's not as serious as it would be if someone cut you open, but it does take effort to keep myself together."

Cat just needed to ask one more thing. "Sorry, Daelen," she broached, tentatively, "I'm trying to find a delicate way of asking this, but when you were inside me, I got the impression…" she trailed off and tried again. "You don't normally show all of your inner light to other people, do you? I mean your people. Routinely."

"Not routinely, no," he agreed.

He explained that his people, the Shadowkin, could make their outer shell semi-translucent to display an aura – the equivalent of facial expressions and body language. A way of conveying emotions. How much they chose to display was governed by complex social norms. Revealing their true inner light, however, was something quite different, and certainly not acceptable in public.

"But you might choose to show it to someone…special?"

"Usually only one. Not always."

"Oh, Daelen, I'm so sorry," Cat offered, eyes glistening. "You shouldn't have had to do that."

"Don't be sorry," he replied, placing a reassuring hand on her arm. "For me, it was little more than breaking a taboo of intimacy – uncomfortable, but not life-changing. You're actually the third person to see my light, which would raise a few eyebrows among my people – if my people had eyebrows. The implications for you were potentially much more serious. I'm just glad you don't seem to have suffered any ill-effects."

"I'm fine," Cat assured him. "It's unlikely either of us would have chosen to do it under other circumstances, but things being as they were, we both fully consented, we both knew what we were doing, and I have no regrets."

"Well if you don't, then neither do I," Daelen agreed. Changing the subject, he remarked, "If you don't mind me saying so, I was impressed with how you handled the pain."

"It was pretty similar to the pain of shapeshifting," she replied.

"It's that painful for you?" he gasped in astonishment. "You seem to do it so freely."

She shrugged. "Pain is part of nature. I simply don't let the pain stop me, just as you don't let yours stop you. Besides, it's mostly outweighed by the joy of being some other creature for a while."

"Well, I'm still sorry I caused you more."

"But Daelen, you've also given me so much knowledge, and that gift is precious to me. Part of my reason for being on this quest with you is to understand you better. Understanding your power, your nature, your pain…it's all the same thing. It's the nature of the Balance."

*****

They reached the harbour at last and left their 'borrowed' horse in the stables. They had no idea when Justaria might be able to reclaim her horse, but Daelen gave them enough money to cover the costs for a whole year, if necessary. If the missing sorceress hadn't returned in that time, then frankly it was highly unlikely she ever would. Catriona wrote a pair of quick notes, one for the Council of Wizards and one for Justaria personally, taking responsibility for the theft of the horse and the damage to her property. She didn't dare risk saying too much beyond 'emergency circumstances,' but she vowed to volunteer herself for a Conclave when she returned.

"In the interests of increased understanding," Daelen ventured as they walked down the harbour in search of the ship he kept on retainer, “before your staff nearly killed me, I was thinking I have seen it before, but I haven't been able to quite remember where.”

“Well, it’s possible you were around one of the times in history when my Angel showed up and made the stars shift.”

“Yes, I suppose that could be it. Anyway, as long as you don’t touch me with it again, I’d be happy to take another look, maybe see if I can unlock its power for you.”

Cat looked troubled by this offer, however.

“If you have information, I will listen, of course, but if you intend to unlock the power itself, then I must refuse. That's not the way – it's not my way. No doubt an agent of Darkness would jump at the chance to increase her own power, and an agent of the Light would be glad of the prospect of using this power to save the world in the coming battles. But I am neither of these things. As an agent of the Balance, I do not seek power for its own sake, and I have no interest in becoming a hero. The edicts of Balance teach that power without context is dangerous, whether used with good or evil intentions. Even the best of intentions can cause great harm. The best way to fight that is with knowledge. For what purpose was the staff created and imbued with this power? Why was the power hidden and the knowledge scattered? Why is it that this power has never been used in the centuries that this staff has existed? Why did my Angel give it to me? I find it hard to accept that only I have the necessary skill and resourcefulness to put the pieces together.” With a smile, she added, “Frankly, I'm not that conceited. When I have a complete understanding of the power of my staff, then I will be qualified to choose how, and indeed whether, the power should be used.”

“Well, it's your staff and your business, so I won't interfere,” Daelen promised. “You must do what you believe is best, but I want to help if you’ll let me.”

“The best way to help is to do what we already planned: let me stop off at Calin's Tower.”

“Why is this place so important to you?” Daelen asked.

Catriona was only too pleased to explain.

Calin was a sorceress of the Balance, who had sacrificed all pursuit of magical power, dedicating her life instead to collecting knowledge. Hers was the ultimate collection of rare magical texts in the whole world. She was also a strong proponent of druid magic being given equal status to wizard magic. Wizard, druid, cleric or just the curious, Calin did not discriminate. Her policy was free access to information for all.

"I could happily get lost in there for weeks, but I know we have our quest to think about, so I will just pay a flying visit."

Cat already new the volumes she wished to borrow, and her staff had a way of drawing her to any others she needed.

"I'm used to studying as I travel, so I won't slow us down. Since I'm the one who insisted on being your shadow, I won't be the one to separate us. You can accompany me in your guise as a wizard. We can use the same rumours that have no doubt spread from the *FaerWay Tavern*, and say you are my current love interest."

"Alright, we'll do as you suggest," Daelen agreed. "I would be honoured to be at your side…my love."

Giving him the side-eye, Cat's only response was, "I don't think there's any need to get into character just yet, Daelen."

"Cat," Daelen began, haltingly, "I know we've only just met, but…"

Before he could finish the thought, he was interrupted by the keening cry of a giant albatross, which promptly came in to land. Cat knew, without looking, who was riding this bird.

"Uh-oh," she remarked. "Here comes trouble."

Mandalee dismounted and sent the bird away, while Daelen, acting on instinct, flew into the air, powering up rapidly. Cat could feel Mandalee gathering her own powers in response.

"Go away, assassin!" he commanded. "Or I'm going to smack you so hard it'll take you a month to fly back. If you survive."

Her green eyes were glowing with fierce anger. "I'm not here for you!" she shot back. "Be thankful for that. I'm here for Catriona."

"No!" Daelen thundered in response. "You will not harm her!"

"I have no intention of harming or even hurting her, I simply need to talk to her. Alone!"

"Request denied, I will not allow it! Go now, while you still can."

Alone and ignored, Catriona looked upon the scene with dismay. They were both her friends, and she couldn't bear to see them tear each other to shreds.

'*But how can I protect one without offending the other?*' she wondered.

Pyrah, sensing her friend's thoughts, observed sympathically, '*Not good.*'

'*I know,*' Cat sent back, '*I've got to stop it.*' Then she had an idea. '*Well, a certain someone's always telling me I have a flair for the dramatic. Maybe I should embrace that.*'

Sensing Catriona's plan, Pyrah wished snakes had eyelids so she could close her eyes to shut out what she feared would be a very messy scene.

Cat used her Windy Steps power to create a staircase of dense air which she then ran up, placing herself high enough to stand directly in the path of any attacks, magical or otherwise. If they wanted to fight each other, they would have to go through her. She pulled out her staff and asked the blue crystal to reflect the light more until it glowed, fiercely, for added theatrical effect.

"I command it;" she declared at the top of her voice, "there will be no battle between you here!" She allowed her words to echo for a moment. When she continued, her voice lost some its fire, but none of its steel. "Mandalee, shut up and calm down. I have sworn not to use my powers to harm you, but I can always restrain you to prevent you from harming yourself." Turning to Daelen, she added, "As for you, what's this you say? You 'will not allow' us to talk? Who the hell do you think you are to decide what you will or will not allow me to do? I am my own woman, and I will talk to whomever I please. Your permission is not required. Power down this instant – and don't flatter yourself that I won't use my magic to restrain you if I must," Cat let her words ring in the air for a long moment, before continuing in a softer tone. "Now, let's all just calm down and try to be sensible about this, shall we?"

Daelen powered down but refused to float back to the ground. Catriona calmly walked down her invisible steps, taking her own good time as a sign that she was still very much in control of this situation. Mandalee was still smouldering but kept a lid on it. She hadn't seen Catriona in this mood before and even with her oath of friendship, she knew better than to push her luck.

“Alright, Cat,” Daelen smoothed, trying to regain some dignity and control. “Talk to your friend, I won't interfere, but I will stay to listen.”

A furious Mandalee shouted into the air, “No. You will not listen. There are some things in this world you need not know. If you know that she and I are friends, then you should also know that she’s completely safe with me.”

Then, looking at Cat, she told her, “I need to talk. If you truly believe there’s a chance of rekindling our old friendship, then come and see me. Alone,” she emphasised. “I do not want ears other than yours and mine to hear. My business is not his. Send me a sympathic message when you’re ready.”

With that, she invoked her super-speed and streaked away.

At last, Daelen floated down to the ground.

Cat wasn’t happy that they’d made such a scene, but replaying their words in her mind, she was at least thankful Mandalee had not used Daelen’s name. With a bit of care, she realised she could quite easily spin the narrative.

To Daelen’s astonishment, she wrapped her arms around his neck and kissed him full on the lips.

“Don’t worry, lover,” she reassured him, raising her voice just enough to be overheard, “she’s just jealous. Let me go and smooth things over with her.”

She leaned close again and whispered, “Play along. Support the story. This is just Catriona Redfletching in the middle of a love triangle. Nothing to do with Daelen StormTiger.”

“Alright Cat,” he acquiesced, matching her tone, following her lead. “I’m sorry about what I said. Of course, you can talk to anyone you want to. I guess I was jealous, too.”

“Nicely done,” she whispered, “and I forgive you.”

*****

Catriona left Pyrah with Daelen. Neither Shadowkin nor Ysirian was happy about it, but Mandalee had insisted on being alone. The druidess wasn’t sure if Mandalee would have a problem with Pyrah, but she didn’t want to risk losing this chance to mend bridges because of a technicality.

Cat sent a sympathic message to Mandalee, asking her location.

Mandalee was rusty at this and returned the image of an anchor, which Cat mistook to mean she was on board a ship. After a couple more goes, Cat finally realised she meant she was at an inn *called* the Anchor. She asked directions of a passer-by, and soon enough she found it. Her old friend was sitting outside. There was a bottle of beer in her hand and another on the table.

Cat sat down opposite and quipped, "Is this drink for me or are you just saving it for later?"

The assassin granted her a half-smile and stated, "It's for my friend."

"It's nice to know I'm still that," Cat replied removing the cap and doing 'cheers' with Mandalee before taking a sip.

"You came when I asked," Mandalee replied, pointedly, "which is an improvement on last time."

"Mandalee, I really am so sorry about what happened. Where is Shyleen, anyway? I trust she's OK?"

The assassin assured her that her feline friend was fine and on her way.

Cat was much relieved to hear it.

"It was two years ago," the assassin shook her head. "Forget it."

"No," Cat refused, resolutely. "I don't want to forget it. I was a terrible friend, and I want to remember it for the rest of my life so I never, ever do anything like it again."

"It just hurt so much when she got zapped by that wizard, I couldn't see for the haze of pain."

"When someone you love is hurt, you feel it, too," Cat agreed.

"It's more than that." Mandalee shook her head and took another long drink. "She's a part of me."

"Of course she is," Cat affirmed, but her friend insisted she still wasn't getting it.

For Mandalee, it wasn't just a metaphor, but it took another half bottle of beer to explain. She became a Cleric of Nature thanks to Shyleen, because Shyleen was no ordinary leopard, just as Pyrah was no regular snake. Although she wasn't from a plane anywhere near that high, in the scheme of things. "Just one level up, in fact," she concluded.

"One level up?" Cat puzzled over that until her brain realised, "Wait, Shyleen's a god?"

"Well," Mandalee replied with another half-smile, "she doesn't like the term – says it's pretentious – but she's from the Pantheon, yes. She was a follower of Blessed Alycia, and as far as Shyleen was concerned, it was Alycia who was a god, not herself."

"Because sometimes even the gods have gods," Cat mused.

"Exactly!" Mandalee gasped. "That's a great way of putting it."

"Just something someone said to me recently," Cat explained dismissively. "So, she came down here because…"

"…Because Blessed Alycia did. According to the legends, anyway."

There was, in fact, much more to the story, but this was neither the time nor the place to tell it. For the moment, she simply explained that Shyleen gave her affinity with nature and access to clerical powers in the faction of Light.

"In exchange for…?" Cat knew these things always came with a price.

"The only thing that would allow her to fully manifest here."

"Which was what?"

The answer to that required the rest of her bottle of beer.

"Half my soul," she admitted quickly.

Cat had no idea what to say. Selling one's soul was traditionally more the province of a Dark wizard in exchange for power.

Mandalee was adamant that she absolutely did not sell her soul. It was an equal share.

"It's a completely different thing," she insisted.

It was a lot to take in, but in the end, it seemed to Catriona that there was only one question of relevance.

"Have you ever regretted it?"

"Never for one fraction of a second."

"Then who the hell am I to judge?"

When they stood up and embraced, Catriona felt as though her heart had just restarted after a two-year break.

"Anyway," Mandalee continued finally, as they sat back down, "the point is, Shyleen forgave you and, I suppose…much as I tried not to…so have I."

Chapter 13

Mandalee explained that it had taken her a while to track down Catriona, using her network of animals. As soon as she realised her friend was heading for the port, she knew she had to act fast if she was going to catch up before Cat boarded a ship. Otherwise, she would have to rely on the intelligence of seagulls. Never a wise move. Unfortunately, there was no way to get a leopard to ride on the back of an albatross.

They both laughed at the idea and just for a moment, it felt as if the friends were slotting back into familiar patterns, but the awkward silence that followed belied that.

After a few minutes, Mandalee asked, "What can you tell me about Daelen?"

"Still want to kill him?"

"Honestly, I don't know what I want. My assignment has become less and less clear. I don't even know who my client is, yet I still have their voice in my head telling me I have to stop Daelen before he destroys the world. Shyleen reckons I need to pick up what I left behind when I walked away from you, you've teamed up with him, and it's all so confusing! What I need…" She trailed off. A moment later, she started again, "What I need is some more pieces to the puzzle."

Cat reached out to place her hands on Mandalee's. "But that confusion is good," she told her. "It means you're thinking for yourself, not just accepting what your mysterious client tells you." She sighed heavily. "Mandalee, maybe this time you're not supposed to kill your mark. There are many ways to stop someone besides killing."

"That thought has occurred to me," Mandalee huffed sullenly, "but what else am I to do? Human relations aren't exactly my area. I'm a bloody assassin for hell's sake!"

Cat offered her a crooked smile, "Well Daelen's not human, and no-one's asking you to have relations with him – he's mine, so hands off."

"What?" Mandalee gasped.

Cat giggled. "No, not really."

She assured her friend that it was just a cover. People knew her, now, so she was trying to generate a rumour that she was off on some wild, romantic quest together with a mysterious and powerful wizard lover. She also talked about Daelen's perception filter, disguising who he really was. A combination of their sympathic link and the fact that she already knew Catriona was with Daelen, meant it didn't work on Mandalee.

"Low profile. Got it." Mandalee nodded. "Actually, I have heard rumours like that about you."

"Excellent, it's working already," Catriona enthused before getting serious again. "An assassin is a hunter. A hunter doesn't always hunt to kill. Sometimes, a hunter hunts for a person or animal that is lost, hurt or in danger, so she can help, not harm, and sometimes people join together to hunt a mark which neither could attempt alone."

The assassin ordered another drink from a passing barmaid. She was going to need it.

"All of which brings me back to, 'What can you tell me about Daelen'?"

*****

By the time Shyleen arrived, Catriona had managed to convince Mandalee to return to the docks with her, where Daelen and Pyrah were waiting in uneasy silence.

Cat asked her old friend to hang back for a moment, while she prepared the way with the shadow warrior, explaining that she hadn't given details of the deeply personal things they had shared, but what she had told her had been enough to convince Mandalee that trying to kill him was not the answer. He was somewhat placated when she explained about the prophecy about him destroying the world.

"To be fair," he accepted, "if my actions were going to destroy the world, I would want someone to stop me, by any means necessary. You don't need to worry, though. Even I don't have that kind of power. Perhaps if I were still whole, I might. Kullos might, too, if he has 'outside help,'" he added, obliquely referring to the void-creature.

Cat introduced them properly, then, and while they were still tense and wary, at least their relationship stopped short of explosive.

They walked along the docks until they finally found Daelen's ship, the *StormChaser*. She was a tall sailing ship with an ornately carved tiger figurehead, three-tone-stained oaken deck, and red and gold sails attached to the three masts. It was by far the most impressive ship in the harbour.

"Isn't she beautiful?" Daelen declared, beaming with pride.

Testing Daelen's sympathic sensitivity, Cat projected the impression of boys and their toys. Then on sudden impulse, she added a rather rude comment, connecting a grown man's need for oversized toys as compensation for a lack in other departments. She couldn't be sure if he got the message since the link was one way, but she was almost certain she saw him blush slightly. She found that gave her a rather perverse sense of satisfaction.

Meanwhile, Mandalee's lips twitched with suppressed laughter and tears formed in her eyes. "You can't possibly be serious!" she blurted out.

Daelen looked hurt. "What's the matter with you?"

Mandalee's laughter was like a dam bursting. She just couldn't hold back the tide any longer.

"Loving the low profile!" she laughed. "You sail in that, nobody's going to suspect a thing!"

Cat, making a supreme effort not to tease him any further, looked up at the shadow warrior who clearly still did not see the problem. She sighed and tried to be as diplomatic as possible.

"Oh, Daelen," she sighed, "this is precisely what I've been trying to tell you. Your power leads you to make basic mistakes. Your problem is, you're not used to thinking strategically. You've never needed to. You just go into a situation at full power and blast your enemy. Look, your ship is magnificent, and I would be proud to sail in her, but as Mandalee says, it's not 'low profile' is it?"

"But *StormChaser* is the only ship that can get us to my secret island base, due to the perception filter."

Cat shook her head. "Ah, you see, it's not," she disputed. "It's the only *crew* that can get us to your secret island base."

"Wait!" Mandalee exclaimed, turning to Daelen with a stunned expression. "You have a secret base on an island?"

"Nope," he replied, with a grin. "I have a secret island with a base on it."

The assassin rolled her eyes. "Figures."

Ignoring the exchange, Cat fished out her notebook and pen, opened it to a blank page and with a look of concentration on her face, sketched a diagram, occasionally crossing out a line and drawing a new one.

At last, she declared, "It's fine, it's no problem. I can work with this, use it to our advantage. Here's the plan."

She walked them through her idea, using her diagram as an aid. When she finished, she asked, "What do you think?"

"I think it's the least ridiculous radical plan I've ever heard from you," Mandalee answered. "I'm disappointed."

Cat raised an eyebrow. "Mandalee, I'm crossing the ocean to a continent I've never seen before and travelling to a desert I know nothing about, to go up against the most powerful and dangerous being in the world that I've no clue how to stop and his growing army that I have no way to fight."

Mandalee considered that for a moment before replying, "Well, that's a relief."

Daelen was incredulous. "How is that a relief?"

"Her ridiculous radical plans have a way of always working out in the end," she explained, "but if she starts trying to use serious ones, that's when I worry."

"I'm always serious about what I do," Cat disputed. "Just not necessarily the way I do it."

*****

My mother's plan, gentle reader, went like this: Daelen had considerable resources to his name, with an entire ship and crew at his beck and call. He could easily afford to charter a second one. A small, nondescript one. One that wouldn't be noticed. He gave Mandalee the money to do the transaction entirely in her name. That way there was nothing to connect it to him.

Meanwhile, Daelen and Cat found a dark, secluded alleyway in which to change. Daelen dropped his disguise and Cat became a rat. She'd never shapeshifted into something that small before, and it hurt like hell, but as ever, she did not let that stop her.

As for Pyrah, she'd just have to put up with being in a pocket dimension for a short while. Daelen picked up the rat and put her safely in his pocket. Then he put on a show, appearing over the docks with his usual accompanying storm, making sure there were plenty of witnesses.

He flew down from the sky to land on the *StormChaser*, where he was greeted by the captain, whom he immediately ordered below decks for a private word. He retrieved the rat from his pocket, and she swiftly changed back to her natural form. If the captain was surprised, he didn't show it. Daelen told him that Catriona's presence must remain a secret and he needed to split his team, running *StormChaser* with a skeleton crew.

When Catriona quipped that she'd heard there was a ship out there, somewhere, run by a crew of actual skeletons, the captain simply agreed that he'd seen it. She was never sure whether he was joking or not.

The rest of his crew would handle the other vessel: the *Dolphin*. This part of the ocean was often home to a pod of the creatures. The assassin had chosen it both because it fitted the bill of having virtually no distinguishing features, and because it was a simple name to transmit sympathically.

The crew transferred in ones and twos, taking different routes, so as not to appear suspicious. Everything was designed to minimise any chance of a connection between the two ships. Once ready, the *StormChaser* set sail for Daelen's secret island, which he called StormClaw. A few minutes later, after two or three other ships had departed, the *Dolphin* got underway on a very different heading, as if they were going to Esca, which they were…just not right away.

Far away from the harbour, the *Dolphin* slowly, gradually changed its heading. It wasn't a direct course for StormClaw, but rather it looked like it was merely a pleasure cruise that happened to be going in that general direction. Happened all the time. In fact, Mandalee and the crew even waved to the people on another ship, passing the other way, on a *genuine* pleasure cruise. Still absolutely nothing to connect the *Dolphin* and *StormChaser* in any way.

If all went to plan, the *StormChaser* would make landfall at StormClaw, and pick up supplies, while Daelen used his self-copy ability to make it look like he was still aboard the ship. In reality, he would sneak ashore. Catriona wouldn't be in his pocket when he did that – he wasn't sure if it would be safe. It wasn't a problem. Who would notice a single rat deserting a not-at-all-sinking ship? Maintaining his copy at extreme long range would be taxing, Daelen admitted. He could do it but, he warned, he might be a little distracted. He would maintain it until *StormChaser* reached the shore.

After a while, the ship would set sail once more, heading for Northern Alloria, apparently with Daelen still on board. Hopefully, any prying eyes would watch the *StormChaser* and pay no attention to the *Dolphin* as it casually, obliquely drifted close to StormClaw. Daelen was strong enough to swim to the *Dolphin*, while Cat would take the aerial route as a seagull – one of many such birds that would be flying around.

The *Dolphin* would quietly pick up its passengers – Catriona Redfletching and her 'wizard lover' – and set sail for Esca and Calin's Tower. After their visit there, they would return to StormClaw: A bird in the air, a swimming 'wizard' and a Cleric of Nature hitching a ride with an actual dolphin.

They would stay there for a while, as Daelen planned, and then head on to their rendezvous across the ocean, slipping in quietly on a simple pleasure boat that nobody would even notice, let alone remember.

That was the plan.

Still, you know what they say about the plans of mice and men, don't you, gentle reader? Technically, this was a plan of rat and woman, but the point still stands. What really happened was this…

*****

Cat couldn't find her sea legs, but she didn't have to worry about seasickness – her druid magic could suppress that without too much effort. That was fortunate because, in case of prying eyes, she and Pyrah would have to stay below decks for the duration of the voyage. Just over a week in one small cabin adjoining Daelen's. Still, the ship and the waves seemed to be conspiring to send her hurtling into Daelen's arms at embarrassingly regular intervals.

After the middle of the first day, she barely moved around at all unless she was practising her new leopard form. When she first did it, Daelen surprised her with a shape-changing ability of his own that she hadn't known about. The only animal he could do was a tiger, which she supposed explained why he was called Daelen StormTiger. Truthfully, it wasn't a particularly good tiger, but Cat saw no reason to risk hurting his feelings by saying so. Besides, her leopard form was hardly up to standard at the moment, and she wouldn't dare use it in front of Shyleen for fear of offending her.

The rest of the time she spent studying. She still had reference books in her pocket dimension, but she confined the study of her staff to the theoretical. She didn't want to risk Daelen getting his hands on it again.

Her upcoming visit to Calin's Tower was on her mind, too. It was somewhere she'd wanted to go since she was very young, but she'd never had the resources to travel beyond the shores of the continent of Elvaria before. Now she had the chance, she knew she couldn't stay long. To maximise this opportunity, Catriona wanted to make sure she was clear about what she was looking for, and what she was willing to give. Calin was Faery and offered knowledge according to the traditions of her people – something precious given freely. Cat didn't often get the chance to interact with people from her father's side of her nature. (Apart from the obvious, and she was hardly a traditional Faery.) She did value her Faery heritage, though, and was eager to show that when she met Calin. Therefore, she felt compelled to freely give knowledge that was precious to her.

Trouble was, there were so many things she could not share. Nothing she had learned about Daelen and nothing relating to her staff, that was for sure. The principles of her druid magic, however, she was more than happy to share, in the hope that other druids might come to push the boundaries of the art as she had. Then maybe they would start to gain more equal status with the Council. Eventually, perhaps there could be schools of druid magic, just as there were for wizards and clerics.

*****

One morning, Cat woke with a start and sat up in bed, due to a sudden flurry of noise and activity in her room. That night was to be their last aboard ship and, since there was absolutely nothing to do, they ended up talking for hours about this and that into the small hours of the morning. At some point, she supposed she must have fallen asleep. From Pyrah, she learned that Daelen had put her into bed and pulled a cover over her. Then he sat down in a bedside chair, saying he'd go to his own cabin in a minute or two, except he'd fallen asleep in the chair.

That had been the situation until the captain came banging on the cabin door, saying he needed help, urgently.

Daelen had woken instantly and told the captain to come in.

"Yes, Captain, what is it?" he asked. Stretching as he got up from the chair, he spared a smile and a wink for his friend who was still trying to piece events together in her just-woken-up state of mind.

"Sir, it seems that we've sailed into a bad squall and there's worse heading this way. We might need you to use your powers to control this one. Some of the crew are even worried that your dark clone might be behind it. Shortly before the clouds started to form out there, a dark streak flashed across the sky and…"

Before he could finish, Daelen was gone, leaving Cat alone with the captain, who was suddenly embarrassed at being in a lady's bedchamber.

Catriona flashed the captain a sweet smile, to try and reassure him that she understood he never would have barged into her room like that, except in an emergency.

Attempting to lighten the mood, she wondered, "Do you suppose it's a Law of Balance, that as one's power increases, one's good manners must decrease as a result? A simple 'excuse me, Catriona' – that's not too much to ask, is it? Maybe even a 'thank you, Captain.' I mean, how long does that take?"

The captain returned the smile but chose not to comment.

Trying another tack, she commented, "Maybe one of these days, he might actually remember that he's not the only one who can control the weather. My druid magic is less draining than what he does because it's more subtle and uses nature rather than coming from within. If he'd just stopped to ask, I could have told him,

'Don't fret, Daelen. I can sense that the storm is perfectly natural. No need to panic, just leave it to me.'"

As she was speaking, the storm ended and Cat rolled her eyes.

"He didn't need to put the storm out," she sighed, shaking her head, "just move it. We could have caught the trailing winds in our sails and used the storm to our advantage. Tell me, is he always so impulsive? Is it always act first, think later with him?" Once again, the captain kept his own counsel.

Seeing she was going to get no conversation, Cat asked the captain to please excuse her, as she was going to take a shower. The captain bowed and immediately left her cabin.

Moments later Daelen landed on the deck of the ship breathing just a little harder than before, and even as she showered, Cat could sense that true to her prediction, Daelen had wasted a significant amount of power to stop the storm, unnecessarily.

"Oh well," she muttered to herself as she enjoyed the feeling of the water on her body, "I suppose I've got a few weeks to try and train the shadow warrior to pay attention to me and think before he acts."

She heard Daelen say, "Well, Captain, you should have smooth sailing from here on out, but if not, you'll have to handle it yourselves. I need to gather my strength for what is to come. Once I've checked on Catriona, I intend to go back to sleep to try and recharge as much as possible. Do not wake me except in an absolute emergency."

"As you say, sir," the captain acknowledged.

Daelen walked into Catriona's cabin just as she turned off the water and stepped out of the shower. Seeing her standing there, naked, dripping with water, he seemed to freeze, staring right at her.

"Ahem!" Cat coughed. "In case you're unfamiliar with our mortal customs, this is the part where you turn around, apologise for accidentally walking in on me like this and immediately go back to your own cabin."

He did not move.

"OK, let me put it more simply: Get out!" she demanded.

Still, he did not move.

Her anger rising, she yelled, "Daelen, if you don't get out right now, I'll…"

She trailed off as she received something from Pyrah via her sympathic sense: '*Pain*' and '*Apologies.*' Then, just as she was trying to piece things together, Daelen began to keel over, and Cat had to rush to catch him before he hit the deck.

A pair of puncture marks on his left leg caught her eye and all at once, Cat realised what had happened.

When she got up, she had simply thrown the bedsheets on the floor, not realising Pyrah was entangled inside. Daelen, still not fully recovered from the incident with her staff and drained from stopping the storm, had entered her cabin just to check on her, not realising she'd got up. He had stepped on what he thought was just a pile of bedsheets and accidentally trodden on Pyrah, who simply lashed out on reflex.

If Catriona didn't act fast, Daelen StormTiger was going to die.

Chapter 14

Ignoring her protests, Cat immediately shoved Pyrah into her pocket dimension where she could do no more harm. She rushed over to Daelen and managed to lay him on her bed while she forced herself to think her way through the panic. Poisons were something of a druid speciality. Most toxins, she could simply take into her own body, bit by bit, and then filter it out before absorbing a bit more and cleansing that, and so on until the poison was all gone. But Pyrah's venom was no ordinary poison. If it could paralyse and kill an albeit split and weakened shadow warrior, what would it do to a mortal girl like her?

She searched her brain for anything she had learned that would help her. What use was all of her studying if it couldn't help her when she needed it? For a moment, she couldn't see past the irony that both Mandalee and Dreya had wanted to kill Daelen and she had stayed their hands. Yet she had almost done it once already and by the looks of it, the second time might be the charm.

"Wait!" she gasped out loud. "That's it! That's the answer!"

She quickly put the pieces together, threw her robes around herself and ran up on deck, yelling frantically for the captain with her voice at the same time as calling desperately for Mandalee with her mind.

The captain came running. "Lady Catriona! Master Daelen said, according to the plan, you can't be on deck."

"I know, it was my plan, but to hell with that now. There's been an accident, and we need to rendezvous with the *Dolphin* as fast as possible. Faster, even."

"But we don't know where they are!" the captain protested. "It was part of the plan that we wouldn't know."

"I'm getting their co-ordinates now!" she snapped, "I just need to know ours."

When she felt Mandalee in her mind, Cat projected '*location*' '*co-ordinates*' and '*come here: emergency*.'

There was a pause as Mandalee consulted with the *Dolphin's* crew before sending over what Cat needed. Cat shared the co-ordinates with the captain and sent over theirs in return. Cat gave both verbal and sympathic orders for the two ships to come about to exact opposite headings as fast as possible.

Mandalee projected her intention to call for her giant albatross to give her a lift, but there was no guarantee that it would be any quicker than if she came by ship. There wasn't anything they could do about the speed of the *Dolphin*, but Cat could certainly do something about the *StormChaser*.

"Captain, tell your crew to batten down the hatches or whatever it is they do in extreme weather," she urged him.

"Why?"

"Because, well, you remember that storm Daelen just got rid of?"

"Yes?"

"Well, I'm about to bring it back again, and it's going to push us to the *Dolphin*."

Even as she spoke, the wind began to pick up, blowing harder and harder.

The captain's eyes widened. "But Lady Catriona, if it's too much, I don't have a full crew, we may not be able to handle it. You could tear the ship apart."

"Better Daelen's ship than Daelen himself." Cat was out of patience. She was beginning to see why Daelen acted the way he did. She rounded on the man, eyes blazing. "Look, Captain, when Daelen gives you an order, do you stand there arguing with him?"

"Well, no, of course not, but—"

"While he is incapacitated, I am in charge, and you will do as I say! If you have a constructive idea, I will listen, but question or debate with me one more time until this crisis is over, and there's a life raft with your name on it. Alternatively, I may decide to do this." She shifted to leopard form, advancing on the Captain, teeth and claws on full display. She changed back. "Now, will you comply?"

The terrified man declared, "Yes, Ma'am!" and with a salute, he ran to relay orders to the crew.

Cat may not have had her sea legs when she first boarded the ship, but she found them pretty quickly when it mattered. The red and white sails furled in the winds that battered the *StormChaser*. The crew were running around, trying desperately to hold the ship together under extreme pressure. It was difficult for Cat to keep the wind blowing consistently in the right direction, but one of the crew, she didn't know his name, called out to her whenever they began to stray off course, so she could correct it.

At last, the lookout spotted another ship at extreme range. A quick sympathic communication with Mandalee confirmed it was the *Dolphin*. Communicating further, Mandalee told Cat her lift had arrived. In response, Cat allowed the high winds to move away and calm down, slowing their momentum to make it easier for the giant albatross to approach and land on the *StormChaser*, safely.

Mandalee vaulted off the bird onto the deck, and Cat took her below to her cabin where an unconscious Daelen lay still on her bed.

"What did you do to him this time?" the assassin wondered.

"I didn't," Cat answered. "Pyrah did. I have a plan, but it's going to need all four of us."

"Four?"

"You, me, Shyleen and Pyrah." Seeing Mandalee hesitate, she demanded to know what was wrong. "We have to act fast." she insisted. "Daelen's nature will hold the venom back for a while, but not forever. He needs our help."

"Maybe this is a sign," Mandalee considered. "Remember my contract?"

Cat nodded, no idea why she'd bring that up now.

"My client appeared to me again on the *Dolphin* and told me I would soon have another chance to stop Daelen destroying the world. Maybe this is how: we let him die."

"But if he dies, what about Kullos and his army?" Cat challenged her. "I'm not saying Daelen's a hero – to be fair, neither does he – but I honestly think if he dies, we all die. If Daelen lives, with your help, we can stop him from doing anything too rash. We can't do anything about Kullos. Only he can. Plus, as I told you before, you're forgetting who and what you are. You're not just an assassin or a hunter, you're a cleric, and right now, that's what I need. Forget past contracts, forget future visitors. This is the present, and it's your choice: kill or cure?"

"This is what Shyleen was trying to tell me," Mandalee realised. "She said I needed to reclaim the parts of me that I left behind two years ago." After a moment, she made her decision.

"I'm with you, Cat. No matter what's happened in the past, no matter what happens in the future, I'm with you. How do I help?"

Cat took Pyrah out of her pocket dimension and explained what she'd put together: Clerical magic had a temporal element. Clerics healed by returning the body to its pre-injured state. Trouble was, Mandalee didn't know enough about Daelen's physiology to do that. But thanks to her link with Shyleen, she understood well enough how a mortal body worked. Including that of a half-Faery. Through their shared sympathic link, Pyrah could provide exact details of her venom. Therefore, as Cat extracted venom from Daelen and took it into herself, Mandalee would have to simultaneously counteract the toxin and reverse the damage to Cat's body.

The whole procedure took about an hour, after which time both young women were drained with the effort, but the venom was gone, and there was nothing to do now but wait.

Cat decided her original plan was well and truly scuppered now. If Kullos or her Monster were indeed watching the *StormChaser* for signs of unusual activity, they had just waved and shouted, and held up a big sign that read, 'Hi, we're here, look at us!' So there seemed no harm in allowing the two ships to pull alongside each other so Shyleen could come over and rejoin Mandalee. At the same time, Pyrah, seeing that her services were no longer required, chose to remain aboard the StormChaser in the cargo hold, out of harm's way.

Cat decided they should travel directly to Daelen's secret island. "There might be…" she searched her mind for the unfamiliar words, "technology there that can help him recharge."

"There might be what there that can help him do what?" her friend asked, confused.

"Best as I understand, a kind of magic-that-isn't that will help him regain energy."

Mandalee considered that and offered a weak, mischievous smile, even as her eyelids drooped over her eyes.

"That explanation made a surprising amount of sense…by your standards."

With that, she passed out.

Cat could feel herself going, too, but fought it off long enough to call for the captain who she knew was hovering nervously outside the door.

"Best speed to StormClaw," she ordered. "Forget us. Help Daelen, understood?"

The druidess barely saw the salute or heard the, "Yes, Ma'am," before she was out. The last thing she did hear was that eerie voice again:

White faction second attempt gone. One attempt remains.

*****

Morning came much like any other day, and Catriona noticed that she and Mandalee had been moved to adjacent beds in a strange room filled with more of this technology that seemed to always consist of tiny lights that flashed, sounds that bleeped and screens that displayed incomprehensible information that somehow meant something to somebody. Beside the bed, there hung small, transparent bags of a colourless fluid that dripped into a clear, flexible tube that alarmingly seemed to be stuck in her arm.

Beside her, Mandalee stirred. Her eyes fluttered open and began to assess her surroundings as Cat had done a moment ago.

"Don't panic, Mandalee," Cat called out gently.

Mandalee turned her head to face her. "Why is it that whenever someone says, 'don't panic,' it just makes me want to panic? What's all this…stuff? What's it doing to us?"

"Well, this 'stuff' is technology. Beyond that, I'm not sure," Cat admitted, "but I don't think it intends us any harm."

"Really? Because I have to say, from what I've seen of this 'technology' so far," the cleric looked pointedly at the tube in her arm, "I'm not a fan."

"Well, you're attuned to nature at least as much as I am," Cat pointed out, "so you tell me: what do you think is in these bags?"

Mandalee sent out her magical senses and replied. "Water, mostly, with a bit of salt dissolved in it."

"There, you see? Harmless," Cat reassured her. "You know how, when we're healing, sometimes we have to rebalance the patient's body fluids?"

Her friend nodded. "You think it's like that?"

"It makes sense. Given what we went through, I'm sure we needed it."

"True," Mandalee agreed, "but I like our way better."

"So do I." Catriona nodded.

"Sorry, ladies, but I don't have your magic," came Daelen's voice from the doorway. He stepped between their beds. "Welcome to StormClaw Island. Not the first impression I would have liked to give you, but under the circumstances…" he shrugged.

After checking what he called 'readings' on the 'instruments,' he asked how they were feeling.

"Don't your 'instruments' tell you that?" Mandalee asked, still not sure she liked or trusted him and his 'technology.'

"They do, but it's always good to see if they match up with what the patient says."

Mandalee had to admit she felt better, other than a slight discomfort where the tube went into her arm. Cat echoed the sentiments, so Daelen declared them fit to be 'discharged.'

"Wait!" Mandalee cried, "You're going to take our energy? We only just got it back!"

Daelen didn't understand, but Cat felt she was getting a better handle on the language and explained that 'discharged' in this sense wasn't the opposite of how she'd described 'recharged' earlier. Daelen confirmed he just meant to release them from their treatment.

The two friends got up, and Daelen turned his back while they dressed. He apologised for stripping them down to their underclothes while they were unconscious, but it had been necessary to examine them properly and put in the drip.

Mandalee reassured him that she understood, and he could turn around now.

He did so, explaining, "Your arms might be a bit sore for a while."

The cleric snorted. "I think you're forgetting you're talking to a pair of magic healers, Daelen."

Cat nodded. "We already took care of that."

"Or you could do that," Daelen agreed.

He also apologised to Catriona for bursting in on her when she came out of the shower.

Mandalee took the opportunity to remind Daelen how dismissive he had been when they first met, and point out that the shadow warrior had, in fact, needed healing from a mere mortal, after all.

"Lesson learned, I trust?"

Looking suitably admonished, Daelen replied, "Believe me, you two are making me revise my opinions on many things. I was rude and obnoxious to you, and I can only apologise."

"Well, I think being bitten by one of the deadliest snakes in the cosmos is probably punishment enough," the assassin allowed.

"Congratulations, by the way," Cat added, "you have the honour of being the first person in history ever to survive a bite from one of Pyrah's species. But unless you want to try for the record of surviving a second bite, I suggest you apologise to her, too, the next time you see her."

"Me? Apologise to her? She was the one who nearly killed me, remember?"

Catriona shrugged. "How would you react if a giant stepped on you the way you stepped on my poor snake?"

"I see your point – I don't think the giant would be so lucky as to survive. How is she, anyway? I'm surprised my power didn't fry her."

Cat shook her head, and told him, "As you know, Pyrah's Ysirian. She absorbs power from anyone she bites. You gave her the mother of all headaches, but she'll be even more dangerous than she was before."

Daelen's eyes widened. "In that case, I'll definitely have to apologise."

Cat smiled, and in a conspiratorial whisper, confided, "Actually, she wants to ask a favour, that you don't tell a soul about what happened. She's got a reputation to maintain, you see – she'd be the laughingstock of the nest if word got out that she'd attacked someone, and they still lived."

Given this new perspective, Daelen agreed, "I can relate to that. Her secret is safe."

"In that case, she's willing to call it quits. On the plus side, I'm willing to bet that if her venom is so effective on you, with her increased power, she could be a serious threat to Kullos. We have gained knowledge and survived. By my reckoning, the balance comes down on our side."

"Easy for you to say," Daelen grumbled, "after you nearly killed me…again."

On sudden impulse, Cat hugged Daelen and planted a kiss on his cheek. "I know. Let's make a pact to have no more accidents, shall we? I'm glad you're OK."

"So am I," Mandalee agreed, though she wasn't going to kiss him.

"First you try to kill me, then you save me," he remarked.

"What can I say?" Mandalee shrugged. "I'm fickle like that."

"Then I'll try and keep on your good side from now on!" Daelen chuckled. "I'm glad to have you with us. It's obvious that you two are going to make a formidable team."

Mandalee smiled, remembering the old days when they went demon hunting together and factored in how much both their powers had advanced since then. "You have no idea," she declared.

Daelen led them out of the medical wing of his facility, to his training centre, where he practised and honed his fighting skills. Next to that was a dining area where he invited them to sit while he brought them meals that cooked in just a few minutes in something he called a 'microwave.'

"OK, now this is technology I can get behind," Mandalee approved as she sampled her meal. Catriona was in full agreement and bombarded Daelen with questions about how it could cook so fast. She quickly lost interest, however, when she learned it had nothing to do with temporal magic.

Getting them both a drink, he left them to it while he resumed his training routines. As they watched him through the window, the shadow warrior stripped down to the waist, showing a toned, muscular body. He began doing flips, twists, and other well-timed stunts. Catching Catriona's eye, he winked at her.

She just smiled and shook her head. "I didn't realise Daelen had such a playful side," she remarked, momentarily forgetting she wasn't alone.

Her friend leaned close and asked, "Do you want me to leave, so you can stare at his body in peace?"

Cat whirled her head around to face Mandalee's crooked grin. "What are you talking about? I'm just…looking, that's all!"

"Yes, looking intently – also known as staring," she teased. "Or if you don't like that word, how about this one: flirting?"

Cat, blushing deeply, protested, "I am not! I'm just…getting into character, you know, for when we go to Calin's Tower."

Her friend nodded knowingly. "Right," she deadpanned, making it clear she didn't believe a word of it. "Getting into character. Got it."

*****

When he saw they were done eating, Daelen rejoined them and announced that he wanted to show them 'something special' before they left for Esca and Calin's Tower.

Mandalee whispered in Catriona's ear, "If his 'something special' is what I think it is, I'm leaving you to your perverted desires."

"I do not have desires," she whispered back. "Perverted or otherwise."

"Come off it, Cat, he probably wants to put part of himself inside you again."

"How do you know about that?"

"Sympathic link, remember. When you called for help, a few things leaked out. Hey, is that what happened? Did his essence just sort of 'leak out'?

The druidess was turning an ever-deepening shade of red. "Are you going to be like this all the time from now on?"

"Oh, yes," Mandalee replied nodding. "All the time."

"What are you two conspiring about?" Daelen wondered.

"Nothing!" Cat replied too quickly.

"Just speculating on what your 'something special' might look like."

"Shut up!" Cat hissed.

"Make me!" Mandalee shot back.

Daelen led them to what he called his portal room. Upon opening the door, all banter momentarily ceased as they saw half a dozen shimmering blue Prismatic Spheres, identical to what he typically used to transport himself across the face of Tempestria.

“These are my doorways to other worlds,” he declared, dropping the concept into the conversation as casually as he might have introduced his wine cellar.

“Other worlds?” the two women gasped.

“Oh, have I impressed you two at last?”

Cat gave him a playful shove for his trouble.

‘*Flirting!*’ Mandalee sent, sympathically.

“So, there *are* other worlds,” a distracted Catriona mused, more to herself than anyone else, pointedly ignoring her friend. “She's been right all along.” Dreya would be extremely interested, she knew. “I can't wait to tell her about this.”

“Who's that?” Daelen wondered.

It was an innocent question, but Catriona's expression was one of shock and anger at herself, for giving away free information she hadn't intended to. With the magically backed promise, such a mistake shouldn’t even have been possible. Unless the effects of these other worlds were disrupting the magic, somehow. She recovered quickly, though and dismissed the question with a wave of her hand. “Oh, just someone I'm acquainted with.”

“All part of your million research projects, Cat?” Mandalee suggested, inadvertently coming to her rescue. “Or part of your project to impress your new shadow warrior boyfriend, perhaps?” she added under her breath.

Rolling her eyes, Cat nevertheless grabbed the lifeline and agreed, “Yeah, that’s it. You got me.”

Daelen explained that this was where he disappeared to for long periods in between battles with Kullos and ‘Aden.’

On the other side of each portal, lay a similar facility on a different world. One was a world ruled by dragons, while in another world of high technology, the dragons were themselves hunted down. Another portal led to a world filled with a myriad of strange sentient creatures, where the essence of magic itself was dangerous. One world was mostly aquatic, while another was home to a sentient forest. But the one in which he spent most of his time was a world without magic called Earth. The latter was where he intended to take them so they could train for just under a month, before returning to complete their voyage.

“We don’t have time for that,” Cat pointed out. “We’d be late for our rendezvous with Michael.”

Daelen shook his head. "That's the beauty of it. Time doesn't work the same there," he explained. "We can spend nearly a month on Earth, and that's only about seven days here."

"Why is their time so different?" Cat wanted to know.

Again, Daelen shook his head. "You don't understand. Earth isn't weird – Time there is just the same as everywhere else on the mortal plane, as far as I can tell," he clarified. "It's Tempestria that's different."

"What?" his two guests demanded.

Daelen shrugged. "I've no idea why, but your world is out of sync with the rest of the universe."

Before Mandalee and Cat had a chance to come to terms with Daelen's revelation, he portalled them all to the *Dolphin,* which was now moored on StormClaw. The shadow warrior thought the combination of the unremarkable vessel and his perception filter was the best way to visit Calin's Tower. Their cover may have been blown in terms of their voyage across the sea, but that was no reason to cause a stir on Esca by turning up aboard the *StormChaser*.

Catriona rewarded his clear thinking with a hug. She was excited at the prospect of finally getting to see the place and thanked him for taking her with another kiss on the cheek, which prompted another round of teasing from Mandalee.

Chapter 15

Calin's Tower, gentle reader, had been standing for more than a century and a half, by my mother's time. It was situated then, as now, in Ellinsford, the capital city of Esca. While StormClaw was a tiny island, easy to hide without anyone missing it, Esca was the third largest island in the world and these days home to a united island nation, but it wasn't always so.

The Tower itself was accessed by way of Red Street, which was neither red, nor a street. It was a narrow passageway, which forced the companions to walk in single file, Catriona taking the lead. My mother knew the history well and felt compelled to explain that the reference to the colour red came from the many bloody battles fought on this soil. In times past, there was a river running through Ellinsford which divided the city and island, both geographically and politically.

The river was called the Ellin – hence the name of the city – but according to myth, at the height of the conflict, it became known as the 'Red River' because it was stained permanently red due to all the blood.

In time, she explained, the climate changed, and the river dried up. With the river gone, the people extended the buildings on either side, so the street became a narrow passageway. Formerly, it was called 'Red River Street,' but over time it was truncated to 'Red Street.'

No-one is sure precisely how the hostilities started, but they lasted, on and off for more than a century. What is certain is that it was perpetuated by ignorance. Both sides accused the other of committing atrocities, desecrating each other's dead. Both sides vehemently denied the charges. It took a long time for the truth to come out and reveal the cultural misunderstanding at the heart of the conflict: Both cultures believed in a soul that escaped the body soon after death, flying out in the direction the deceased was facing when laid to rest. At this point, however, their belief systems diverged.

Those on the Eastern side of the river believed the body must be laid face up, allowing the soul to fly into space and explore the cosmos for eternity. If the body were laid face down, the soul would be trapped forever. Something that was viewed as sacrilege.

Those on the Western side believed the souls of their people were fragments of the soul of the world. From Tempestria they came and to Tempestria they must return, so the body must be laid face down to allow the soul of the deceased to become one with Tempestria once more. They believed that if the deceased were laid to rest face up, the disoriented soul would fly out of the body and become lost in space, doomed to wander for eternity, never to find its way home. To them, *this* was sacrilege.

During the war, then, each side in their ignorance, treated the enemy fallen according to their own customs, not realising how this would be viewed by the other side. Not until a third party got them to agree to talks.

Calin grew up in the latter stages of the conflict and when she chose this site for her Tower, dedicated to free access to knowledge, she decided to make Red Street the only approach to the main entrance. She encouraged people to learn the origin of the name of the street, recall the battles of old and realise the price of ignorance and misunderstanding. That suited her philosophy and indeed, the philosophy of the entire Order of Balance. Calin also thought it was appropriate since Red was the symbolic colour of the Balance as recognised by the Council. The red helped the Balance stand distinct and separate from both the Light and Dark orders, not merely a blend of the two. Their core philosophy being that power wielded in ignorance was dangerous, regardless of intent.

Calin's interest wasn't limited to magic. Her vast library was considered the finest in the world on any subject one might care to name. It was a researcher's paradise. However, mages were her core group of patrons.

A law was passed to protect Calin and what she represented. To that end, she would always have the services of three mages called Custodians, one from each order. They were not just guards, but her personal staff, there to do what she could not. To maintain the balance, Calin swore a magically backed oath to never acquire power or use the knowledge of her Tower for personal gain. For example, suppose a wizard was researching a powerful spell. Calin could retain only the theoretical understanding of how it was done.

A magical block prevented her from casting all but a few rudimentary spells.

Catriona finished her lecture with a sigh of admiration for this individual. As much as she valued knowledge and insisted 'power isn't everything,' the idea of sacrificing the ability to use the things she learned was horrifying to her. She couldn't imagine being unable to work with nature as she did, unable to use her pocket dimension magic. Perhaps worst of all was the idea of sacrificing her ability to shapeshift…

…My mother had no idea, gentle reader, that events were already in motion that would force her to do exactly that.

*****

The door to the callers' office was opened by one of the many acolytes Calin hired to help run the Tower. "Is your Mistress available, please?" Catriona asked. "I have heard that she is seeking to increase her section on druid magic, and I've brought some contributions as a gift."

"Yes, certainly," the girl replied, "if you'll come with me, I will introduce you."

The girl led the companions through seemingly endless corridors. As they reached a pair of large wooden double doors, they heard a bell chime magically behind them. Without being touched, the doors opened to reveal a sizeable gothic chamber with a high ceiling and lit by magelights that gave the appearance of candles without the potentially disastrous fire hazard. Calin herself was a Faery woman of considerable beauty and noble bearing. Despite her age of approaching two hundred years, her hair was mainly night-black, with just a few strands here and there lightened to grey, which only increased the sense of wisdom one could see in her grey-blue eyes. Behind her, ever watchful, sat the three Custodians.

Calin rose to greet her visitors, a kind smile on her face.

"Welcome, my dears," she greeted them. "My Tower is yours. If you need assistance, please don't hesitate to ask. Now, what's this I hear about a gift?"

Catriona stepped forward and dropped to one knee, kissing Calin's ring finger.

"Mistress Calin, I am honoured to meet you. I have waited too long."

Daelen was stunned by this, and even Mandalee was unprepared, having never imagined Catriona Redfletching would kneel to anyone.

Calin seemed a little taken aback herself, saying, "Please, get up. I'm no hero that you should kneel to me."

"I would not kneel to any mere hero, Mistress Calin," Catriona replied. "You will forever be a revered figure in history, and it will be a privilege to one day tell my children that I met you in person. I am merely giving you the honour you rightly deserve."

Satisfied, Cat got up and introduced herself.

"You are Catriona Redfletching?" Calin wondered. "I have heard of you. Your reputation is growing. There are formidable mages who respect and fear you. Tell me: how do you replicate Holy Water? I had a group of orthodox clerics of Light in here a few months ago complaining about your 'blasphemy.' They swore they were going to burn you at the stake if they caught you."

Catriona smiled darkly. "Some of them tried. I granted them a visit to their god."

*****

Rather than attack her directly, they had used their clerical magic to instil a kind of blind faith in the minds of a section of their congregation, including children. This effectively turned them into a cult that would fight Catriona even at the cost of their own lives. It had taken all of Cat's ingenuity to restrict, snare and disarm her attackers. Pyrah not being with her at the time didn't matter. They were linked no matter what. Besides, Cat had enough mental strength of her own to establish a sympathetic link with one of her attackers. As a rule, she didn't impose a sympathetic link without permission, but under the circumstances, she decided it was warranted. Besides, it wasn't as if she could read minds as such. But she could clearly sense the waves of hatred emanating not from them, but through them.

She would not impose her will on these people who were obviously being used. Instead, focussing on one man, she projected an overwhelming sense of '*Freedom*,' encouraging him to break free of the conditioning. As soon as he did, the man told Cat he remembered everything and asked if there was anything he could do to help free the others, many of whom were friends and family. Cat urged him to keep thinking '*Freedom*' in his mind. Not just the word, but the concept, the idea.

"Think about what freedom means to you," she coached. "Focus on that and imagine shouting it at me without actually speaking."

He did as she asked, which helped her to free the next one with less effort. Not every person she released added to her chorus. Some just wanted to go home, and she wouldn't stand against that. Many did join her, however, and pretty soon, the attack was over, but Catriona was far from done. The druidess wanted to deal with the clerics at the heart of this assault. If she didn't, they would just do it again to others, and their next attack might be something the druidess was less equipped to deal with. When she cornered the trio of clerics, she was resolved not to give them a chance to attack anyone ever again.

She knew that some of her past actions had ruffled feathers, to put it mildly, and her association with Dreya the Dark seemed to bring out strong feelings in some people. So, she had prepared. People who harboured a powerful hatred were usually absolutely convinced of their own rightness. Therefore, Cat had been working on a kind of sympathic version of her Nature's Mirror. Taking the raw material of hatred in these clerics, her power reflected it. She turned their hatred back on them and redirected their sense of rightness so they would be susceptible to her suggestions. The more they hated, the more they snared themselves until Cat decided that since their Holy Water was such a vital connection to their gods, they should sacrifice themselves by drowning in it.

"I do this not out of hatred or malice," she pronounced. "Not even because you attacked me. But because you robbed others of their free will; used them when they wanted no part of your vendetta. I do it to protect them and your future victims."

They could have stopped it at any time. All the clerics had to do was let go of their hatred. Then they would be safe. But they didn't. They kept on hating, and so they kept on believing Catriona was right when she said they should drown. And so they did.

The Council ruled that Catriona had acted in defence, to end a threat, and no charges were brought.

*****

"Their kind seeks to perpetuate ignorance," Calin fumed, "and that is against all I stand for. I shall not mourn their loss."

"Me neither," Catriona agreed, "and to answer your original question, what the clerics call a Blessing is just a transfer of magical energy with a specific frequency. That can be analysed and replicated, just like any other form of energy."

"Fascinating," Calin acknowledged. "Now," she continued, changing the subject, "will you introduce me to your companions?"

"This is Mandalee," Catriona began, "a good friend of mine."

It felt so good to be able to say that again after more than two years.

"The White Assassin," Calin remarked.

"The what?" Mandalee wondered.

"Didn't you know? It's a title you seem to have picked up."

Mandalee didn't like it. "What's next – the Red Druid? The Grey Wizard? The Purple Flower Arranger? I mean, I can't be the only assassin who ever wore white or belonged to the order of Light. Unless there's some rule that you can't have more than one magic user of the same colour."

"No rule that I know of," Calin agreed, "and I would know if there were."

Moving on to Daelen, she inquired, "And this young man would be—?"

"My lover, Dan," Catriona lied quickly, moving close to Daelen's side, taking his hand in hers and flashing him a loving smile.

Somehow, Mandalee had found a way to make sympathic kissing noises in Cat's mind. The druidess made a supreme effort to rise above it.

Calin studied him carefully for a long moment, before saying, "A pleasure to meet such an interesting individual, young sir. This truly is a day for extraordinary guests."

Before Daelen could think of a response, he heard her voice in his mind, '*I know how to see through a perception filter, shadow warrior. Don't worry, it's working for everyone else.*'

She turned her attention back to Catriona. "He is your lover, you say? I have heard rumours that you are in a relationship with a powerful wizard, though there is some debate as to who that is. I even heard one claim that you were romantically involved with Dreya the Dark."

"Yes, I've heard the same rumours," Cat answered simply, neither confirming nor denying it. Denial was often the surest way to make people believe a rumour was true. "Who knows how they start?"

"Indeed," Calin agreed. "As if Dreya the Dark does romance!"

"Well, quite," Cat replied, noncommittally.

"Besides, the Red Druid only has eyes for Dan. Right, Cat?" Mandalee put in.

Catriona ignored her in favour of talking to Calin. "Before I forget why I asked to see you, Mistress Calin, I should give you this."

She produced a notebook from her pocket dimension and handed it to her.

Calin opened it, and her eyes lit up. "New druid magic. This is exactly what I have been looking for. Thank you, Catriona."

"As your knowledge is given freely, Mistress Calin, so is mine."

"Only a slice of what you can do, I'm sure, but on a personal level, your respect for Faery custom is appreciated," Calin accepted, "I'm delighted to know a half-human keeps one foot in her Faery heritage."

"More like half a foot, if I'm honest. I'd like to do more, but time pulls me ever forward."

"Indeed, your life, what I know of it, is ever the adventure, but before I leave you to your research, if you can spare but a moment, there is something I would like to show you."

"You mean the Mystery of Calin's Tower?" Cat asked.

"Exactly," Calin affirmed.

Chapter 16

My mother had read all about Calin's Tower and knew the legend well. You see, gentle reader, the reason I gave earlier for the location of the Tower was only half the story. The other half had become known as the Mystery of Calin's Tower, although that was something of a misnomer since the Mystery pre-dated the Tower by centuries. The Tower was simply built around it.

There was a mysterious inscription set in the stone floor at the exact centre of the Tower. Despite its age, it had not suffered from any erosion or damage. In fact, nothing could even mark it. Anything placed over it was either moved or destroyed by forces unknown. The inscription, just three bold symbols, was as clear as if it had been carved yesterday. Unfortunately, no one knew what it was supposed to say. It was utterly unlike any known language form. If indeed it was a language at all.

As I'm sure you've realised by now, gentle reader, my mother loved a puzzle, and she had wanted to see the Mystery since she was a little girl. Now that she was here, though, she at first resisted the impulse to be drawn into another mystery when she already had so many and a mission with Daelen to think about.

Daelen, however, maintaining his cover as 'Dan,' encouraged her, "Don't worry, sweetheart, we can afford the time. It can't hurt to just take a look. Then we can grab the books you need and be on our way."

After stealing a staged kiss (at least, she told herself it was just staged) Cat asked Mandalee if she agreed.

"Sure. It beats standing here watching you two lovebirds snogging all the time," she teased.

So, together, the three accompanied Calin to the site of the inscription.

It was located deep in the shadows, but Catriona took her Crystal Mage Staff out of her pocket dimension and caused the crystal to glow, banishing the darkness. As soon as her eyes adjusted, she gasped, "How? How is this possible?"

"How is what possible?" Daelen asked.

Mandalee, who knew her best, instantly ceased any hint of making fun as she grew worried about Cat's pale, wide-eyed expression. “What's up, Cat?” she asked. “You look like you've seen a ghost.”

“Maybe I have, Mandalee, or at least the work of one.” To Calin, she declared, “Dig hole here.”

“Yes, well, obviously, we’ve tried that, but we’ve never been able to even scratch it.”

“No, you don’t understand,” Cat pressed. “That’s what the inscription says: ‘Dig hole here.’”

“Astonishing!” Calin breathed. “What language does it say that in?”

“That's the bit that's got my heart racing… it's my own personal shorthand. It's what I use to make notes that I don't want anybody reading.”

“Where did you learn this shorthand?”

“I didn’t learn it from anywhere. It’s based on a secret language that I made up when I was a little girl. There is literally no way that anybody else could know it. Not unless you believe in huge cosmic coincidences.”

“I don’t,” Calin insisted.

“But this inscription is almost a thousand years old,” Mandalee objected, “it can't possibly be your shorthand.”

“Yeah, and besides,” Daelen added, “I think you'd remember if you wrote it.”

“Unless I haven’t done it yet,” Cat suggested. “Look, it seems to me that the only way to solve this is to obey the instruction and dig a hole, with your permission, Mistress Calin. Trust me, I can do this without damaging your Tower in any way.”

“But as I said, it’s been tried before. No-one can even scratch it.”

“Has anybody tried it with druid magic?” Mandalee asked, supporting her friend.

She understood what her friend was thinking, and it was ridiculous, but she knew how Cat’s ridiculous radical ideas usually turned out.

“Not to my knowledge,” Calin conceded.

In the end, she agreed to let Catriona try. After all, if it didn’t work, nothing would happen, and if it did, Calin had dedicated her life to the pursuit of knowledge. She could hardly forbid archaeology under her roof.

Catriona asked the others to stand back, and then she concentrated, using her staff to aid her focus.

At first, the rock seemed to resist her reshaping efforts, but then on pure impulse, she commanded, "Open up; it's Catriona Redfletching. I have come."

The rock seemed to respond, the resistance ended, and it began to grow molten. The molten rock flowed, creating a hole in the centre, large enough for a person to fit inside.

When it was about six feet deep, Mandalee called out, "Cat, stop, I think I see something!"

Cat stopped digging, cooled the rock and used her staff light to see down the hole. At the bottom, the air shimmered, and they could see nothing beneath it.

"What is it?" Calin asked.

"It's an open pocket dimension," Catriona replied. "You'll find the details in the notes I gave you. I use one all the time."

She put her staff safely on the ground away from the hole. She reasoned she might need two hands for this, but she didn't want to risk anyone else touching it. She could put it away, but she wasn't sure what the effects might be of opening a pocket dimension close to another one – it had never come up before.

She lay down and tried to reach down into the pocket dimension in the hole, but it was too far away.

"Oh well," Cat sighed, "I've always wondered what it looks like inside."

She asked her two friends to grab an ankle each and lower her down, imploring them not to let go.

They lowered her slowly until everything from her waist up disappeared inside the pocket dimension. After a few moments, Mandalee felt her shake her leg, which she took as an instruction to pull her back up until she was back on her feet again, holding a small airtight silver box, which she handed to Daelen. Retrieving her staff, she invited Daelen to open the container while she closed the empty pocket dimension and put the stone floor back as it was, complete with redundant inscription.

"Extraordinary," Calin breathed.

Cat shrugged and pulled a face. "Thought it quite boring myself. Would you believe the inside of a pocket dimension looks like a completely ordinary night sky? How rubbish is that?"

She was hoping the silver box might contain something more exciting. Inside the box was a piece of parchment – a letter.

"It's addressed to you, Cat," Daelen told her.

"It's OK, just read it out loud," she replied. "I don't intend this to be a secret."

So, Daelen read:

Dear Catriona Redfletching,

There's no easy way to say this, but basically, I'm here in the past, but from the future. Sort of. Things have gone horribly wrong on my world, and I'm giving you a chance to fix them. Not for us – it's too late for that – but for you, for your Tempestria. So, yeah, no pressure. Sorry.

In your future, I have gained the power to manipulate Time. Thus, I was able to whizz back a few centuries and leave this letter for you. This is my second Intervention, having laid the groundwork with my first, although if everything goes as planned, you'll experience them the other way around. (Time travel is complicated.)

There are some major events unfolding in your life right now, but the test that is to come is greater than you realise, and you must be prepared. As ever, knowledge is the key and knowing you as I do, you've already borrowed most of what you need from Calin's Tower, but there's one other reference you cannot afford to miss, and you won't find it here. I put it all together too late, so I'm giving you a clue.

You recognised the 'unknown language' on the ground in Calin's Tower. Besides your notebook, it exists in one other place. You saw it once, but you weren't paying attention. Don't blame you, neither was I, but you can't make that mistake again. You need it in your hands before you face Kullos, and you can't delay your mission. You have connections: use them.

I also offer you some advice: Keep Mandalee close, for she will play an essential role in your future. The three of you are bound by Time and Magic. More than this I cannot say, for to do so would break the laws of time...may the cosmos forgive me, I have already stretched them to their limit.

Aye, ever yours,

"Who is it signed?" Cat asked, already knowing the answer – there was only one person she knew who signed off like that.

In a slightly shaky voice, Daelen answered, "Catriona Redfletching."

Cat brightened, "Oh well, that explains that, then. Time magic."

Daelen couldn't say anything for fear of blowing his cover, but telepathically, he told Cat, '*I have made portals into the past, but it takes a lot of effort, and even I couldn't do something like this.*'

Underneath Catriona's signature, there was a postscript.

p.s. Tell our boyfriend, he was adorable when he was younger.

Cat and Daelen turned matching shades of red, while Mandalee burst out laughing.

"Dear gods, it's totally a love across the ages!"

Just then, a voice came out of the air, instantly sobering the mood:

Red faction first attempt gone. Two attempts remain.

*****

A pair of acolytes were already waiting with the books Cat had requested. She immediately put them safely in her pocket dimension.

On sudden impulse, Cat asked Calin if she had a camera on the premises. She replied that she had indeed introduced a small photography studio as a new way of communicating information.

Calin led them there and showed her how to take a clear photograph of her letter. As she did so, she couldn't help but marvel at how the parchment was in pristine condition and the script so clear, apart from a few spots that looked as if they had been made by droplets of water. Had she been crying when she hid this letter, she wondered?

Satisfied with her photograph, Cat explained that she needed 'a contact' to see it, but she didn't dare risk losing the original, and she wasn't confident that sympathic communication would be precise enough. She asked Calin to keep the photograph safe until someone came asking for it. She had already sent a sympathic message, and they would be along shortly.

"How will I know this person is the right messenger?" Calin asked.

"There is a three-word code phrase. The same words that are written in stone."

Calin gave a sharp nod of understanding.

"Mistress Calin," Catriona declared, formally, "thank you for sparing your time for us. When our quest is over, I plan to return here and get lost in your Tower for at least a year."

"And you will be very welcome, my dear," embracing Cat and each of her other companions. "I hope I live long enough to witness the birth of time magic first-hand, but if that is not to be, I pray only that the knowledge will be brought here to my Tower."

With that, she escorted them to the exit and wished them a safe journey.

Mandalee, who had been reading the letter for herself, suddenly spoke up, "Erm, guys, a p.p.s. just appeared on the back of this letter."

"What?" the others exclaimed at once.

Mandalee read it out:

p.p.s. Get out of there fast. Daelen's dark clone is searching for you, and you need to be well away from Calin's Tower before he strikes. The Tower must be protected.

Cat rolled her eyes, and remarked, "Next time I write that note, I swear I'm going to give us more time. Let's go."

Needing no further encouragement, the three companions ran back to the waiting *Dolphin* and as soon as they left the harbour, Cat whipped up an excellent tailwind to take them back to StormClaw as quickly as possible.

Chapter 17

Out there, in open water, Aden appeared amid his signature dark lightning and accompanying unnatural storm. He flew down to hover above the *Dolphin*, and greeted Daelen with his customary, bright and cheerful, "Hello, you!"

"Hello, you," Daelen returned, darkly.

"What's this, brother?" Aden wondered. "You have two pets now? Hey, is this how they reproduce? Just split apart, and suddenly there's two of them? It would explain why there's so many of them infesting this world. You know, I tried to get a pet of my own, but she bit me. Ungrateful witch."

"What do you want, 'brother'?" Daelen asked in a wearied tone. "Actually, forget that question, here's a better one: what happened to you?"

From his energy reading, his dark clone was as critically drained as he'd ever seen him.

"Send your pets away, Daelen," Aden ordered him. "I want things back how they used to be – just you and me, as it should be."

"Alright," Daelen agreed and told his friends, "I'm going to send you on ahead while I deal with him safely."

"But we can help!" Mandalee insisted. "Right, Cat?"

To her astonishment, Cat just shrugged. "I'm sure Daelen knows what he's doing."

As Daelen's power teleported them away to StormClaw, Mandalee just stared at her, in utter disbelief.

*****

"Look," Aden sighed, "I don't have the energy to argue, and for once, I'm not here to fight. Just to talk. I want to…what's that term these mortals use…parley?"

Daelen was suspicious. "We've been fighting for centuries, and suddenly you want to parley? You've never been interested in that before."

"I've never had my aura kicked by a mortal before, either," Aden pointed out. "If it makes you feel better, we can fly away from your ship, and talk out in the middle of the ocean, well away from your precious little mortal crew."

Still wary, but intrigued, Daelen was torn for a moment. Ultimately curiosity won out.

"Very well," Daelen acknowledged, "I accept your terms of parley. Let's go."

With that, the two shadow warriors flew away from the *Dolphin*, away from Esca, and closer to StormClaw. As soon as they were clear of the main shipping routes, they initiated their signature storm powers to deter any vessels from straying too close. Only when he was sure they were alone out there, with just the seagulls for company, was Daelen prepared to parley.

For the first time ever, thanks to Daelen's new mortal friends, and Aden's mistake of taking on Dreya the Dark, Daelen had a clear advantage. He could afford to be patient for once and listen to what his dark clone had to say.

It would turn out to be a momentous occasion. One might even say a meeting of minds.

*****

Meanwhile, in Daelen's base on StormClaw, Catriona pulled a book out of her pocket dimension and sat down.

She looked up at an annoyed Mandalee and, with a sigh, asked, "What's up now?"

"I used to think I understood you," Mandalee replied, shaking her head in disbelief, "despite your ridiculous radical ideas, but this is unbelievable. After everything you've gone through to protect Daelen, even talking me into saving his life, you're just going to leave him to fight Aden alone?"

The druidess gazed out of a window that looked out to sea in the direction of Esca. There was a storm on the horizon. A tempest of incredible power and magnitude. A storm that was utterly impossible without some kind of build-up.

"Yup," she answered simply.

"Look at that storm, Cat! They must be going all out over there. Daelen could be hurt, badly, and you're just sitting there like you don't care, which I know for a fact isn't true."

Catriona's feelings were bleeding out through their sympathic connection. She was only winding her friend up about them because she knew there was a truth to them.

"Yes, of course I'm worried about him," Catriona replied, "and OK, I will admit I've felt a certain…attraction, but don't you dare tell him I said that."

"Ha!" Mandalee cried. "I knew it! I knew I was right about you two!"

"There is no 'us two'!" Cat snapped. "Just because I love him, that doesn't mean I want to do anything about it."

She winced. She hadn't intended for the L-word to slip out.

"Why wouldn't you want to?"

Catriona thought for a moment, choosing her words carefully. "Let's just call it personal honour and leave it at that."

The White Assassin knew better than to push Cat into revealing more than she was willing to, so she returned to worrying about Daelen.

Catriona glanced out at the darkening sky with disapproval, before settling down and using her light from the staff's blue crystal to illuminate her reading.

"I don't know how you can be so calm about this," Mandalee grumbled, pacing restlessly. "I can tell he's alive out there, yet at the same time, he's not."

To her magical senses, it seemed like his power was both fading and growing. Waxing and waning at the same time. Shyleen was equally baffled. The disruption to nature was playing havoc with her nerves, and she knew Catriona must feel it, too, in addition to her emotions regarding Daelen himself. Yet the druidess continued to ignore it in favour of studying her books.

"You know more of Daelen's past and power than I do. If you know what's going on, tell me. Please!" she implored her. "Something major is going down out there, and I don't know what to do about it."

"So don't do anything about it," Cat suggested. "Please, Mandalee," she continued, exasperated. "I don't mean to sound heartless, but I've got a lot of studying to do, and you're being very distracting."

"What? You can't study at a time like this!"

"Why not?" Cat wondered, absently.

“Have you lost your mind? Daelen could be in all sorts of trouble, his power’s all over the place and the storm’s coming closer.

“Well, as to the first two,” Cat replied, turning a page in her book, “there's very little I can do about them right now. Daelen teleported us here; if he needs our help, I'm sure he's perfectly capable of teleporting us back again. As for the storm, it's nothing I can't keep under control. It may be magically generated, but what he continually fails to understand, just like wizards, is that no matter the cause, the effect is a simple storm. A thing of nature. Therefore, it makes sense to use druid magic – the power of nature – to control it. If Daelen ever comes down from his lofty, arrogant perch, he might actually realise that himself and quit wasting his own power on things that I can deal with in a much less draining way. Right now, it seems to me that I can either spend the waiting time fretting and worrying, or I can stay calm and study these priceless texts. Please, Mandalee,” she implored her, a wearied expression on her face, “do us both a favour and learn to relax.”

Mandalee directed the full force of her ire and frustration at her friend.

“Well, excuse me! You’re the one who dragged me into this, and I seem to remember you telling me that you were Daelen’s shadow, and you weren't supposed to be separated!”

“Huh?” Cat wondered. “Oh that – that was before I got my note at Calin's Tower. It's not so important now. I have what I need. And I didn’t drag you anywhere, your client did. I just made you question the terms of your contract. Whatever happens, we’ll deal with it together. For now, sit down or go for a walk, but either way, please relax.”

Mandalee made a show of controlling herself, but she was still tightly wound.

Catriona smiled affectionately and shook her head in mild exasperation.

“First you tried to kill him, then you saved him, then you started to like him, and now you’re worried that the dark clone that has singularly failed to kill Daelen for a thousand years when he was at full strength, is suddenly going to find a way to do it in his weakened state. You think I don’t make sense? You’re not exactly a rock of consistency yourself.”

The White Assassin had to admit when she put it that way, she had a point. There was just too much going on that Mandalee didn't understand, and she didn't like it.

She decided a walk was the preferable option, Shyleen at her side, leaving Catriona to her book. A book on photography, of all things. Mandalee had no idea why Cat would want to study that at a time like this, but then she'd never understood half of what her friend was interested in.

*****

When at last Daelen returned, appearing high above StormClaw Island, his power level was far beyond anything his mortal companions had felt before.

"Catriona!" he boomed, "I want to begin your training right now. Come on, do you really think that you can 'deal with me,' or are you all talk? Just look at the powers you have – none rival mine, and nor do yours, Mandalee. You two think you can beat me? Then come on, get your butts up here. Now!"

The building shook as if Daelen's voice was an enormous thunderclap. Powerful gusts of wind seemed to come from every movement of Daelen's hands and feet.

"Come on! At least give me a taste of what little powers you have. I mean, you say that you can deal with me, so come on and try it!" Daelen boomed.

Mandalee and Shyleen rushed to Catriona's side. "What's happened to him?" the assassin whispered.

Daelen heard her.

"Something amazing!" Daelen bellowed. "I'm more powerful than I have been for centuries, which means I don't need my pets anymore!"

Calmly, without hurrying, sitting in a bubble of serenity, untroubled by Daelen's storm, Cat put her book away in her pocket dimension.

Leaning on her staff to help her to her feet, she demanded, "What the hell is wrong with you, Daelen? This is not like you. Is your dark clone too powerful for you to keep in check, now that you've merged?"

"They've done what?" Mandalee gasped.

Cat did not reply.

"You look down on our powers, shadow warrior," she continued, "but at least we can control ourselves. You can't even do that. You've lost it Daelen; get a grip."

"How do you know about our joining?" Daelen thundered.

"You just don't learn, do you? Knowledge is my business. You think you can dismiss me with a wave of your hand, but you can't. It's time somebody taught you some respect for others. You come here, issue your orders and expect us to jump to comply. Well, forget it. I am on this mission for my own reasons, but now that I have the information from Calin's Tower, maybe I don't need you anymore. Now I know my destiny, I can choose to walk away. If you kill Kullos by yourself, that's up to you, and if he kills you…well, right now, I'd say that's no great loss."

"Just as I thought – a weakling and a coward."

"Oh no, it takes courage to choose not to fight and strength to walk away. It is cowardice for you to join with your dark clone just because you're scared you won't be able to defeat your enemy. It is weak to join with someone and allow them to dominate you. Ha! When I join sympathically with Pyrah, it's on equal terms even though she's powerful enough to kill a shadow warrior. I, a 'mere mortal,' have more willpower than you do. You're pathetic."

With that, Cat deliberately turned her back on Daelen and calmly walked away.

Livid, Daelen roared, "Don't you dare turn your back on me!"

Cat just ignored him, and Daelen's rage got the better of him. Without warning, he powered up his beam cannon and fired, killing Catriona on the spot.

"No!" Mandalee screamed, running to her friend's side. "To think I was just beginning to like you!" she spat at Daelen, cradling Cat's lifeless body in her arms. "You think you're some kind of hero, but you're just a filthy, stinking monster – I should have fulfilled my contract and killed you when I had the chance!"

Daelen didn't respond; he was too stunned.

'*How could I do this to her?*' he wondered, floating down to the ground.

Had he spoken that aloud? He didn't know; he didn't care. In blackest despair, he did what few people had ever seen him do – he sat down and wept.

"She was so beautiful and smart and funny. She helped me at great risk to herself, and I killed her. She was right, I'm a weak coward, allowing my dark clone to achieve by joining what he couldn't in combat. I let him dominate me and use me to destroy her.

"If you're going to kill me, Mandalee, do it. I won't try to stop you. But if you let me live, I swear I will keep my dark side under control long enough to kill Kullos. After that, I don't care what happens to me. Either way, it's your choice."

Mandalee was torn as never before. She didn't know what to do. Fortunately, she was saved from the choice when a wolf slunk out of the shadows. Both Daelen and Mandalee looked on in disbelief as it changed into Catriona Redfletching.

"So, does this mean we've got the real Daelen back, or what?" she asked, in the same tone she might use to ask the time of day.

"Cat!" both her friends exclaimed at once and wrapped her in a three-way hug.

"Be careful," she laughed, "or you'll kill me for real this time, by suffocation!"

"But how?" Daelen asked.

With a wave of her staff, the dead Catriona vanished.

"A simple Mirror Image spell," she answered, as if that explained everything.

*****

My mother was three steps ahead, as usual, gentle reader. She had been working on the spell since she found out Daelen could copy himself. It seemed like a natural extension of her Nature's Mirror. If she could reflect beams of light, then surely, she could reflect an image of herself in a similar way to taking a photograph. Couple that with her Windy Steps spell, making air solid enough to stand on, and she could make her copy seem solid and real, too. She already had experience of the workings of photography; she just needed a little more detail. A quick look at the book on the science of photography provided the final piece of the puzzle. When Mandalee had left the room, Cat had cast the spell, leaving her copy sitting right there while her real self took the form of a seagull and flew out to investigate what was going on with Daelen.

*****

"So, the Catriona I killed was just an illusion!" Daelen gasped, much relieved.

"That's right, and now that I've successfully used such a simple trick against you, maybe it's time you swallowed your ego a bit."

Mandalee demanded some solo attention then, hugging her friend tight, saying, "I'm so happy you're alright." Then she stepped back and slapped Cat across the cheek. "And that's for letting me think you were dead."

To Daelen, she warned, "You have some serious making up to do before I will ever trust you again."

"I swear nothing like that will ever happen again," Daelen vowed.

Cat inclined her head in acknowledgement. "So, what exactly happened to you out there? I didn't get much from my spying."

Daelen promised to explain all about Aden's request to parley, but he wanted to take them somewhere first. They followed him to his portal room, where he ushered them through the one he had told them led to Earth. There to retreat, recover and train. Also, to buy time, almost literally.

He reasoned that no matter what powers of detection Kullos might have, he surely couldn't spy on them on another world.

"What about Shyleen?" Mandalee asked.

"Up to her," Daelen replied, simply. "If she comes, she'll have to stay in my grounds – can't have a leopard running around in the city. Otherwise, she can stay here on StormClaw. There's plenty of wild prey out there so she won't starve. Remember, it'll only be a few days for her."

Shyleen chose to stay on StormClaw, and just admonished Mandalee to be mindful and take special care of her half-Faery friend during her 'difficult time.' The White Assassin tried to press her on what she meant by that, but the leopard kept her own counsel and would say no more.

*****

The portal room on the other side was inside a facility that was virtually identical to his base on StormClaw. As they stepped out into the corridor, Cat pointed out the photographs that were mounted all along one wall. Head and shoulder shots, each with a name underneath. A few appeared human, while others were species that she couldn't identify. They were all from different worlds, Daelen explained. None from Tempestria. His bases didn't run themselves, clean themselves, maintain themselves, stock themselves with food and supplies. So, he usually kept two or three people on as his personal staff. Presently, he had two young women in his employ: Sara and Jessica.

"They're out at the moment," he informed them. "I haven't had chance to forewarn them like I normally do. I'll text them – send them a message – and ask them to come in to help out with a few things tomorrow."

"And they're from one of those other worlds?" Mandalee wondered.

Daelen confirmed it. "Their stories are not mine to tell. Suffice to say they're refugees of sorts. They're happy to take care of my base here and elsewhere, in exchange for the chance to escape and see other worlds."

Cat nodded; she could see how that would be appealing.

"Can they pass for human?" Mandalee wondered.

"Hardly!" Daelen laughed.

"Not that I'm worried about how they might look," Mandalee assured him, quickly, lest there be any misunderstanding. "I'm just wondering how they fit in out there."

"Or are the people of Earth used to seeing aliens?" Cat suggested.

Daelen smiled as if at a joke he knew his companions wouldn't get. "Not normally, no," he replied. He told them that, as a rule, whenever they went out into the wider world, Sara and Jessica wore a device called a perception filter. "But if I'm right about where they've gone today…" he opened a door into a bedroom and peered around the door for a moment. "Yep, I'm right. They've left them behind. Today, they don't need to worry about it."

"Why not?" Cat asked, unable to work it out.

“For the same reason you don’t need to worry about your clothes or your markings looking too conspicuous when we go out.”

His explanation did little to answer Cat and Mandalee’s confusion. All he would say was that they would see what he meant when they went out to a place he called a ‘shopping mall.’

“Sara and Jessica are at an event in an adjoining building:

“A sci-fi convention.”

Chapter 18

The two young women had never seen such crowds before. Even a busy marketplace in Walminster couldn't compare. The speed of their road transport – a horseless carriage called a car – took some getting used to, as well.

Laughing, Daelen joked that if they thought that was fast, they should try a rollercoaster.

As they travelled, Daelen talked about his meeting with his dark clone.

They had agreed to communicate telepathically, to maximise privacy, and Aden had made a surprising amount of sense. After his defeat at the hands of Dreya the Dark, he'd thought of a way to use his much-drained power to his advantage: to spy on Kullos through astral projection.

Daelen admitted he'd done much the same thing when he was suffering from the effects of Pyrah's venom.

"That's news to me," Cat objected.

Mandalee nodded in agreement.

Daelen apologised but assured them he had always intended to tell them when they got here and could talk without risk of sensitive information being overheard.

Mandalee had to concede that made sense and given how many times Catriona had criticised his lack of strategic thinking, she could hardly complain. She did find it interesting, though, that he and Aden had both had the same idea under similar circumstances.

"He and I were split from the same shadow warrior," Daelen pointed out, "so it's not too surprising that we think along similar lines, sometimes."

"And now that you've remerged, I guess you're literally of one mind again," Mandalee supposed.

Daelen shook his head. "Not so. We're still separate, despite our merging. That's why he was able to dominate me for a while. I will have to battle him for the rest of my life, same as ever. Only the battlefield has changed. I can never again be what I was – what the original Daelen was. Complete. Whole."

"You've glued the two halves of the box back together again," Cat mused, thinking of his analogy for his people as being 'light in a box,' "but the damage cannot be reversed."

Daelen smiled, grimly, "Not unless you really can turn back Time a thousand years. But even if you could, I suppose we'd lose everything we both experienced in that time. That's not a price I would ever pay. Maybe if I could return home…" he trailed off, and then dismissed the idea, "but that's impossible. Anyway, for the moment, it's just as well," he added, "because I can compartmentalise certain information that we don't want my 'other half' to know."

Cat nodded, recognising his oblique warning to be careful not to mention certain things, such as the presence of the being that killed her parents. Michael might call it a 'void-creature,' but to Cat, it would always simply be the 'Monster.'

Daelen returned to his story.

*****

'*Kullos wasn't paying attention to a power signature as low as mine,*' Aden told Daelen. '*He was too busy watching you, which wasn't difficult considering all the noise you've been making. What have you been doing out here, anyway? I'd have thought you'd be sneaking up on him.*'

'*Believe it or not, that was the plan,*' Daelen admitted, ruefully. '*Things got a little out of hand.*' Not wishing to discuss it any further, he asked what Aden had found out from his spying, wanting to see if it would match what he had observed for himself.

'*Well, I must admit your distraction proved quite useful,*' Aden conceded, '*because I was able to snoop around for ages and I found out where Kullos was getting all his extra power from. You know, don't you?*' he asked.

Daelen had learned a lot about information trading from his question-for-a-question game with Catriona, and he wasn't going to blurt everything out just because Aden might already know.

Instead, he simply replied, '*You tell me.*'

'*He has his dimensional control device,*' Aden told him. Even though the communication was still telepathic, Daelen could still detect fear creeping into his words. '*Or most of it, at any rate.*'

'*Yes, I saw that, too,*' Daelen agreed. '*But how? It was destroyed a thousand years ago when we were split,*' he objected.

'*Was it really?*' Aden gasped. '*Well, goodness me, I had no idea. I mean, it's not like I was there at the time or anything. Oh, wait – yes, I was.*'

Having got that out of his system, he went on to say he'd gathered that Kullos must have been in the process of finding the lost fragments for some time.

Again, Daelen objected that even if he could find them all, it wasn't as if he could glue it back together and expect it to work like new.

Aden pointed out that Kullos had already got it working well enough to access the energy from that part of himself that was still in the shadow realm. Aden didn't understand where he'd found the technology to do it, but he had.

'*Someone's been interfering with events that really ought not to be tampered with any more than they already have been,*' Daelen quoted.

'*What?*' Aden wondered.

Daelen decided to add Time Intervention to the list of information to be shielded from his dark clone.

'*Just something I read in a sci-fi novel on Earth,*' he lied.

'*Why would you bring that up now?*' Aden frowned.

'*Just popped into my head,*' he shrugged, dismissing the issue.

It was all just speculation, anyway. Kullos had always been a skilled engineer, so it was conceivable he'd figured out a way to do it all on his own.

Aden conceded they might have underestimated Kullos' technical skill.

'*It could even be an application of some kind of new magic,*' Daelen supposed.

He had expected Aden to scoff at such a suggestion and was surprised when he didn't.

'*Before my run-in with Dreya the Dark,*' he replied ruefully, '*I might have dismissed such an idea, but now…*' He trailed off and then admitted something Daelen never thought he'd hear his clone say. '*Daelen, I was scared. Me, a shadow warrior, scared of a mortal wizard!*'

'*They're on the verge of something,*' Daelen offered. '*Me, you, Kullos and Michael we can't go on, the four of us like it's business as usual. Things have changed, and we need to do the same.*'

Daelen had to hide a smile when he realised, he was paraphrasing Catriona. She had made quite the impression on him already. He wondered how strong that influence might yet grow.

Aden agreed, '*I think Kullos figured that out a while ago and he's left us scrambling to catch up. Think about it: he must have enough of his control device assembled by now to re-Ascend, but he hasn't. Why?*'

'*Because that's not his intent,*' Daelen realised.

*****

"So, what *is* his intent?" Mandalee asked as they reached the shopping mall itself.

Cat nodded. She wanted to know the same thing.

As they stepped towards the doors to the shopping mall, they opened automatically, as if in welcome invitation to the treasure trove of wonders that lay beyond. It was by far the largest single building they had ever seen. Even the Council building in Walminster could fit inside it. Either side of wide aisles, were densely packed shops, selling all manner of clothes, shoes, bags and jewellery. The smell of food mingled with that of perfume, and the noise was deafening: A million conversations, constant background music, announcements and strange sounds made by technology and gadgets at whose function neither my mother nor Aunt Mandalee could begin to guess.

True to his word, the presence of people from the 'sci-fi convention' did seem to provide excellent cover for their Tempestrian clothing and Cat's half-Faery features. Indeed, there were several people – native humans, they assumed – dressed in outfits far more outlandish than Mandalee's white leather and Catriona's red robes. Catriona's usually feint Faery spots seemed to glow under the strange lighting, but people just thought they were done with make-up. Most of the crowd never even gave them a second glance, although there were a few smiles, and several people asked to perform what the girls assumed must be some kind of religious or cultural ritual known as 'taking a selfie.' Keen to fit in with local customs, they saw no reason to refuse. When these people showed them the end result of their 'selfie,' Catriona recognised it as a form of photography, but clearly far in advance of what their world had yet developed.

Mandalee was quite happy to soak up the atmosphere and enjoy the experience, while Cat had to restrain herself from continually asking how things worked. She was especially interested to learn that these people had taken Calin's core concept of making knowledge accessible to all, to a whole new level. They had found a way to make knowledge instantly available from anywhere, as she understood it, by storing all their information in clouds in the sky. The sky that, she realised as she looked through the glass dome in the ceiling, was totally free of void storms.

Catriona filed that away in her mind under 'things to discuss later.' For now, she needed to focus on what Daelen was telling them, and his answer to Mandalee's question definitely brought her mind back down to, well, Earth, she supposed.

Daelen spoke two words, "Heaven's Surrender."

"What's that when it's at home?" Mandalee wondered.

Whatever it was, Catriona was positive of one thing: it did not sound good. Still, she was momentarily distracted by her friend's turn of phrase.

"'When it's at home'?" she asked, with a puzzled frown.

Mandalee explained that she'd been trying to discreetly listen to snippets of conversations in the crowd, and she'd overheard that expression.

"Did I use it right?" she asked Daelen.

The shadow warrior grinned and nodded.

"Spot on," he assured her, "and if you're interested in learning Earth expressions, you're going to love Jessica. She uses them all the time."

Bringing the conversation back to more important matters, Mandalee repeated her question.

"So, 'Heaven's Surrender'?"

Daelen reminded his friends that Kullos had once been both his people's Chief Engineer and their greatest Champion.

"Heaven's Surrender was a weapon he devised in a desperate attempt to win our ongoing war."

It had been his responsibility to deploy the weapon against their enemy, only their enemy found out about it and took it from him before he could use it. He was severely injured in the process, and while he was evacuated to a medical facility, his shadow warrior unit tried to wrest the weapon from her. The weapon was damaged in the struggle, and a fraction of its power was unleashed. It wasn't enough to harm their enemy, but the entire two-dozen-strong shadow warrior unit was totally obliterated.

"Any further development on the weapon was banned from that moment on," Daelen explained. "It was deemed too dangerous."

"So, how can Kullos use it, if this enemy of yours took the only one?" Mandalee asked.

"Because there was a prototype," Daelen explained as he continued to guide them around the mall. "There was no known safe way to dispose of it, so it was entrusted to, guess who?"

"Kullos!" his friends chorused.

Daelen nodded. "He kept it safely locked away in his own personal vault."

"Don't tell me," Cat groaned, shutting her eyes and cringing at the thought. "A pocket dimension."

Again, Daelen nodded. "Right."

"And with a repaired control device thing, he'll be able to pull that prototype out of mothballs and use it," Mandalee deduced. "That's why you recombined with your dark clone? So, you can get there quick and stop him before he gets all the pieces?"

Daelen shook his head.

"It's too late for that, isn't it?" Cat surmised.

Daelen confirmed it.

"He already has enough pieces to activate the weapon; it'll just be unstable. Trouble is, *he's* unstable. If I confront him before his device is complete, he'll just use the weapon anyway. But if we wait until he *does* have all the pieces, at least the weapon will be controllable."

"Oh great, he'll be in control when he blows us all to bits," Mandalee sniped.

"My clone and I agreed we'd have only one chance: our recombined power might just be enough for me to take it from him and use it to destroy him, or least the part of him that's in this mortal plane. Nothing I can do about the rest of him, but if I can re-shatter his control device – assuming it doesn't blow itself apart anyway, due to Heaven's Surrender, he will be cut off just like the rest of my people."

"As you are cut off from them," Cat realised. Of course, she already knew that Alycia's Barrier prevented all travel between the mortal realm and the higher planes. She just hadn't framed the thought in quite that way to see it from Daelen's perspective. She knew what it was like to lose a home. She was lucky – her 'Angel' had given her a new one. "With Kullos gone and you recombined, you'll be the last of your kind in our world," she realised, further. "The last living shadow warrior."

Daelen nodded. "I'll be alone."

Cat hugged him tight, tears in her eyes.

"No," she insisted. "You won't."

Daelen smiled, weakly, at the sentiment.

Even Mandalee, though she still wasn't sure she should trust him, at least felt sympathy and refrained from any remarks about her friend's feelings for him.

Instead, she asked something that had always puzzled her about his kind.

"You've explained how, when you and Kullos came down to our mortal plane, you had to leave part of yourselves behind, but you haven't explained what that means for that part of you." Convinced she was once again failing to make any sense, she tried again. "What I'm asking is: while this part of you is running around down here, is the other part of you still running around up there?"

Daelen shook his head. "When my people used to do this all the time – before they were cut off – it was like going to sleep. In fact, once upon a time, long ago, before our understanding grew, my people used to believe the mortal realm wasn't real."

"What?" his companions demanded.

Daelen smiled reassuringly. "It was a very long time ago, but they honestly used to think their dimensional control devices were dream enhancers and the mortal realm was just some kind of shared dreamscape." He chuckled, as he continued, "Even when they began to accept that this was a real place they were travelling to, there was a school of thought that suggested we'd dreamed you into existence."

"Maybe you did," Mandalee considered. "There are a few creation myths on Tempestria that say the world was dreamed into being. Maybe your people were the dreamers."

"Philosophy aside," Cat put in, "in the case of you and Kullos, you've both been asleep for a very long time."

"Once again, putting it in mortal terms, we'd both be classed as being in a coma."

"Can your people survive being in a coma for that long?" Mandalee wondered.

"I honestly don't know," Daelen admitted. "Nor do I know how long the part of me that's 'running around down here' as you put it, can survive without the part that should be 'running around up there.' Plus, you know time works differently on Tempestria compared to Earth, so imagine trying to relate either of those to how it works on my home plane of existence."

"I imagine you can't," Cat replied.

"Exactly," Daelen confirmed. "All I can do – all anyone can do – is live my life for as long as I'm alive. My people call you 'mortals' and I use the term out of habit myself, even though I know it's a misnomer. After all, it's not as if shadow warriors are immortal. The nature of our existence is different, but still, we are born, we live, we age, and we die, just like you."

Once again choosing practicalities over philosophy, Cat pressed, "Anyway, going back to Heaven's Surrender, what can we do about it?"

"Well, I'm the only one who knows enough about the weapon to shield your world from the overspill of power."

"How?" Cat asked.

"I was working on a different angle in our war because Kullos wasn't the only Champion of our people with technical expertise. Not a weapon, but a shield. Some way to keep our enemy out of our plane of reality forever. I can adapt that shield to contain the power of Heaven's Surrender and protect your world."

"But how can you access it, if you can't reach your home plane of reality?" Mandalee wondered.

It was Cat who answered, "Because it's already here, isn't it?" she realised. "In Michael's Tomb."

Daelen gasped in astonishment, "How on Earth did you figure that one out? Oh, no, don't tell me: You used your special ability of paying attention."

"Well, isn't it obvious? That place is full of technology. Some of it keeps Michael in…what's that word again…stasis? But that wasn't its original purpose. It couldn't be. It was built before Michael even existed. Besides, there's an entire lower level to the place. I'm guessing that's where this shield of yours is kept, yes?"

Daelen confirmed it. "In a way, Kullos was partly right all those centuries ago: there was a sort of weapon being built down here. It seemed like the best way to keep it out of enemy hands. She was too busy with our war to even notice the mortal realm. In fact, I don't believe she even knows it exists."

"And what fancy name did you give this shield power of yours?" Mandalee asked.

"The only thing I could call it. To my mind, it was a final roll of the dice. There was no way to know if it would be successful in keeping the enemy out. When I came to deploy it against her, in mortal terms, I was just going to close my eyes and make a Wish."

"So, in a nutshell," Cat recapped, "you're planning to steal this ultimate weapon from Kullos, use it against him, and protect our world with a Wish?"

Daelen nodded pensively.

To Mandalee, she remarked, "And you think I have ridiculous radical plans."

There followed a profound silence, penetrated only when the assassin declared, "Dear gods, I need a drink."

"Me, too," Catriona agreed.

"I think we could all use one," Daelen approved. "Let's take a break from our mission. We've been through a lot already, and there's plenty more to do, but for now, for the next few hours, I officially veto any conversation about wars, our fight against Kullos and higher planes of reality. There's loads to do in this place, so let's just try to forget about it for a while, agreed?"

The two young women glanced at each other, then looked back at Daelen.

"Agreed," they chimed in unison.

Chapter 19

The three companions spent the next few hours eating, drinking, and shopping. Mandalee was more interested in the clothing and jewellery stores, than was Catriona. She was especially pleased that there didn't seem to be any issues relating to her gender identity while she was shopping.

"Well, I'm not going to stand here and say there's no such prejudice in this world," Daelen sighed. "Sadly, that would be a lie. But in a big city shopping mall like this, frankly, you're nothing people haven't seen before."

The only slight incident was when Mandalee helpfully told a sales assistant that a pair of jeans she was going to try on were damaged. She pointed out the rips and tears on the legs, but apparently, they were meant to be like that. The assistant pointed out other 'non-ripped styles' that actually cost less.

A very confused Catriona tried to make sense of it. "Why would clothes that look damaged cost more than clothes that don't?"

Daelen tried to explain it was called fashion, but neither Mandalee nor Cat really understood.

Several hours in, Mandalee was still thoroughly enjoying the experience and ended up with more bags than she could carry, so Daelen had to help her out as well as pay for everything with something called a 'credit card' under the human name 'Daniel Storm.' She had already changed three times. The only constant, a pair of silver sapphire earrings that caught the light as they dangled from her ears. They had been her first purchase – love at first sight.

By contrast, Catriona's initial curiosity in technology and books had quickly evaporated, until enthusiasm had been replaced by irritation and ultimately a nasty temper. She seemed intent on finding reasons to dislike everything she saw. In the end, she refused to buy all but a few basic cotton clothing essentials. Otherwise, her acquisitions were limited to a single black dress made from a synthetic velvet, which she had only accepted because Mandalee picked it out for her, insisting it would look perfect on her. Not wanting to upset her friend, she did her best to wear a fake smile and seem grateful.

In truth, she hated it: The fabric reminded her of Dreya. She was already feeling cut off from her world and this reminder of how much she missed the woman she loved, while at the same time having feelings for Daelen, was like pouring salt into an open wound. But her magically backed promise kept her from explaining the pain this experience was causing her and that made her lash out.

At last, she declared she'd had it with the place and flatly refused to walk another step in any direction other than the exit.

"I'm going back outside to read," she decided. "You keep wasting your time if you like, but I'm not wasting any more of mine!"

"But you've barely bought anything," Daelen objected. "I thought you'd want to be able to fit in with this world when you go out."

Cat insisted it didn't matter. She didn't need to fit in because she had no intention of setting foot outside Daelen's place again while they were on Earth.

When Mandalee asked Cat to put some of her stuff in her pocket dimension, her friend snapped, "I can't! All my connections with our world are severed here, so I can't access my pocket dimension, and even if I could, it's not there to be cluttered with stupid, frivolous stuff like your shopping!" Scowling at Daelen, she growled, "Let me know when you're ready to go. We've got more important things to do – or at least, I do."

Mandalee tried to ask what was wrong, but Cat just turned her back and strode away towards the exit.

*****

Later that evening, back at Daelen's house, Cat was sitting in a corner, her nose in a book, while her companions chatted on the other side of the room. They occasionally glanced her way, but they treated Cat in the same way one might treat her namesake animal when its claws were out, its tail was wagging, and its fur was standing on end. They sensed that even asking what was wrong was likely to get them scratched, so they simply gave her a wide berth and hoped she would come to them when she was ready.

When Daelen and Mandalee decided to retire for the night, Daelen approached her, but a glare stopped him from approaching within three feet.

"What do you want?" she demanded.

She knew she was being rude, but somehow, she just couldn't stop herself. From her shapeshifting, she thought she understood what pain was. This place was proving her wrong about that.

"I was just suggesting to Mandalee that we should go to bed now. The time difference in this place can throw you off, but it's good to try and establish a routine for the next few weeks."

"Thank you so much for your opinion," she replied acidly.

"Look, if this is about before, I swear I'm back under control now."

Cat's only response was a stony silence.

"Tomorrow, we start training properly," he told her, "so you'll need to be wide awake for that because I promise you, you're going to have to use every trick in the book."

"My tricks aren't in the book yet, Daelen," Catriona countered, closing the book she'd been reading to punctuate her statement. "Good night," she offered; a phrase with no emotion behind it. Refusing to even look at Daelen, she walked away.

*****

Dawn came, and the two girls woke to the scent of cooked eggs, bacon and sausages drifting towards them from the kitchen.

As they rose, drawn to movement from outside, Mandalee offered her friend a "Good Morning," and got nothing but a "That remains to be seen," in return. The White Assassin chose not to comment.

There came a polite knock on the door, and a female voice sang, "Heya, loves! Are you up?"

When Mandalee invited her in, the door opened to reveal a young woman standing there. If she were from Tempestria, Mandalee would guess she was in her late teens, no more than two or three years younger than Cat and herself. However, she was clearly not Tempestrian, so she couldn't be sure. The girl had dark purple skin, golden eyes, catlike ears poking through her dark hair and a tail swishing behind her. Skin tone aside, her face was mostly human-like, but with just a hint of something feline. That was OK. As she'd once told her friend beside her, she'd always got along really well with cats.

"I'm Jessica," she beamed with a small wave. "I work for Daelen here. He asked us to come and help out while you're with us. Just wanted to tell you, your breakfast is ready if you'd like to follow me…"

The pair walked with her, through to the dining room, where someone was just finishing up preparing a table for them. Her skin tone was ever-so-slightly paler, Mandalee thought, but otherwise she looked remarkably similar to Jessica. She hoped that wasn't racist. Just because they were 'alien' from her perspective, she'd hate to be one of those people who thought they 'all looked alike.'

Her fears proved unfounded, however, as Jessica introduced her as, "Sara – my twin sister."

"Nice to meet you both," Mandalee offered.

"Likewise," Sara returned.

Cat remained silent. Jessica and Sara's eyes flickered towards each other but otherwise did their best to pretend they hadn't noticed. "If you'd care to sit down, loves?" Jessica invited them. "Cheers," she smiled when they complied. "Right now, first thing I need to ask: do you have any food allergies I should know about?"

"Food allergies?" Cat wondered.

"Not that we know of," Mandalee agreed, looking equally blank.

"Well, it's always good to check," Jessica opined. "We wouldn't want to poison Daelen's visitors on their first day. It's bad manners," she laughed.

Then, noticing that her sister seemed to have zoned out for a moment, she declared, "Earth to Sara!"

Sara gave a start. "Hmmm?"

"Shouldn't you be getting back in the kitchen, love? Before you burn something?"

"Oh, yeah. Sorry," Sara apologised to their guests, "still recovering from the afterparty," she explained. "Two hours' sleep."

"Hey, it's the same for me," Jessica objected, "but I'm proper bright-eyed and," she flared out the end of her tail, "bushy-tailed as always. You're just getting old, that's what it is." she teased.

"I thought you said you were twins?" Mandalee put in, enjoying their banter.

Jessica was about to say something, but Sara cut her off. "This is the part where she says she's younger by, like, ten minutes."

Jessica grinned, "You're as old as the person you feel, dearie. Speaking of which, how old was that elf boy you were snogging in the corner last night?"

"You saw that?"

"Sara, love, *everybody* saw that! They put it up on the big screen. Was he really an elf or just a human dressed up?"

"Jessica!" Sara admonished her sister. "You know I never kiss and tell." With that, she excused herself, saying, "I'll be in the kitchen."

As she walked away, Jessica turned back to the two guests and whispered, "To be honest, loves, I'm cream-crackered myself. I just hide it better.

"Now," she continued, "normally I'd ask what you'd like, but we weren't sure what you're used to where you're from, so we figured it'd probably be best if we were to give you a full breakfast and then you can leave anything you don't want. We won't be offended. OK, dears?"

Mandalee agreed that sounded reasonable. Cat just nodded, which left Jessica hesitant.

"You sure?" she pressed gently.

"Yes, fine!" Cat affirmed in a belligerent tone.

Jessica flickered a nervous smile and glanced at Mandalee, who offered a small shake of the head in a silent, apologetic, 'please ignore my friend.'

"There's water and orange juice on the table," Jessica told them. "Anything else you need, just give us a nudge, OK, loves?"

"Thank you, Jessica," Mandalee replied, doing her best to reassure her. "It smells delicious."

"Well, we'll do our best," she replied and left for the kitchen.

When she'd left the room, keeping her voice down, Mandalee rebuked her friend, "Cat, that was rude. Whatever your problem is, I'm pretty sure it's not Sara and Jessica's fault. If you want to be grumpy with Daelen and me, fine, but don't take it out on them."

Cat's eyes flashed for a moment, but the fire faltered, and with a sigh, she admitted, "You're right." She still wasn't forthcoming about what her problem was, but she did apologise when Jessica returned. "And say sorry to Sara for me, too, will you?"

"No problem, love," she replied with a smile on her lips and a twinkle in her eye as she placed their cooked meals in front of them. "That was nothing. You should see Daelen when he's in one of his moods." She shrugged. "It's part of the job."

"Well, it shouldn't be," Cat insisted, frowning. "I was wrong, it won't happen again, and next time Daelen's rude to you, make sure you tell him it's unacceptable."

"Maybe I will, at that," Jessica, her cheeks taking on a golden sheen. Her species' equivalent of a blush, Cat supposed. "Anyway, I'd best not keep you talking. Don't want you leaving a bad review on the 'net cause your breakfast was cold, do I?" she laughed. Then, seeing the blank looks, she dismissed it with a wave of her hand. "Don't mind me. I'm not from around here – obviously," she added with a giggle, indicating her body, "but I've been here a while and picked up a lot of the lingo with the way I talk. Sara's not so into it, but I don't even realise I'm doing it, half the time. Anyway, I'll leave you guys to it. Give us a nudge if you need anything else, OK, dears?"

With a fresh smile and a wink, she left the room once more.

"I like her," Cat remarked, as she tucked into her breakfast, smiling what Mandalee thought was, without doubt, the broadest smile she'd seen on her face since they came to this world.

"Well, she's perked you up, that's for sure," the cleric observed, between mouthfuls of sausage, bacon and eggs.

"Yeah, sorry," Cat nodded. "It's just this place." She waved a fork in the air to vaguely encompass their surroundings. "Don't know if it's the world or just because we're in a huge city full of concrete, but I've never been so cut off from nature, and I don't like it."

Suddenly, Mandalee realised that must be what Shyleen meant about taking 'special care' of Catriona during her 'difficult time.'

"Shyleen knew you'd feel this way," she realised, "I just didn't think."

Catriona recalled how, years ago, back on Tempestria, her father had ventured into a human city and hated it so much, he never again left his forest home. Catriona had never had that problem, "but maybe I inherited some of that from my Dad, after all. You're a Cleric of Nature – I'm surprised you can stand it."

"It's OK for me. Half my soul is still on Tempestria," she reminded her friend.

"Of course," Cat understood. "But even the clothes – all those synthetic fabrics. I appreciate the technical skill to create them, but—"

"—But you don't want to wear them," Mandalee finished for her. "That dress I got you – you really hate it, don't you?" she sighed, looking slightly crestfallen.

"Yes," Cat admitted. "I'm sorry, but yes, I do. Wearing it would be…painful," she went on, choosing her words, carefully. "Can't really say why."

"You don't need to. I should have realised. At least you're talking to me again."

"Yeah, Jessica helped, despite how rude I was to her. Wherever she's from, I get the impression that she's somehow close to nature. She seems to radiate something that feels similar to my druid magic."

"Yes, I sensed that, too," Mandalee agreed. "It's different, which I guess is to be expected since she's from another world, but it's only as different as…" she floundered, looking for an analogy.

"As different as this food," Cat suggested, indicating their breakfast.

"Exactly," Mandalee nodded, enthusiastically, delighted that her friend was engaging with her like this again. "I mean, we have pretty similar things in our world, but…"

"…but it's like a slightly different flavour. Like using a different combination of spices," Cat concluded.

"Well, then," Mandalee declared, raising her glass, "here's to diversity: the spice of life!"

"The spice of life!" Cat echoed, raising her glass, too, adding in a fair approximation of Jessica's voice, "Cheers, love!"

Chapter 20

Sara returned to the dining room just as they were finishing up.

"Message from Daelen," she announced. "He says he's giving you an hour to let your breakfast go down and warm-up, then he expects you in his training centre."

Cat arched her eyebrows. "Does he now?"

"Jessica's gone to get you a combat suit each. It's a lightweight, magically resistant body armour made from—"

"—Made from some kind of clever synthetic fabric, no doubt."

"Uh-oh," Mandalee remarked, knowing how her friend would react to that.

"Well, Daelen can 'expect' what he likes, but there is no way in hell I'll be wearing any such thing."

Sara offered an apologetic smile. "He's used to getting his own way."

"I bet he is," Cat agreed.

"If it helps," Mandalee put in, trying to smooth things over, "I'll give it a try, and I'm quite looking forward to a physical workout with a shadow warrior. Maybe he'll even teach me some of his powers."

Cat shrugged. "His major destructive powers don't interest me much, except on a purely academic level. They're overrated and disruptive to nature. I'm a little surprised you would consider using them yourself." She breathed deeply as she stood and stretched out the kinks in her muscles. "Ah," she remarked, "I can feel my stubborn streak surfacing. Daelen is going to find me very picky about what I choose to do today."

"Well, as my sister would say," Sara offered, "'Don't shoot the messenger, love'."

"Not at all," Catriona assured her. She was unfamiliar with the expression, but the meaning was plain enough. "That won't happen again. Thank you for the message, Sara. What happens after you deliver it is no fault of yours."

"Anyway," Mandalee spoke up, "since we have time to kill, why don't we talk about you for a while? You and your sister, what's your story?"

"You mean, 'What's a nice pair of girls like us doing in a place like this'?" came a voice from the doorway.

They turned and saw Jessica walk in, wearing an outfit that covered her from her neck down to her ankles, leaving only her tail sticking out. It seemed to cling to her skin, smoothing every contour. Mandalee was immediately fascinated by it. In many ways, except for the colour, it wasn't all that different, in principle, to her own leather outfit. Something designed for maximum flexibility while, she suspected, offering more protection than the thin fabric would suggest.

Turning back to Sara, she wondered, "Is that one of those combat suits you were talking about?"

Sara agreed it was, and Jessica obligingly did a pirouette to show it off.

"You like?" Jessica asked.

"I do," the assassin agreed. "My friend's not keen."

"As I said, though," Cat reiterated, "I do appreciate the technical skill that can create such fabric." She walked over to Jessica and moved to feel the fabric on the girl's arm. "May I?"

"Sure thing, dear," she replied. "Maybe it'll help you change your mind."

As soon as Cat's hand touched Jessica, she yelped in pain and snatched it back.

"Maybe not," Sara remarked, rushing over to examine Cat's hand. The skin had turned red and inflamed with small, raised white patches of swelling. "Looks like an extreme allergic reaction."

"It's OK," Cat assured them. "It's nothing serious, I'll have it healed in no…time…" she trailed off.

"What's wrong?" Mandalee asked.

Cat reminded her that she couldn't access her powers in this world.

"We should get you to the medical bay." Sara offered.

Mandalee shook her head. "I'll do it," she volunteered. "My deal with nature means my powers work fine no matter where I am."

Cat held up her uninjured hand and asked her to wait. "I want to test a theory," she insisted, wincing with the pain, "in the portal room."

They walked through the maze of corridors and opened the door to the room with the permanent portals to other worlds. Catriona could immediately sense which one was Tempestria. Breathing deeply, she reached out her senses to receive the Blessing of Alycia, Mother of Nature. Connection restored, it was a simple matter to heal the inflammation of her skin.

"As I thought," Cat mused. "All I need is a doorway to our world, and I can do everything here that I can do there."

"That link's important to you, isn't it?" Sara observed. "Not just for your magic, but to who you are."

Cat nodded.

"Believe me, we can relate," Sara sighed with a wistful smile. "My sister and I come here often, just to be close to our world. A world we can never see again."

"Why not?" Mandalee asked. "If you don't mind me asking. Feel free to tell me to mind my own business."

"Aww, rubbish!" Jessica chimed in dismissively. "There's no harm in telling 'em, is there, sis?"

Sara agreed. "It's not like we get to be ourselves around many people. 'Hi, I'm really a purple Chetsuan girl from another world that I can never go back to' isn't the best chat-up line."

"Who needs chat-up lines? Some of us just find the nearest cute elf boy and stick our tongue down his throat," Jessica teased.

"But seriously," Sara continued, refusing to rise to it. "If you want our story, we're perfectly happy to share. There's no point in making it a secret."

"As my sister says," Jessica explained, "we're Chetsuan girls. That's our name for our species: Chetsuan. Our world, Phitonia, is that one there," she pointed to the second portal from the right. "Unfortunately, we shared our world with these flying lizards called dragons. They had a different name for us: dinner."

"In the old days," Sara took up the story, "our people found ways to defend themselves and build a civilisation, despite not being top of the food chain. Then, a few decades ago, the red dragon Mallax rose to power. We don't really know the details."

"Yeah," Jessica agreed. "Dragon politics wasn't big on the school syllabus, was it, love? Back when there was a school. But as far as we understand it, even other dragons were scared of him and sort of fell into line or else. Now, by all accounts, Mallax had what I guess you might call a food allergy."

"Specifically, to Chetsuans," Sara put in.

"Yeah, even proximity to us brings him out in hives something rotten, poor dear. So, he decided, if we were no good to him, we were no good for any dragon, and suddenly we're off the menu. Which might seem like a good thing, except…"

"…Except that meant we got downgraded from dinner to vermin," Sara explained. "Their determination to exterminate us destroyed everything our people had built. Civilisation gone, our people were forced underground to live with the rats."

"All vermin together. Vermin United!" Jessica declared, punching the air, her voice dripping with sarcasm.

"We spent our early teens moving from one hole in the ground to another. We grew up fast, until one day, when it was our turn to gather food. Always a risk, but obviously a necessary one."

"That's when we got snatched," Jessica revealed, "and taken to the black dragon, Zacar. I guess you'd call him a scientist. Working alone as he did, even Mallax didn't know half of what he got up to. Zacar was looking for a final solution to their infestation problem, and under his orders, there were dragons constantly on the lookout for stray Chetsuans to become his laboratory rats."

"Longest year of our lives," Sara lamented. "Which was a hell of an achievement because not many lived that long."

Mandalee exchanged a glance with Cat. She was beginning to wish she'd never asked.

"What…erm…" the druidess began tentatively, "…what did he do to you?"

The way the two sisters looked at each other at that moment, the shared suffering in their eyes spoke volumes without them ever speaking a word.

In the end, Jessica shook her head emphatically. "No. Don't want to talk about that. Sorry, love."

Sara reached out and held her sister close. "You wouldn't thank us if we did," she whispered, a haunted look in her eyes.

Mandalee spoke up to say, "I am so sorry for making you relive this," she apologised, reaching out to them both. "I never imagined…"

"Nothing to be sorry for, dearie," Jessica assured her. "You haven't made us do anything, and as for reliving it, it's not like we're ever going to forget. We've just learned to get on with our lives."

"But you can't get on with your lives with your people?" Cat wondered.

"No, never," Sara shook her head, emphatically. "You see, the reason we survived was that we were Zacar's successful test rats."

"Oh, yeah, a real eureka moment for him, it was!" Jessica remarked. "We're carriers."

"Carriers?" Mandalee frowned, not understanding.

Catriona did. "Plague carriers," she clarified, tears in her eyes at the horror of the idea.

"Don't worry, you're perfectly safe." Sara assured them. "It can't jump species. Zacar made sure of that. He snared more of our people from across our world for lab trials. Other than caging them up, he didn't do a thing to them. He didn't need to: we did."

"Yep, we killed them all, we did. Every single one. We couldn't do anything except sit in our cages and watch them die slowly. Zacar was understandably delighted with us."

"True to the scientific method," Sara took up the story, "having successfully proved the formula under laboratory conditions, we would have been released back into the wild as field tests. Then, once our people started dying all around us, he would move on to mass production and create more of us carriers all over our world."

"Eventually, the carriers would be the last of our species, and if all the carriers were sterilised before they were released…"

"You couldn't reproduce," Mandalee realised, "so there would be no need to hunt down the carriers in the end. Give it time and extinction would happen naturally."

"Thank the stars it never got that far," Jessica put in.

"What happened?" Mandalee wanted to know.

"Daelen StormTiger happened," Jessica beamed.

"We'd all heard of him of course," Sara told them with a smile, "but to be honest, I thought it was just a myth. A story people told to give them hope. That one day, without warning, this superhero would drop out of the sky and save us. He'd done it before, hundreds of years ago, or so the story went. Beaten back the dragons, given our people a chance." She shrugged. "It obviously didn't last, so as I said, I never believed he was real."

"I did," Jessica put in. "I always did." A golden flush spread across her face as she continued, "It's kind of embarrassing, now that I know him, and please don't tell him I said this, but I used to pray to him. Or at least wish for him. And then, one day, my wish came true. He burst into the lab, tore open our cages, killed Zacar and destroyed every last bit of his research before setting fire to the place and opening up one of his blue portals to this world."

Sara took up the story. "He made sure we understood what would happen if we ever set foot on our world again. Two carriers might not be enough to wipe out our whole species, but we'd kill anyone we came into contact with. So now, the only Chetsuans we'll ever see in our lives are each other."

"Yeah, and I'm sick of the sight of her already," Jessica remarked, clearly not meaning a word of it.

Sara smiled and gave her a shove. "It's not so bad," she asserted. "We live here, mostly, but we've been through the portals to other worlds, too."

"Not to yours," Jessica interjected. "He was always worried about that Kullos bloke detecting our alien presence, and through us, learning of StormClaw Island, and finding the open doorways to these other worlds. After a year in a cage, having the run of a handful of worlds is pretty cool. Even if we have to wear a perception filter so no-one can see the real us. Except when we go to sci-fi conventions to snog elves."

"You're not going to let that go, are you?" Sara laughed.

"Nope."

"You're only jealous!"

"Too right, I'm jealous. He was cute, not that I could see much of his face when it was locked onto yours. Nice arse, though."

Going back to her policy of ignoring her sister's remarks, Sara explained, "In return for such freedom, all Daelen asks is that we keep his bases running for him. Seems like a small price to pay, really."

"OK, I admit Daelen can be a bit arrogant and act without thinking," Jessica allowed, "and I suppose he does see us as serving girls at his beck and call, but it's not a bad job."

"And as we said, we have a lot of free time to do whatever we want."

Mandalee didn't know what to say, but she certainly wouldn't have gone with what Cat asked.

"You don't resent us, do you?"

The two Chetsuans and one human frowned.

"Resent you, dear?" Jessica gasped. "Why on Earth would we do that?"

"Because Daelen is on a mission with us to save our world from Kullos. Does it never occur to you to wonder why, when he could be on your world, saving the Chetsuans from the dragons?"

"Maybe he will, one day," Jessica shrugged. "Even he can't be everywhere at once."

"My sister's faith aside," Sara reasoned, "as I understand it, if Kullos wins, he won't stop with destroying your world. He's got the whole mortal plane in his sights."

"The dragons reckon the Chetsuans are vermin," Jessica growled. "Kullos reckons all mortal life forms are vermin: Chetsuans, dragons, humans, Faery…" Her scowl morphed into a smirk, which she directed at her sister. "…Elves who get snogged at sci-fi conventions."

"And it's not just the half dozen worlds through these portals, there are loads more. Point is, there's a bigger picture. So, no, Catriona, we don't resent you. Not a bit. Do we, Jess?"

Her sister shook her head. "No way! In fact, Daelen filled us in on the situation on your world when we came in this morning, and we've already told him we want to help, even if that just means serving your breakfast and having a chat."

"Whatever you need from us, it's yours," Sara agreed.

"And what you need right now," Jessica advised, checking the time, "is to get back to your rooms and change for your training session with Daelen."

"Oh yes, the training session," Cat echoed with a distinct lack of enthusiasm.

"Well, obviously the body armour is out of the question for you," Sara realised. "And synthetic fabrics in general. We'll have to try and find something else for you."

"No need," the druidess insisted. "I'm fine as I am."

"He won't like it," Jessica warned her.

"That's OK," Mandalee, insisted. "I'll distract him by being his star pupil."

Chapter 21

Sara led them to Daelen's training centre, located in a separate outbuilding, and knocked on the door before entering. Mandalee, as promised, was wearing the one-piece combat body armour that Jessica had laid out for her. She was actually really pleased with it. Clinging to her like a second skin, it was predominately white, with purple and silver highlights, matching her regular outfit very well. It was just so much lighter, far more flexible and, best of all, it seemed to give her curves that, if she was honest, she didn't really have, and hide parts that Mandalee *wished* she didn't have. Her friend, however, was dressed in her usual red robes. Jessica had taken the suit away from her room to make sure Cat couldn't touch it by accident and suffer another adverse reaction. The druidess was giving Mandalee a wide berth for the same reason. Almost as soon as they left the portal room, she lost the connection to her world and her magic, and she felt herself losing her temper again along with it.

Once they were inside, Sara made herself scarce as quickly as possible. She knew there were going to be fireworks and she wanted to be far away when they started.

Daelen was wearing only the bottom half of a two-piece combat suit, sweat pouring from his muscular torso. He was breathing heavily when they entered, but it soon abated, demonstrating his high fitness level.

He scowled at Catriona. "Why aren't you wearing your combat suit?" he demanded.

"When I touched it, my hand swelled up. If I put it on, it would probably kill me. Never thought about my Faery physiology, did you?"

"Oh, no, I didn't know that would happen. Maybe if it had a natural cotton lining or something?"

"Doesn't matter." Cat shook her head. "I wouldn't wear it, anyway."

"Well, you can't train in your robes," Daelen insisted.

Cat shrugged and turned to walk away.

"Where do you think you're going?"

"I can't train in my robes, apparently," she shot back. "Therefore, I can't train, which is fine because I've no intention of doing it anyway."

"I do," Mandalee volunteered. "If it helps."

"There you go," Cat declared. "You've got one willing victim – I mean student – you don't need two."

"But if you want to help save your world, you have to train."

"Not your way," Cat countered.

"But my way is better!" Daelen insisted.

"No, it is not better, it is simply different. In many ways, it is inferior because it is crude and predictable, as I have tried to point out before, though I don't know why I waste my breath. Our ways of doing things will always be different, and in that diversity, there lies strength. Do not presume to make me your pupil because I will have no part of that."

So saying, she planted her feet and folded her arms, as a silent challenge of 'move me if you dare.'

"What are you talking about, Cat?" Daelen demanded. "This is why I brought you here. To train you to fight properly! To help you be more powerful! What's your problem?"

Cat stepped close and faced him with feral ferocity.

"My problem is you!" she yelled, pushing him back a step. "The way you just assume I will be training your way. Fighting your way. I already fight 'properly,'" she pushed him back another step, "I just don't fight the way you do. I *will* not fight the way you do. I fight my way. You keep forgetting, I am not a shadow warrior," another step, "and I have no desire to act like one. I keep telling you I have no interest in fighting power with power," and another, "but you don't listen!" One more. "You never listen!" She kept pushing, her voice growing louder and louder with every sentence. "For the last time: I don't like your training, I don't like your world, I don't like your weapons, I don't like your rules, I don't like your decor and I DON'T LIKE YOU!" With her last push, she stormed off, running away from the training centre.

She re-entered the house, darted around a corner and almost collided with Sara, but the Chetsuan girl flattened herself against the wall beside the old grandfather clock, out of Cat's way, in an impressive display of agility. A little way further on, and Jessica, rummaging in the large linen cupboard, stuck her head around the door to see what was going on, just in time to see Catriona collapse in a heap on the floor.

*****

Catriona Redfletching woke up in a bed in the portal room. Mandalee by her bedside. Cat could tell she'd been crying.

"What— What's going on?" the druidess croaked.

The smile on her best friend's face was like the sun bursting out from behind the clouds. She stood over Cat's bed and gave her a gentle hug before returning to her bedside seat.

"Oh, Cat!" she gasped. "I've been so worried about you. You've been out for hours."

"What's wrong with me?" asked the half-Faery. She felt so drained of energy.

"It's my fault," Mandalee asserted.

"I bet it's not," Cat returned. She knew that doubting herself was a well-worn Mandalee trait.

"It is," she insisted. "I got so caught up in how much I'm enjoying it here, I never gave enough thought to why my best friend was so miserable. I'm a Cleric of Nature – it should have been obvious."

"If it helps," Cat replied, "I'm a druid, and it's not obvious to me, so why not just explain?"

"You're half-Faery," Mandalee stated, as if that explained everything.

Cat made an effort to give a wry smile. "Thanks for the confirmation of my species, but I already knew that."

The assassin shook her head in a self-deprecating way. "Sorry, explanations aren't really my area. I generally leave them to Shyleen."

Cat reached out a hand to touch Mandalee's. "I wish you'd give yourself more credit."

"I'll try," Mandalee promised. "OK, well, you know how you told me your father couldn't leave the forests without becoming ill?"

Cat nodded. The one time he'd tried to visit her mother's city home, he'd collapsed.

“As with anything else, some Faery are more affected than others. Add your human half, and you’re less affected than most full Faery. In the time I’ve known you, the most you’ve ever really got is a kind of homesickness for the wildlands. Spend a few nights sleeping under the stars, and you’re right as rain.”

“Do I detect another Jessica expression there?” Cat wondered. Mandalee nodded. “I like it. Rain is good; water is life. So, what, you’re saying I’m homesick?”

“Literally sick from being away from home, yes. I guess even a half-Faery doesn’t fare too well away from her world. You haven’t just been cut off from your druid magic – you’ve been cut off from everything your Faery half needs to survive. In short, being here is killing you. Your reaction to synthetic fabrics was an acute symptom of a wider problem. I wanted to take you home, but Daelen was worried about the time difference between the two worlds and the possible stress of transition. Then I remembered that when we were chatting to Sara and Jessica, here in the portal room this morning, you quickly healed up, so I hoped letting you rest right next to the portal home would help you recover.”

Mandalee had refused to leave her friend’s side until she showed signs of improvement.

“Well, it’s working,” Cat assured her, “but I’m still a bit shaky.”

“You just need time, and the one advantage we have in being away from Tempestria is that it does buy time.”

“Yeah, that’s weird, the time thing,” Cat pondered with a puzzled frown.

“Well, don’t waste your energy trying to figure out how the cosmos works right now. Just focus on getting stronger again so we can take you back home.”

Catriona sat up quickly and immediately regretted it when the room started spinning. “Back home? We can’t go back already!”

“We have to. Cat, we’ve just been through this – this world is making you ill.”

“I know, you explained the problem just fine,” she assured her friend. “What I’m interested in now is the solution. Come on, Mandalee. How long have you known me? You can’t honestly believe this is going to stop me from achieving my goals. Besides, now that I know there are other worlds, I want to see them.”

"You haven't been a fan of this one so far," the assassin reminded her.

Cat dismissed that, pointing out, "I'm not a fan of anywhere when I'm sick. This place isn't going to beat me. My body's limitations aren't going to beat me."

"So, what's your magical solution?" Mandalee asked.

"Essentially, the same thing I figured out years ago: I need our world's nature to use my druid magic. Now I know I need it just to survive. The problem is the same, so the solution is the same. I need to carry nature with me at all times. Mandalee, I need to talk to Daelen. Where is he, anyway?"

"Taking his frustrations out on his training centre."

"Well, that's constructive," she snarked, rolling her eyes.

"Cut the guy some slack – he brought you to Earth, and it nearly killed you."

"I've nearly killed him twice, but I didn't start beating up furniture. I focussed on the solution. Go to him, please, Mandalee. Tell him I want to see him, and tell him…" she trailed off, trying to remember the Earth expression she was looking for. "Tell him to 'get his arse in gear.'"

Mandalee left the room, and a few minutes later, Daelen StormTiger took her place at Catriona's bedside.

He immediately started to apologise, but Catriona cut him off. "No, Daelen," she refuted softly, reaching out to caress his arm. "It's me who needs to apologise. Don't get me wrong, some of what I said was valid, and we'll address those things later, but I went too far. I was unkind and unfair, just lashing out without knowing why."

"It's already forgotten."

"Thank you, but there is one thing in particular…of all the things I said I don't like…just to set the record straight." She could see what Daelen was waiting for. "The truth is…I do quite like…" She faltered for a moment, as if uncertain how to continue. Then she grinned and finished, "your decor."

Daelen smiled. He understood what she was saying without saying it.

"As for your training, there is one thing I want you to teach me when I'm on my feet again: your Prismatic Sphere portals."

She wouldn't do it the way he did, but if she could study how he made one, up close, she was sure she would be able to create her own version. A smaller, portable one that she could tether to herself at all times when on another world. With a permanent link to Tempestria, she would not only survive but also have access to all the druid magic she had at home.

Daelen agreed that he'd be glad to show her, but for now, she needed to rest.

Catriona was satisfied with that, so she lay back down. Daelen pulled the covers over her and then, on impulse kissed her gently on the forehead.

Rather than merely leaving, as she expected, he took a piece of paper from his pocket, unfolded it and began to sing:

Angels among us, stars in the night,
Watch o'er your sleep, shining so bright,
Safe in their light, as you close your eyes,
Love will surround you, 'til morning you rise.

Angels among us, shed you no tears,
Bright Angels guard you, quiet your fears,
Nature's embrace, is gentle and strong,
Love will surround you, all your life long.

Cat smiled. It was such an unexpected, touching thing for him to do. Thinking about it, she decided that, if she was completely honest, contrary to her words earlier in the day, she did like him, too. In fact, she was concerned that she was beginning to like him maybe a little too much.

It also briefly occurred to her to wonder where he'd managed to find that Faery lullaby, considering they were on another world, but sleep overtook her before she could think any more about it.

*****

Later that evening, after a strenuous training session with Daelen, Mandalee found Jessica in the magnificent great hall at the heart of the mansion house complex. Seeing the White Assassin come in, the Chetsuan girl greeted her with her customary, "Heya, love!"

"Jessica," Mandalee began, "do you mind if I raid your kitchen? I need to do something for Cat."

"Sure thing, but are you sure it's not something that I could do for you? Sara and me, we're here to help, you know."

Mandalee smiled at the helpful, eager girl. The Cleric of Nature couldn't imagine she'd be so chipper if she were cut off from her world with no prospect of ever seeing it again without killing everyone she met.

"No, thank you," she chuckled. "I just want to bake some cookies for my friend. I'm sure the end result would be a lot better if you did it, but—"

"—But that's not the point, is it?" Jessica finished. "They wouldn't be from you, then, would they?"

Mandalee smiled and shook her head.

"Aww, that's so sweet!"

Linking arms, her broad grin wrinkled her nose as she led Mandalee out of the hall. "Just come with me, dearie, and I'll show you where everything is."

*****

A couple of hours later, deciding her friend had slept long enough, Mandalee stumbled back into the portal room, her clothes soiled with flour and egg white, with some hot tea and a fresh batch of half-burnt cookies.

Seeing that her friend was indeed awake, she set the tray down on the bedside table.

"Here, Cat," she croaked, having made herself hoarse while swearing at her inability to cook, "I made you something."

She banged one of her cookies on the table, to demonstrate how hard they were, then throwing one across the room, it broke a vase. "They're completely inedible, but as you can see, they make brilliant weapons."

She threw another one at lethal speed right through a pillow.

Catriona sat up and burst out laughing.

“Oh, Mandalee!” Cat beamed, once she managed to calm down. “Whatever did I do without you? I’m so glad you joined Daelen and me.”

Mandalee smiled and hugged her friend.

Just then, Jessica entered with a fresh plate of cookies.

“Heya, loves!” she greeted them. “These ones you *can* eat,” she assured them. “Good to see you’ve got some colour back in your cheeks, Cat. Your friend tried – a lot – but in the end, I had to step in before she ran out of ingredients…or burned down the house.”

“It was only a small fire!” Mandalee protested. “I had it under control!”

“Yes, dear, of course you did,” Jessica replied, voice filled with sarcasm.

She was going to clear away Mandalee’s attempts at baking, but Cat stopped her. “Leave them. Like Mandalee says, they’re great weapons. I want to practice throwing them from my bed, ready for the next time Daelen annoys me.”

Jessica cocked her head to one side as she considered that. “Tell you what, love,” she remarked, conspiratorially, “I reckon you should aim for his ego.”

The other two could see where she was going with this and laughing together, they all chorused, “It’s certainly a big enough target!”

Then Jessica taught them an Earth custom called a ‘high five.’

*****

After another full day of bed rest, Cat began to feel strong enough to try out a few simple druid spells, starting with fixing the vase and pillow that Mandalee had broken with her cookies. While she was in the portal room, she was once again able to access her pocket dimension and resume studying, which alleviated the boredom that had begun to set in.

The day after, she decided she was ready to leave the confines of the portal room. She told Daelen she really wanted to spend time in his library, so it would be best to learn to open a portal there. She'd figure out how to make a small, portable version later.

When Daelen showed her his technique for opening a portal, she realised it was not unlike opening her pocket dimension. By analogy, she compared it to using her stoneshaper magic to create a tunnel, rather than a cave. The only difference was that the tunnel needed to penetrate through to the other side, which meant she needed to know where she was going. The other way of looking at it, she supposed, was a dressed-up teleportation spell. Teleportation was something she hadn't attempted herself, but from her technical discussions with Dreya, she was reasonably sure she could do it if she put her mind to it. It had just never been a priority for her. She'd rather fly.

At first, Cat found she needed to pop back to the portal room to recharge with the magic of her world, in between attempts to open a portal of her own. After a few hours, though, she could open and close portals at will. After another couple of days of experimentation, she reduced the size of her portals until they were so small, they could not be seen with the naked eye, beyond a point of blue light if one was acutely observant. But she could still feel Tempestria on the other side.

She experimented with going outside into the garden to practise more druid magic, including shapeshifting. Everything worked well – at least after the first time when she narrowly avoided a potentially nasty accident.

Cat was in leopard form when she gave Sara a bit of a shock, enthusiastically jumping out of the bushes at the Chetsuan girl who thought she was about to be mauled to death. Quick as a flash, she brought out a pair of daggers from her boot tops. Cat knew Sara and Jessica weren't just domestic help – they were security. They trained a lot, both with and without Daelen and were perfectly capable of defending themselves and Daelen's home. Cat hastily jumped away from her and shifted back.

"What the—?" Sara began. "Cat?"

The druidess gave her a sheepish grin. "I guess I should have told you I could do that. Sorry."

Sara sheathed her blades and laughed. "Wow, that's amazing! I mean, I know Daelen does a tiger, but to be honest," she looked around and shared in a whisper, "it's not very good."

Cat nodded. “I haven’t had the heart to tell him, yet.”

Sara asked if she could do any more animals, but when Cat offered to show her, she stopped her.

“No, wait. My sister has to see this, too. Can you go back to leopard form and hide? Only fair you give her the same scare you gave me. Don’t worry, I won’t let her hurt you,” she assured her. “I can’t wait to see the look on her face.”

“If it’s anything like yours, you won’t be disappointed,” Cat promised her and agreed to do it.

A few minutes later, Sara returned with her sister, and leopard form Catriona leapt out at her. True to her word, Sara was quick to stay her hand when Jessica reached for weapons.

Cat shifted back, and Sara burst with laughter at Jessica’s reaction.

“You set me up deliberately, didn’t you?” Jessica mock complained.

“I got the shock of my life, and you’re my sister – we share everything.”

With a cheeky grin, her sister pointed out, “Not everything: You didn’t share that elf boy you were snogging.”

“What? You think he could have handled us both?”

Jessica considered that, then agreed, “No, you’re right, love. Fair point.”

Chapter 22

The next few days fell into a pattern. Mandalee trained with Daelen, often alongside one or both of the Chetsuans, while Cat split her time between studying in the library and working on her magic in the garden.

Then, one evening, about ten days into their stay on Earth, when Cat and Mandalee went to look for Daelen, he was nowhere to be found. What they did find was a note on the dining room table.

Dear Catriona and Mandalee,

There's trouble on one of the other worlds I keep an eye on and I need to nip it in the bud now.

Tomorrow, in my absence, I have instructions for you. I expect you two to train hard all day. That means you, too, Cat. You're far enough behind as it is. Just because I'm not around, that does not mean you get to slack off.

Sorry to run out on you like this, but if I leave it, things will only get worse in the long run. Better to take a day out of our schedule and sort it out now.

Thank you for understanding,
Daelen.

"There he goes again," Cat complained to her friend, "giving us his orders and expecting us to jump to follow them. Well I, for one, am going to do nothing he 'expects' me to do. I hate it when he gets like this."

Mandalee grinned and goaded her friend, "Maybe, but you still love him, right?"

Catriona's look shot her down in flames. "Love?" she wondered. "Who said anything about love?"

"You did, actually. Just once."

Cat snorted, "I couldn't possibly have been sober, at the time. Infatuation perhaps, but love is something quite different. In fact, I've had just about all I can stand from him right now. It's been days since I yelled at him and despite me telling him I thought some of my points were valid, he still hasn't found time to talk to me about them. Mandalee, you train tomorrow if you like, but I'm…how do they say it in this world? Oh yeah, I'm on strike. I swear, one more thing, and he's going to find my staff rammed up somewhere very painful."

"Your confused feelings aside, you do have a point, Cat," Mandalee admitted. "It does always seem to be his rules, his way. Alright, I'm on strike, too. Tomorrow, I'm having a day out, exploring the city. You want to come?"

Cat smiled apologetically and reminded her friend that she still had nothing to wear. Having just recovered, she didn't want to risk a setback by trying to wear any of this world's clothes.

When Sara and Jessica brought dinner and sat down with them, Mandalee grilled them for recommendations of where to go and what to see on her 'day off,' and Cat wondered if there would be any problems going out at night in owl mode. Other than the possibility of confused bird watchers, they both thought it should be OK.

So, the next day, Catriona continued her usual split of study and magic, while Mandalee spent the day sightseeing, returning in the evening. Before the druidess could take her turn to go out, however, Daelen returned.

Striding into the great hall where the assassin was telling Cat all about her day, he launched straight into, "Have you been training hard in my absence?"

The two friends looked at each other and then turned to him.

"Nope!" they chorused.

"What do you mean 'nope'? My instructions were quite clear; I told you what I expected you to do."

Cat leapt to her feet, lips and eyes narrowed in barely suppressed anger. "That's just the problem," she snapped. "Your instructions, your expectations, your training, your way, your rules."

She took a step forward, and Daelen found himself once more stepping back in the face of her fire.

"You stand there and say, 'you will train now,' 'you will be doing my style of training,' 'you will wear body armour,' 'you will do this,' 'you will do that,' 'you will do as I say.' Well, I'm sorry to burst your bubble, Daelen, but I will not do as you say! For the last time, I am not your lackey, I am not your student, I am not your soldier, and you are not my commander. You have absolutely no right to stand there and give me orders or leave notes telling me what you 'expect.' I will not tolerate it. If you want me to do something, you *ask* me. You *discuss* it with me. Is that clear enough for you, or do I have to write it down?"

"Cat, I never meant–"

"No, you never do, that just makes it worse."

Daelen reached out to her, apologetically, "Look, Cat, if I'm getting this all wrong then I'm sorry. It's just that I'm not used to working as a team. I'm used to either working alone or having students and soldiers under my command. Giving orders is what I do…it's a hard habit to break."

Catriona was unmoved. "Try harder," she suggested. "Otherwise, if you can't accept me as your equal partner, if you don't start showing me more respect, consideration and courtesy, I'll go back to my world and walk away."

She took a few meaningful steps to put distance between them.

Turning back, she added, "Maybe I don't need to go on this quest anymore. Maybe my time would be better spent at Calin's Tower, training my mind and my magic."

"I thought you were committed to saving your world with me," a confused Daelen protested.

"I'm committed to saving our world *from* you!" Mandalee quipped, trying to lighten the mood. It didn't work.

Cat shook her head. "No, I told you I had my own reasons for joining you, which essentially boils down to knowledge. In my time with you, I've learned a lot about you. Come to that, I've learned a lot about myself. I've been to Calin's Tower, I've unlocked all but a few layers of the security of my staff, and I've learned how to open portals to other worlds. Maybe I've learned all I can from being with you.

"But you're right; I have pledged myself to this cause, and it is a matter of honour that I see it through. Still, I will only put up with so much in the name of honour."

"Look," Mandalee ventured, standing between them, trying to calm things down. "I think we all understand Cat's objections, right, Daelen?" she asked, pointedly.

Daelen nodded.

"And, Cat, you don't really want to leave, do you?"

Catriona shook her head.

"Good," Mandalee breathed. She then suggested that Daelen let Cat go flying that night for as long as she wanted. She thought it would do her friend a world of good to get out of the house for a while in a way that worked best for her. Then when she returned, all happy and relaxed, they could all sit down calmly together, talk, and discuss what they might do the next day.

"Does that sound like a reasonable plan to both of you?" she asked.

They both agreed that it did.

"Excellent," Mandalee declared, much relieved. "In that case, I guess we'll see you later, Cat."

Cat hugged her friend. "Thanks, Mandalee. You're the best."

Stepping away, she shifted to Tawny owl form and flew straight out of an open window, into the cool night air.

*****

Later that night, Daelen and Mandalee were doing some cooldown stretching exercises together, when Mandalee noticed an owl glide silently behind Daelen and shift to Catriona's natural form. Cat pounced on Daelen, but his reactions were faster, and a moment later a bewildered Catriona was sitting in the pond. To Mandalee's dismay, she still looked annoyed. She hoped there wasn't going to be another fight.

"Cat, I'm sorry, please forgive me?" Daelen gasped. "I didn't mean to throw you in the pond. It was just a reflex."

To the assassin's relief, Cat smiled and told him it was OK.

"You just looked pissed off."

Cat shook her head. "For once, Daelen, not at you."

She explained that she'd been having a great time until she ran into a male owl who took a shine to her markings and wouldn't take 'no' for an answer. "By the gods, Daelen, I swear even you would draw the line at such a macho display!"

The shadow warrior grinned. "So, I wasn't the only guy to ruffle your feathers today, then?" he remarked.

Cat laughed, "You could say that."

That's when Mandalee pushed Daelen in the pond, too, sharing in the laughter just for a moment before unexpectedly joining them. Cat had worked her magic to ask the ground to rise up, suddenly, under Mandalee's feet causing her to lose her balance.

"Actually, Daelen," Cat giggled while splashing the others, "I think the shock of a nice cold bath was just the thing for all of us."

The three climbed out of the water and sat down together. Given the cool night air, they'd have to head back inside the house, soon, so they could dry off and change, but first, there was something Daelen wanted to say.

"Cat," he began, "I really will do my best to treat you better from now on."

"Good," the druidess relented. "Now, would you like to start again? Pretend we just got here tonight, and tomorrow is Day One."

With a supreme effort, Daelen politely asked, "How would you like to spend the day tomorrow? I would like it very much if you would train with me a little. All I ask is that you try a few things that I suggest. If you're not comfortable, if they don't suit your style, then that's completely up to you to decide. If there's anything specific you'd like to learn, please feel free to ask, and if there's anything you want to teach me, go ahead."

"There," Cat approved with a warm smile. "Didn't hurt, did it?"

"Little bit."

"Poor baby," Mandalee snarked.

"Tough," Cat insisted, "and to answer your question, I can see that a certain level of training to improve my physical fitness level could only be a good thing."

"Agreed," her friend nodded, "and I think that once we've had a few more days' training, you and I should combine our skills to take Daelen on and basically kick his arse."

Cat liked that idea immensely.

"Perfect," she agreed. To the shadow warrior, she added, "Together, we can demonstrate that for all your power, you have your weaknesses that can be exploited. Power isn't everything."

Daelen agreed to the plan, so it was settled.

"See?" Mandalee spoke up. "Wasn't that easy once you two stopped yelling at each other?"

That earned her a hug from both sides.

"Can I ask you a question, Cat?" Daelen broached carefully.

Cat nodded and assured him he could ask her anything he liked. It was being dictated to that she objected to.

"Believe me, I've got that message, now," he affirmed.

He pointed out that with her micro-portal connection home, her druid magic was at full strength and with a cotton underlayer, he was confident she could wear the body armour without any ill-effects. "Would you consider wearing it or something similar? Obviously, we'd all monitor you closely to make sure it doesn't affect you."

"As an experiment," she considered, "while I'm in this world, I could try it for a short period, but there's no point getting used to wearing it because back on Tempestria, it's just not possible. I'm sorry, Daelen. I know you're trying to help, and I appreciate that, but the Council of Wizards forbids it. The law is quite clear: '*A wizard mage, or druid mage, shall carry and use but one bladed weapon and shall wear no armour or shield.*'"

"Mandalee uses bladed weapons," Daelen countered, "and seems quite happy wearing armour."

"I'm different," Mandalee explained. "I'm a cleric. We have our own rules. I'm not the mage that Cat is. Primarily, I'm a demon hunter and assassin, and your body armour suits me."

Cat winked at her friend. "In more ways than one."

Mandalee smiled back before continuing to explain that her magic was mostly a way to enhance her physical skills, adding strength, speed, agility. Plus, her affinity for nature expressed itself in different ways to Catriona's. She could talk with animals, treating them like her own personal network of spies. "Because even when people think they're alone, there are often animals around who can see and hear everything," she pointed out. "I don't often fight with magic directly the way a mage does. I can do a bit, but it's not my style."

"But I promise I'll try your body armour, at least once, as an experiment," Cat assured Daelen. "It may be something I can take to the Council for a ruling, once we're done with Kullos. At the very least, given how I reacted last time, it would be a good test, to see if my link to Tempestria is as strong as I think it is. Gaining that knowledge is perfectly in line with the philosophy of my Order so they could have no objections. If I can touch and even wear your armour without a reaction, it would open up other possibilities, too. Maybe I could even give that shopping mall a second go with an open mind and a fresh attitude."

"More shopping?" Mandalee enthused, her eyes lighting up. "Now you're talking!"

Daelen suggested they start to head inside, then, so the girls didn't catch a cold. They both agreed it was a good idea.

Stepping between them and linking arms, Mandalee asked, "So, does this mean we're all friends again?"

"Yeah, I think we can safely say that," Cat agreed.

"An assassin peacemaker," Daelen remarked, shaking his head in wonder. "I thought I'd seen everything until I met you two."

"You ain't seen nothin' yet," Mandalee quipped. "Jessica's been coaching me on more of this world's expressions. Did I say it right?"

"Yes, you got it. Spot on, well d–"

"What did you say?" Cat demanded, suddenly, an intense look growing on her face.

"I was just saying Mandalee got that expression right."

Cat waved a hand dismissively. "Not that – before that."

"Er, I mentioned something about thinking I'd seen everything unt–"

"Yes, yes, yes," Cat affirmed, nodding and snapping her fingers, impatiently, "back up another step."

"Let me think. Oh yeah, I called Mandalee an assassin peacemaker."

"Wow!" the druidess gasped, almost missing a step. "Second time was even better."

"Cat, what are you talking about?" Mandalee wondered.

"Hmm? Oh, I'm sorry, I'll try to explain, but not here. Let's go and clean ourselves up, then meet me in the library. There's something I need to check up on."

Without another word, she changed into her owl form and flew into their bedroom through an open window. The other two had to take the more conventional route through the house.

Chapter 23

Forgive me, gentle reader, if you feel I've been neglecting you for a while. I'm afraid I have once again got so caught up in my writing, that I haven't been interjecting very much to give you my perspective on things. Actually, maybe some of you were pleased about that. If so, I guess I'm sorry to interrupt, but it is necessary from time to time, and there's something I would like to discuss at this point: perception filters.

If we're honest, I think most of us have them. They may not be actual tech devices but we still have them. We use them without even realising it. As I gaze through time to the scene in Daelen's library, in his house on Earth – itself hidden by a perception filter – is, I believe, the perfect illustration of my point.

*****

By the time Mandalee and Daelen reached the library, Cat was already sitting in her favourite leather office chair, surrounded by books and her notes. Sara and Jessica were there, too, eager to help, as always, and keen to be involved in what Daelen's two Tempestrian guests were doing. Daelen recognised that a few of the books arrayed before Catriona were from this very library. The two Chetsuan girls had obviously been helping her find a few things. Daelen hadn't failed to notice how much they had both started to shine in the presence of Mandalee and Catriona. They were similar ages – as far as one could judge such things when they were different species from different worlds where Time moved at a different rate – and he was delighted at how quickly they had formed a bond.

Perception filters were useful things, but how could Sara and Jessica ever make real friends if they couldn't be themselves? Sadly, the way some Earth humans treated even members of their own species with slightly different skin pigmentation, they definitely weren't ready for a pair of purple, cat-like aliens.

Mandalee could relate, too, in a different way, given how some people had problems with her gender identity. None of the people in that room saw it as an issue, but on Tempestria, she sometimes hid the features of her face behind a mask. Features that gave away the fact that she had not been born biologically female, despite her otherwise flawless efforts to 'pass.' That mask was her perception filter.

Even Catriona sometimes encountered casual racism relating to her Faery heritage. Daelen couldn't believe a Tavern called '*FaerWay*,' with that terrible sign, was still allowed to exist. Since Catriona was half-human, her Faery spots were faint, so it wouldn't be difficult for Cat to hide her heritage, but instead, she insisted everybody knew. Her perception filter worked differently: it helped her to create the perception that such prejudice didn't upset her, when, in fact, it most assuredly did.

Daelen still felt guilty about the racist remarks his own dark clone had made to Cat. He hoped that was something 'Aden' had picked up on his own, and not something that had come from the original Daelen StormTiger before the split. He wouldn't like to think he used to be like that. More importantly, now that the two halves were if not exactly recombined, then certainly co-existing, he hoped that didn't mean that such attitudes were a part of him now.

In fact, if you think about it, gentle reader, wasn't he using a perception filter of his own all the time? As he had confirmed to Catriona, this body wasn't really him. It was a shell. He had described his true nature as 'light in a box' and while it was true that it was physically impossible for his whole self to fit inside the mortal realm – impossible without ripping it apart, anyway – he could have easily chosen a form that at least approximated what he truly looked like. Instead, he had chosen the appearance of a human male. He wasn't sure what that said about him. What he did know was that even looking the way he did, it was difficult for many Tempestrians to trust a higher planar being. If he appeared as 'light in a box,' he couldn't imagine that making the situation any easier.

Returning his attention to Sara and Jessica, he took in the good-natured banter between the two sisters. Jessica was still not letting go of the fact that Sara had snogged someone at that party a couple of weekends ago. There was an extra spring in their steps, and their tails were perked right up – a sure sign of happiness in Chetsuans. What would happen when it was just the two of them, again? Would they still be happy here, or could they find a home on

Tempestria? Would the people there be any more receptive to their true selves than the people of Earth? Or would they both have to wear a perception filter for the rest of their lives? OK, they could deactivate them when they were alone with Cat and Mandalee, and he was sure there would be other Tempestrians who would be equally accepting. How many, he couldn't be sure, but whatever the number, was it enough?

Daelen worried about these things now, more than ever, because he was hiding something from all four of his mortal friends. That was another kind of perception filter, in a way. He had created the perception that he had simply brought Mandalee and Cat here to train. In Catriona's case, he had done the job too well and almost pushed her away. Hidden behind that perception filter was the truth: training was only part of it. He had hoped that the Time difference between Tempestria and Earth would give his four mortal friends the time to get to know each other. Bond.

The camaraderie he was witnessing before him was already a vindication of that idea. These four didn't see race, gender or place of origin as a barrier. To them, that diversity was like the strong force that held the material universe together. That was important because, in a couple of months, Earth time – a fortnight on Tempestria – Sara and Jessica were going to have to choose.

You see, gentle reader, Daelen already knew in his mind how his Ultimate Final Battle with Kullos was going to go – even best-case scenario. In the end, it was going to be just the two of them, as it was always meant to be. Kullos was a shadow warrior, and that made him his responsibility and his alone. In case the Wish barrier was not entirely successful in containing the power, he could not risk his friends, nor let any other mortals be caught in the blast of Heaven's Surrender. The only way he could see to ensure that, was to let StormClaw Island be their last battlefield. His ship, his crew, his friends, all would be safe across the water. Since StormClaw was hidden behind a perception filter, no-one else knew it existed. It was empty of all mortal life. No collateral damage…except his own house.

All of his facilities in all of his seven worlds were connected via the portal system, and he was likely to pull power from them. That would be devastating to anyone living there, even fatal if the building fell down. At the very least, the portals would collapse forever. Obviously, Sara and Jessica could not be home at the time, but more than that, whichever world they were on when the moment came, that was where they would have to build the rest of their lives. Of the seven worlds, they clearly could never return to their own world, Phitonia, so that left six to choose from. Of those, at least three were unsuitable long term, leaving three more: Earth, Tempestria and Lavos, the world where dragons were being hunted down. He didn't think they could ever be comfortable in a world with dragons, even if they weren't a threat like they were on Phitonia.

Trouble was, they'd never seen Tempestria. He knew Cat and Mandalee would provide the very best impression of that world – Tempestria couldn't find better ambassadors than those two – but Daelen had no right to force the issue. The choice was Sara's and Jessica's alone. He wasn't going to tell them yet, though. He was worried that that would put undue pressure on their building relationships. It would undoubtedly affect things. How could it not?

Daelen knew the Chetsuan girls had made sort-of-friends on Earth and if he gave them the choice too soon, he was pretty sure that was the world they would choose. As I said, gentle reader, he couldn't be sure whether they would need their perception filters any less on Tempestria, but at the very least they would have two friends who knew and accepted them for who they really were. He wanted them to consider that. In fact, what he was really hoping, was that Mandalee and Cat might invite their Chetsuan friends *before* the moment of the choice arrived. That way, it would be seen as an act of pure friendship, untainted by any sense of charity.

The timing was unfortunate because he didn't want Sara and Jessica involved in any fighting. Trained though they were, there was too great a risk of something happening to one of them for a cause, a world, and a fight that was not theirs. Moreover, he knew that if either one of them were to die, the other would not survive – she would make sure of it. He had taken them from their world so they could live, not so they could die.

The other aspect of the battle he was concealing was that, as far as he could see, there was no possible way he could survive. His dark clone had believed otherwise. That was why he had proposed the merging, thinking the Wish barrier would protect him. It wouldn't. Daelen was convinced of that.

That was OK. Daelen's one regret was that he had no idea what had happened to his home plane of reality since he'd been cut off. Had the enemy continued her attacks? Had his people discovered a way to stop her? Or had she finally won and destroyed them all? He supposed he would never know.

There in the library, Daelen unlocked a small, wooden box and surreptitiously hid a letter inside, before locking it again. The lock was on a timer, set to open on the day equivalent to when he was due to rendezvous with Michael and his team at that ancient temple in Northern Alloria. On that day, Sara and Jessica would receive an urgent message, telling them to come to the library immediately, open the box and read the letter. The letter that would change their lives. The letter that would give them three days, Earth time – less than one day on Tempestria – to choose a world and leave this house forever before it could be destroyed.

According to the schedule, in terms of Tempestrian time, that would be the night before they launched their attack on Kullos and his forces. The beginning of the end. He had planned it that way so he would be able to take a few hours, just before the dawn, to take a walk by himself while the others were sleeping. To think, to wonder about the Chetsuans' choice, and just to enjoy the simple pleasure of one last walk in the woods on Tempestria in this facsimile of a human body.

No battles. No fighting. No interruptions.

*****

If you are thinking back to the beginning of my writing, gentle reader, knowing about my Illegal Time Intervention, sending Aunt Mandalee to interrupt his walk and bring him to our time to help us fight our battles, you will appreciate the irony.

*****

"Ah, there you are," Catriona remarked as if she had been waiting for hours. "Please take a seat, and I'll try to explain some things."

"Is this to do with your staff?" Mandalee guessed as she and Daelen sat down. Seeing Daelen's 'how did you know that' expression, she told him, "She gets a certain look in her eyes when it's to do with her staff."

"Yes, well, that look is part of what I want to explain," Cat replied, with a slightly embarrassed expression. "The straight answer to your question, Mandalee, is 'Yes and No.'"

"That's a straight answer?" Sara piped up.

"It is for her," Mandalee confirmed.

"Must have a different definition on your world, I guess," Jessica shrugged.

"If you'll be quiet for a moment," the druidess huffed with mock irritation, "I was about to explain."

"Well, pardon me for breathing, I'm sure," Sara remarked indignantly.

"Bit touchy about this staff of hers, isn't she?" Jessica offered.

"Ooh!" Mandalee cried, "I've just thought: have I told you guys about the day I met our Cat, stuck in my demon trap, and naked with nothing but a strategically placed staff?"

"No, and now you have to tell us," Sara insisted.

Jessica nodded enthusiastically. "Leaving out no detail, no matter how small."

"Well, it was pretty cold that day, so there was one detail that was quite small, wasn't there, Cat?"

Cat flushed a bit more and agreed, "Just as well – made it easier to cover with my staff."

The others were not following this at all; Mandalee promised to explain later.

In the meantime, Catriona continued with what she wanted to say.

"You've probably gathered that I'm linked with my staff, right?" Her friends nodded. "Well, more correctly, I am linked to the power within the staff. An important distinction because I'm beginning to understand that the staff itself is really quite irrelevant. It's a tool, a vessel, nothing more. Anyway, whenever I learn something significant, something that brings me a step closer to understanding this power, I get a sympathic jolt. It's, erm—" She tried to find a way to describe it other than the one she had in mind, but couldn't, so blushing deeply, she confessed, "It's, well, it's kind of like sex, as a matter of fact."

“They have devices like that in this world,” Jessica quipped. "I could get you one if you'd like."

“Jessica!” Sara exclaimed, genuinely shocked.

“What?” her sister retorted, unperturbed. “It’s alright for you, sis; we don’t all have elf boys we can snog. Some of us have to make do.”

Seeing that Catriona wasn’t offended by her sister’s remarks, the slightly more reticent Sara was emboldened enough to join in. “Yeah, but you know what Catriona’s like. Think about it: synthetic materials you-know-where.” She winced. “Could be nasty.”

“Blimey, you’re right,” Jessica’s eyes widened. “Never thought of that. Sorry, Cat. Better stick with your staff.”

“Anyway, moving on from that,” a bright red Daelen encouraged an only slightly less flushed Catriona.

“Yes, well, this -er- stimulus, is important because most of what I learn is buried deep within magical texts. Most, but not all. Sometimes I find solutions in non-magic-related books.”

“Like you figured out your Mirror Image spell from reading about photography,” Mandalee offered by way of example.

“Exactly,” Cat agreed. “Also, remember this power has something to do with Time. Not the Time travel you know, Daelen, but something new…and yet at the same time, far older. Perhaps as old as the world – my world. Perhaps even older, I don't know yet. So, sometimes it uses events it must know will happen. Maybe it even shapes those events, but whatever the details, it stimulates me in this way to bring about its, erm…” she hesitated before saying the next word, guessing Jessica and Sara’s reactions. “…release,” she finished.

The two Chetsuans screamed with laughter.

“I can’t—” Sara gasped, “—I can’t breathe!”

“Didn’t seem to need to come up for air when you were snogging that elf boy for hours,” Jessica quipped.

Mandalee, knowing her friend was trying to make a serious point, was making a supreme effort to control herself, but Cat could see the tears of laughter forming in the corners of her eyes.

“So, why, erm,” she began, faltering and then trying again. “Why bring this up now?”

“Because when Daelen described you in that particular way, it felt…” the druidess blushed again “…well, it felt pretty good, actually, and I don't think it was just the sound of your sexy voice, Daelen. It's telling me to find a reference to that phrase. That's why I brought everyone in here.

"I've searched through everything I've already got, and so far, nothing. There's something here in this library, I'm sure of it, but somehow it's eluding my usual locator magic."

"Why would it do that?" Daelen wondered, scowling at the two Chetsuans. They were trying hard to calm down, but just as one settled, a giggle would escape the other's mouth and set her sister off again. "If this 'assassin peacemaker' reference is significant, why would it obstruct your ability to find it?"

"My guess is that sometimes it's not just about finding the information," she seemed to wince, slightly, "but *how* I find it."

This prompted Sara and Jessica to sing a chorus of a song called 'It Ain't What You Do, It's the Way That You Do It' followed by an equivalent of a high five with their tails.

"Before we turn your entire library upside down, Daelen, can you think of anything?"

"Seems reasonable," Mandalee told Daelen. "I mean, it was you who said, 'assassin peacemaker,' so maybe it's a reference to something you've seen before."

"Hey guys," Cat called out, looking distinctly uncomfortable. Everyone turned to look at the druidess, her eyes slightly glazed. "Could we avoid saying the actual phrase from now on, please?"

Mandalee suddenly realised that the reason her friend was so flushed wasn't just from embarrassment but from the repeated…stimulus.

"You mean, every time one of us says it…"

Cat nodded.

Mandalee and Daelen apologised, while the Chetsuans went with, "Blimey!"

Daelen had a thought, just then. He couldn't quite isolate it; it was just a vague impression that they were looking in the wrong place.

"Have you tried fiction?"

Cat frowned. "No, why would I?"

"Just an idea," he replied with a shrug. "It feels right. As if it's something I read once, long ago."

"Any chance of narrowing it down?" Mandalee prompted.

“Actually, we can probably narrow it down with some common sense,” Sara suggested. “Daelen said assa—” she caught herself, “—I mean, he used that phrase with reference to you, Mandalee, so I would guess that the kind of character we’re looking for is a bit like you.”

Jessica took up the thread.

“Good thinking, sis. So, the question is, what category would this world put your story in?”

“Fantasy? Sci-Fi?” Sara suggested.

“Action adventure,” Daelen insisted. “I’m sure of it. That’s where we need to look.”

“Well done guys,” Cat commended them. “I knew we’d get there if we worked together.”

The two Chetsuans, knowing the library better than anyone, even Daelen himself, ran over to the relevant section of shelves and began searching through the titles, starting at each end and working their way through so they’d meet in the middle.

A few moments later, Sara called out, “Found it!”

Working backwards from Z, what she had found was the end of a series of books, under the umbrella title:

‘*Melanda: Assassin*’ written by ‘*Rose Storm.*’

Despite their age, they were perfectly preserved, as if untouched by the passage of time.

This final instalment was entitled: *The Assassin Peacemaker* and according to the back cover:

Tired of the infighting, the Assassin has turned Peacemaker. Recent events forced the two gangs to work together, but now that threat has ended, they look set to return to their old ways. Elisabeth Melanda is determined that will not happen. The Red Cats and the Twin Tigers must fully unite before everything is lost. To do that, the Assassin Peacemaker finds she must go back to the beginning, to where this all started, in Training School.

“Training School,” Jessica echoed. “That’s the title of the first novel in the series.”

So saying, she pulled it off the shelf. She also pointed out to her sister that she’d just used the forbidden phrase twice.

Realising she was right, Sara gasped an apology to Cat.

"It's OK," she replied. "Nothing happened, which means you've found it."

The Chetsuans brought the two novels over to where the druidess was sitting.

"Rose Storm," Daelen remarked with misty eyes. "That was the name she used. I should have remembered."

He reminded Catriona that he'd once had a mortal lover from Tempestria, named Rose. They lived there in his house on Earth for a time, and one of the things she liked to do was write fiction. She enjoyed the creative process of putting words in ink onto paper. She wrote a lot, and it had been so long ago that he couldn't remember all the titles.

Mandalee told Daelen she recognised the surname 'Storm' from his credit card – she'd seen it often enough while she was shopping. Come to think of it, she hadn't worn half her new stuff, but they were going to be here for more than two weeks, yet, so she guessed she'd have time.

"And then she used the other half for the name of one of these gangs in her story," Cat realised. "The Twin Tigers."

"The names of her main character and the other gang ain't exactly subtle, either, are they, love?" Jessica put in. "E. Melanda: Mandalee, Red: Redfletching, Cats: Catriona." Then she paused, stunned as the implications hit her. "Hang on – these books were written long before any of us were even born, Daelen excepted. How could she have known your names?"

"Wait," Sara put in, "you mentioned something about Time magic. Is that what this is?"

"Must be," Cat replied, nodding absently while flicking through the pages of *The Assassin Peacemaker*. Nothing leapt out, so she decided the most sensible plan was to do what the back cover said: go back to the beginning, to *Training School*. Opening that first book, then, she read the dedication inside:

To Cat,

Dig deep in your training, and you will find the keys to success.

Aye, ever yours,

Rose

~x~

“What does that mean?” Daelen wondered.

Cat gave him a wry smile. “I guess it means I’m going to be training with you, after all.”

Chapter 24

"Is this how your staff research always works, then?" Daelen wondered.

"Mostly," Cat nodded. "It's about learning specific magical keys to unlock one layer of protection at a time."

"Magical keys?" Mandalee wondered.

"Think of it this way," Cat encouraged her. "Your mark is being sheltered by your enemies in the deepest room of a house like this one. Between you and your quarry are many guards and many doors that are locked and booby-trapped. If you miss one or make one small slip, your enemies will capture you. As a trained assassin, what would you do?"

Mandalee smirked, "Knowing me, I'd probably just have a couple of drinks, get armed to the teeth and go for it."

Her friend laughed, "Not quite the analogy I was hoping for. OK, you can't launch a full-scale assault because before killing your mark, you must make him reveal information that is vital to your sponsors. His death alone will not fulfil your contract. On the plus side, your mark and his friends are not going anywhere so you can afford to wait."

"In that case, I would need to plan it to the letter, know the location and detail of every trap, every lock, every guard. It would be futile and probably fatal to attempt a move without all the information. I would probably also need help from others, but not too many, if only to gather the…" she hesitated, "…intel – is that the right phrase, Jess?"

Jessica nodded.

"Well, that's how I gain access to this power," Catriona explained. "I don't know yet whether the power within this staff is friend or foe, but I have to find out. I need to understand every barrier between me and its release before attempting to use it, or even deciding whether I should. This isn't a solo effort; I need help from others, but only from the right people, not too many. Pretty much just you guys."

Plus Dreya, of course, but she couldn't mention that.

"It sounds pretty complex," Daelen commented, with a newfound appreciation for Catriona's hard work.

"It's certainly a serious challenge – that's why I'm enjoying it so much."

She paused for a moment to determine if there were any more questions or comments – there were none.

It was getting late. She had already seen a few stifled yawns, and she took her own as a firm agreement that it was time for bed.

In the morning, she would, at last, begin her training.

*****

The next few mornings, they enjoyed breakfast together before dividing the day up into chunks. Mandalee would do physical exercise and workouts with Daelen, while Cat spent her time studying. Then Mandalee would train and spar with either Sara or Jessica – they were pretty evenly matched as long as Mandalee didn't use her super-speed. Meanwhile, Catriona would suffer through physical training with Daelen. She wasn't the physical fighter that Mandalee was, and it quickly became apparent that it was never going to be her forte.

By now, the shadow warrior had learned that trying to push Catriona into doing something she didn't want to do was futile, but he could help her to push herself. Cat appreciated the value of improving her physical conditioning, which she had to admit wasn't quite back to where it had been before her illness. Within a few days, though, Daelen had managed to help her push herself even further, so she was in the best condition of her life.

At range, her archery was a match for anyone. Up close, it made more sense for her to shift to leopard, wolf or even bear form. Apart from anything else, in a real battle, her attackers were unlikely to expect that, so that would put surprise on her side.

Away from the training centre, Cat and Mandalee worked on their different forms of magic. Both young women were reminded of the time they had spent hunting demons together, a few years ago. This was really just an extension of the skills they had developed back then.

Their evenings were kept free of work – even Cat put her books away – in favour of going out into the city, soaking up the sights, the culture and shopping. Cat still didn't buy anything and simply used a perception filter. Sometimes, Daelen accompanied them. Other times, he left the four young ladies to their own devices in the name of not cramping their style. The more time they spent together, the less they would want to part later. That meant it was more likely Jessica and Sara would choose Tempestria to be their new home when the moment came.

The pattern held until one day, just into the second half of their planned stay on Earth, when Cat and Mandalee heard a commotion coming from Daelen's training centre. Powerful cannon blasts followed by explosions mingled with shouts and screams from the Chetsuan girls. Racing to the scene, the two friends found Sara and Jessica standing outside the training centre. Jessica was pounding on the door begging for Daelen to let her in and help.

"It's no good, Jess!" Sara implored her, reaching out to her sister. "He won't listen. He never does when he's like this, you know that."

Jessica snarled and swore at her sister.

"You turn your back on him if you want, but I won't!" she insisted. "I'm staying here," she continued, her voice becoming a scream, "until he opens this bloody door!" She resumed her pounding and demanding to be let in.

Catriona was shocked. She'd never heard them say a cross word to each other in the admittedly short time she'd known them.

She shared a worried look with Mandalee, who asked, "Sara, what's going on?"

There came a rumbling sound, as the house shook to its very foundations. The girls had to hold onto each other to keep their balance.

"Oh, hey, you two," Sara greeted them. "It's Daelen. He's having another one of his moods. He gets like this from time to time. Go on, have a look through the glass."

Jessica moved aside, close to Sara, and nuzzled her sister's neck in a Chetsuan apology. Sara licked Jessica's forehead, and all was forgiven.

Inside the training centre, Daelen was pushing himself like nothing they'd seen before. The reinforced and shielded walls strained under the assault of his cannon blasts. He had conjured a copy for the purposes of sparring, but it was like he thought he was fighting Aden in there. Fighting for real. Their attacks were a flurry of movement, each blow strong enough to flatten a mountain and he was accelerating, hitting harder and faster, using ever more powerful cannon blasts, all the time screaming and yelling unintelligibly.

Cat spotted some technology standing in the far corner. In one of their recent trips into the city, Sara had taken them to something called a 'rock and roll bar' which had a music player called a jukebox. The device in the corner looked a bit like that, but it didn't seem to be designed to play music.

"It's a gravity generator," Jessica explained. "It's why we can't get in. It's ten times Earth normal, we'd be killed. Of course, Daelen's not like us so he can take it."

Cat noticed Jessica's usual affectations of speech disappeared when she was upset. She missed hearing them, and she wanted her to be happy again so she could go back to using them.

There came another mini earthquake. It felt as though the whole world shook that time.

"What the hell is he trying to do? Break this world in two or just flatten his own house?" Mandalee wondered.

As she spoke, Daelen's frenzied attack on himself grew in intensity, until he finally managed to knock himself out. At least, they hoped he was just unconscious. His copy vanished. A stray bit of power from his last volley had hit the gravity generator, and the pitch of the hum it was emitting began to rise.

"Oh, no!" Sara gasped. "The gravity's being turned up higher!"

It was already up to twelve G and climbing.

"How much can Daelen take?" Mandalee wondered. Then, when the house shook again, she revised her question. "Actually, never mind Daelen. How much can this house take?" she worried.

The gravity well was already too strong for them to attempt to step into even if they could get through the door, but Catriona had a ridiculous radical plan. Daelen had shielded the room but had made the mistake people always made: he forgot to shield the floor. She used her stoneshaper magic, weakening the floor until it gave way and the device fell through. Cat encouraged the process still further so that the Earth itself swallowed the machine whole. Then she changed the magic to squeeze the gap closed, crushing the machine within. The gravity returned to normal.

The next challenge was getting inside.

"If you can make a small gap," Sara volunteered, "I could get in and shut down the shields from the inside to let the rest of you in."

Jessica backed her up. "My sister's got a pretty good head for tech skills."

Cat agreed and reshaped the floor to create a crawlspace underneath the door.

Borrowing a knife from Mandalee that she said looked ideal, Sara crawled inside, prised off the control panel and set to fiddling with its inner workings. After a minute, she got annoyed and kicked the door. Giving up on the technical approach, she reached for a gun that she had strapped to her leg under her skirt.

"We both have them for security," Jessica explained. "So far, no-one's ever tried to break in from another world, at least as long as we've been here. Still, you never know."

Sara shot the control panel with what Jessica called a laser, but it was shielded against that sort of attack. Moving on to Plan C, she undid the holster strap from around her leg and used it to strap the gun to the knife instead. It took a couple of goes, but she managed to get the knife wedged into the frame of the control panel, preventing the gun from falling down.

"Guys," Jessica fretted, "if she's doing what I think she's doing, I think we'd best stand well back, just in case."

Sara fiddled with something inside the gun's workings and ran away from the door, getting down on the floor to shield Daelen's body with hers. There was a deafening, high-pitched whine, followed by a massive explosion as the gun blew itself up, taking the control panel, the door and half the wall down with it.

It took a moment for the smoke and dust to settle enough to be able to see again, but Jessica was immediately on her feet, calling out for her sister.

"I'm here, Jess," came her reply as the air cleared. "Don't worry, I'm fine."

Jessica ran to her and embraced her tightly, then she pulled away, looked at the gaping hole in the wall and quipped, "Hey, Sara, love. You were only supposed to blow the bloody door off."

The two Tempestrians didn't get the reference, but Sara obviously did, because they did another of their tail-high-fives.

Cat was in there in a flash, holding Daelen in her arms, Mandalee by her side. When Mandalee's healing proved unsuccessful, Catriona tried her way, but that also failed.

"It's not you guys," Sara reassured them, shaking her head. "There's nothing physically wrong with him. He's just drained. Once we get him charging up again, he'll be fine."

She volunteered to go and fetch a trolley so they could wheel him to the sickbay.

"Classic hero behaviour, I'm afraid, dears," Jessica remarked.

Cat and Mandalee shared a smile at hearing her old speech pattern re-emerging, now that the immediate danger was past.

"Every now and then, Daelen gets all het up about his battles, starts to think he's a monster and pushes himself to the edge to try and get even stronger, so he can 'make up' for whatever he reckons he's done that probably wasn't his fault in the first place. Then he comes in here and takes a chunk out of himself, his training centre or, in this case, both."

Cat nodded, pensively. "He told me he doesn't like to think of himself as a hero, but it's a bit difficult to avoid labelling him that way when he plays the part so well."

"This fight you're preparing for on your world, fighting this Kullos bloke. It's a pretty big deal, right?"

"We think Daelen's going to save our world, or possibly destroy it, or both," Mandalee replied. "The jury's still out, as you say here."

"Hey, you're getting pretty good at those," Jessica grinned, then she grew serious. "Anyway, yeah, I get that. Really, I do, but I think it's more than that this time. I reckon, this time, he's not planning on coming back. Sara says not to worry, that I'm imagining it, but I don't think I am. He hasn't said anything – he wouldn't – but I've noticed things. Little things."

"Like what?" Cat asked.

"Well, like throwing us together, for a start. I mean, don't get me wrong, it's great having you here, like proper mates. Sara's not looked that shade of purple for years." She broke off and explained that basically meant she was looking healthy and happy. "Look, all I'm saying is, I think Daelen's thinking about what we're gonna do if he's not around anymore."

"Well, whether that's true or not," Mandalee assured them, "you and your sister are welcome on Tempestria anytime."

"Definitely," Cat agreed. "You know that, right?"

"Yeah, I was hoping you'd say that. Cheers, loves. You go sort out Kullos, and me and my sister are coming over for a visit. For sure."

As they were speaking, they heard the sound of a trolley being wheeled down the corridor, getting closer. From the doorway, Sara called out for Cat to smooth out the floor where the doorway used to be, so she could get the trolley in and out. Cat obliged her.

"Your voices were drifting down the corridor," Sara told Cat, "and I think you should know, there's another thing that drives Daelen to do this, from time to time. I think he's pining for his lost loves."

"Loves?" Cat asked. "Plural?"

"He slipped up once," Sara nodded. "Tried to cover it up quickly, but I wasn't convinced. No idea who the other one was, but I do know he loved Rose with all his heart, and I think your research into your staff in the library the other day brought it all back."

"Thought so," Cat grimaced. "If I'd known where it was going to lead, I would have found another way."

"Don't blame yourself," Sara admonished her as she and the others lifted Daelen onto the trolley. "It would have happened sooner or later, anyway. Especially since you remind him of her so much."

"I know," Cat sighed. "Still, it's pretty tough, competing with a ghost," she remarked, dryly. Three pairs of wide eyes turned towards her, and a blushing druidess, realising what she'd said, tried to cover it. "That is, I would be competing with a ghost if I had any intention of returning his feelings, which I don't, which is fine since his feelings aren't really directed at me at all, but that other girl, not that it bothers me, you understand, I mean…" she trailed off. "I'm really not convincing anybody, am I?"

Three heads shook as one.

"Fair enough."

They began wheeling the trolley, continuing their conversation.

"Thing is, you're wrong," Sara insisted. "He does love you, not just the memory of Rose. Believe it or not, I think what Daelen did today was his idea of therapy. Trying to get over Rose finally, after so long, so he can focus on his feelings for you without them being tainted. I think he was trying to finally bury his lost love deep underground. Underneath his training centre."

Abruptly, Cat stopped wheeling. "What did you say?" she gasped.

"I just said—"

"—No!" she cried quickly, holding up a restraining hand. "That was just rhetorical. Now is really not the time for another one of those, thank you."

"Another one of—" Sara began, confused.

Jessica whispered something in her sister's ear and Sara's eyes widened.

"Oh!" she gasped, understanding. "Another one of *those*."

"What are you planning, Cat?" Mandalee asked.

Catriona grinned. "Well, you know me. I'm always one for study, brain over brawn, and all that. Sometimes, though, I will admit there's something to be said for Daelen's brute force."

Mandalee shook her head, not getting it. "Not with you," she admitted. Then with a wry smile, she added, "No change there, then."

"'*The Red Cat and Twin Tiger gangs have to unite*' *and* '*go back to Training School*,'" she paraphrased from *The Assassin Peacemaker*. "I have to use my druid magic but also use Daelen's approach of brute force and power. Not careful, controlled shaping like I'd normally do, but really rip the place apart like he would," Cat explained. "And in case that's too cryptic for you, the dedication gives it to me straight: '*Dig deep in your training, and you will find the keys to success*.' Literally, dig deep underneath the training centre, and I'll find something I need. You three sort out Daelen. I think this house needs a new garden."

Explaining no further, she shifted to her falcon form and flew back to Daelen's training centre.

Reverting to her natural form, she stepped inside and stood in the middle of the training centre. Along one wall, there lay some technology: monitoring equipment, security systems, lighting.

Facing that wall, she remarked, "That lot can go for a start."

Holding out a hand, she called for her staff, which obediently appeared out of her pocket dimension. She was less reticent about using the staff to focus her magic, now that she'd realised the staff itself and the power within it were entirely separate. She pointed it at the electronic mechanism and spoke a word of magic. The crystal flared as it sent forth a bolt of lightning, shorting out the wiring and circuitry. Her next blast was one of fire, setting delicate parts aflame. Creating a massive hole in the outside wall, she stepped clear of the building. Using stoneshaper and woodshaper in concert, she carved up the building like a roast dinner. A column of fire sprang up in the middle, and she sat down to watch the building burn. Since it was entirely separate from the main house, she didn't have to worry about being careful, so she wasn't. There was no finesse in her magic. She was just intent on smashing it up and burning it down.

When the flames died down, and the wood was reduced to ashes, she switched elements to ice – dry ice – cooling the stonework to the point where it became brittle. Calling on the power of air she found it quite barbaric fun to throw large spheres of superdense air at the walls, to smash them. Once satisfied, she caused a mini-earthquake to rip the foundations apart. She searched and sifted through the rubble, channelling her magic ever deeper until finally, she found it: the sealed access to a pocket dimension. Sealed, that is, until now. For as soon as she lay down in the dirt and reached towards it, it opened effortlessly at her touch. This pocket dimension wasn't like the one in Calin's library. It was tiny. As soon as she reached her hand inside, she felt a cold metal box, which she pulled clear. Sitting down, caring nothing for how filthy her robes were getting, she opened the box and inside was a booklet and note, which read:

Hi Cat,

If you've been doing your homework, then you will recognise the magical keys in this book as those relating to your staff, so I'm not telling you anything you don't already know. But here's the punchline: These keys are not for your staff, they're for something else. If you've solved the Mystery of Calin's Tower, you will have worked out what they're for. If you haven't, then things have gone horribly wrong (again), and you need to go there immediately. Nothing's more important.

Aye, ever yours,

Rose

~x~

p.s. I have no idea why the keys are the same.

"There's always another mystery, isn't there?" Cat mumured to herself. "Thanks, Rose. You've been a big help."

Just then, a voice came out of the ether:

Red faction second attempt gone. One attempt remains.

Chapter 25

Catriona used her magic some more, allowing the ground to gape even broader and deeper so it could swallow the remains of the building and all of its contents deep under the ground, before filling in the hole and smoothing over the top layer. Walking over to some nearby plants, Cat used her love of nature to ask them to give up their seeds. They responded to her gentle druid magic and dropped their seeds into her hand. When she decided she had collected enough, she spent an hour painstakingly planting them by hand, before calling for gentle rain and sunshine to assist her in accelerating their growth. By the time she was finished, in the place where Daelen's training centre once stood, there was now a beautiful meadow. Amid the lush, green grass, stood bright, colourful flowers, dozens of varieties of non-flowering plants and herbs. Butterflies fluttered, bees buzzed, and birds sang their joy of this wondrous new creation. There was just one thing missing, Cat decided, and taking off in her falcon form again, she flew away to find what she needed.

A few moments later, she returned with an acorn in her beak. She spotted Mandalee on the ground – she had come from her bedside vigil to see what her friend was up to. Sending out a sympathic greeting, the falcon circled over the meadow – scaring some of the smaller birds away – and landed in the centre. Without returning to her natural form, Cat gently planted the acorn in the earth and covered the hole. She even chose to use her druid powers, still in her bird form, flying up as a mighty oak tree grew tall and strong. The growth stopped, and the falcon perched on a branch. Mandalee did not disturb her, but simply sat down and waited, closing her eyes to better enjoy the smells and sounds of nature. After a while, she felt a touch on her shoulder and opened her eyes to see a small brown mouse perched there. Mandalee smiled and lifted the mouse gently onto her hand, where she stroked the little creature, which she knew to be her friend Catriona.

It was dark before Cat could bring herself to return to her half-Faery form, but when she did, she told her friend, "This isn't just any old garden. It's a recreation of my childhood home. It's amazing how similar the wildlife is here, compared to Tempestria.

At first, I couldn't cope because this world was so alien, and yet now I've managed to create a small slice of the Faery lands of Quarthonia here on another world. This oak tree reminds me of the one back home, the one my parents were married under all those years ago. A girl could get quite homesick here. In a good way."

Cat was understating her achievement, in Mandalee's opinion. She'd been to Quarthonia herself and seen a view of which this, as far as the Cleric of Nature could tell, was an absolutely faithful recreation, down to the smallest detail. She would never cease to be amazed at what her friend could do when she put her mind to it. Mandalee was also quietly envious – though not in any negative way – of how Catriona's powers could have such creative possibilities. Sometimes it seemed to Mandalee that everything she did was about killing. She didn't regret her kills – those who died at her hands sought to take away the lives of innocent people who had not the power to protect themselves. She took lives to save lives, and she never lost sight of that. Still, she would give much to be able to create beauty, but since she didn't have that gift, she would do the only thing she could: protect the life of someone who did.

"Now, if Daelen wants to rebuild his training centre," Cat continued, "he will have to chop down my childhood home to do it. If he really does care for me and not just this girl from his past, then he won't do that. Maybe from now on, instead of coming here to work himself into the cold grave, he will come to relax and enjoy the beauty of life. This is 'Catriona's Meadow' now; my gift to him. Hopefully, it will serve as a reminder to him that even though I don't love him in the way he would wish, I do still love him, and before you say anything, Mandalee, yes, I am willing to admit that now."

"So, you admit you love him, you know he loves you, and yet you're not going to do anything about those feelings?" Mandalee wondered, puzzled.

"An excellent summation," Cat agreed.

"Why not?"

"Mandalee, you know I don't like keeping things from you, but this is one thing I can't tell you."

"You mean you won't," the assassin countered.

"No, I mean I can't," Cat insisted. "I am prevented by a promise – a magically backed promise. When I was cut off from

Tempestria, I could feel the magic slipping away, but now that I'm connected again, it's strengthened anew."

She explained, as best she could, that her promise could be partially removed via a sympathic agreement that the time was right, but only physical contact could eliminate it entirely.

"So, I meant what I said, Mandalee. I physically cannot tell you why I choose not to have a relationship with him. And please keep any speculation to yourself, OK?"

To Catriona's surprise, Mandalee assured her that she understood.

"Even without the magical element, I wouldn't ask you to break a promise. Just one question: Have you ever regretted it?"

"Never for one fraction of a second."

As far as her friend was concerned, that was all she needed to know.

They stayed there together and chatted for a while until Jessica came to find them.

"Heya, loves! There you are. Wow, love what you've done with the place, Cat. Daelen should be up and ready to go again in a minute or two if you want to go and see him."

Cat thanked her and jumped up, ready to go again, herself, holding out a hand to her friend, who grabbed it and pulled herself onto her feet.

Jessica turned to walk away, but Mandalee called out to her, "Hey, Jessica? You OK, now?"

"Tickety-boo, love," she replied with a beaming smile.

*****

"Where am I? What happened?" Daelen groaned, rubbing his head as Cat and Mandalee walked in. "Oh no, I'm doing the clichés again, aren't I? Man, I feel like my body's been put in a blender."

"Short version: you nearly killed yourself. We rescued you," Cat told him.

"And," Mandalee added in a low voice, checking that the two Chetsuan girls weren't around, "you upset Jessica, which is practically a criminal offence as far as I'm concerned."

Cat nodded. "She was so worried about you, she even yelled at her sister."

Daelen looked suitably ashamed of that, at least.

"Don't worry, they're fine again now," Mandalee assured him. "Nothing's getting between those two for long, and I'd fight anything that tried."

Daelen promised to have a word with her, but Cat admonished him, "Don't you dare. She'd be mortified that we've told you. Besides, she wasn't the only one who was worried about you. Just don't do anything like it again."

"Try talking about your feelings, rather than blasting chunks out of the Earth," Mandalee advised, "or whatever world you happen to be on, OK?"

Daelen smiled grimly. "I'll do my best."

At that point, the assassin left the two of them alone to do exactly as she had suggested.

"Before we do that," Cat began, "there's something you should know about your training centre."

"What about it?"

"You don't have one anymore."

Daelen went to the window, through which he used to be able to see his training centre. He was quite startled to see in its place, a garden, sitting in the shade of a hundred-year-old oak tree that hadn't been there a few hours ago.

"Spending time in that garden will do you much more good than your training centre would," Cat said, by way of explanation.

Daelen just smiled and told her it was the most beautiful gift he'd ever received, and it was at that moment that he tried to kiss her. Catriona turned her head, though, so he only got her cheek, not her lips.

"Please don't do that again," Catriona told him.

Daelen stammered an apology. "I—I—didn't mean…I'm sorry."

"I know. It's OK. There's all kinds of chemistry going on between us, and things just got a little confused, no harm done. But I do think we need to 'put our cards on the table' – is that the right expression?"

Daelen agreed that it was.

"In that case, why don't you start by telling me what you think you were doing, trying to kill yourself like that?"

"Well, I wasn't trying to kill myself, for a start," he insisted.

"Then why did you push yourself to such extremes? There are a few theories flying around, such as pining over your long-lost love, but I'd like to hear your version."

Daelen shook his head. "It wasn't about Rose."

"Are you sure?" Cat pressed. "I mean, are you sure I didn't just open an old wound when my research led me to her?"

"No," Daelen stated, emphatically. "On the contrary, that just made me realise that thinking about Rose doesn't bring me pain anymore. She's just a memory, now. A good memory. Rose will always belong to my past, but memories of the past should not prevent us from living in the present."

"Then, again, we come back to 'Why'?"

"Because my present is you."

"OK," Cat replied, "I know we're on another world, but I'm pretty sure that, even here, that line makes no sense."

Daelen breathed, deeply, trying to find the right words. "This is the eve of my final confrontation with Kullos. Our previous battles were part of what I thought was an endless cycle, but that cycle is now broken. Outside interference or not, Time manipulation or not, it doesn't matter why. It only matters that it is, and I have to be ready. There is one chance to save your world. One. I have to be stronger, faster, more powerful than I have ever been. Heaven's Surrender will be used. The only question is whose finger will be on the trigger. But saving your world isn't an abstract concept, anymore, or some obligation for past actions. It's about the present. It's about you. I will push myself to my limits and then go still further, because that is the only way I know to keep you alive."

"So, it's all about me?"

"Of course," the shadow warrior insisted. "It's true that I needed time to sort out my feelings, separate what I feel for you from the pictures in my mind, pictures from the past. But now, I swear, all I see is you. I know our timing is terrible, but I think that just makes it even more important to embrace the short time we have together. You're amazing, Cat: strong and independent. You speak your mind, you're beautiful, and you have such a good heart. I know I rub you up the wrong way, sometimes, but every time that happens, I understand you a little better. So why can't we seize this moment and be together while we can?"

Catriona took his hands in hers and gazed up at him, eyes pleading for understanding.

"Daelen," she began, "the truth is, I do care about you..."

"I don't want to push you, Cat, but you did say 'cards on the table,' remember?" Daelen said, pointedly.

Cat nodded. "You're right. I set the rules, and I have to follow them." Starting afresh, she confessed, "The real truth is, I don't just care; I love you. You trusted me with a part of your essence, allowed me to see and touch a part of your true self, and I will always cherish that. I am truly flattered, deeply touched by your feelings for me, and that you chose to share them with me, but that doesn't mean I'm looking to get into any kind of relationship with you. It's more complicated than that. The time will come when I can explain more, but right now, this is all I can say. I hope you can respect that because I still think it's important that we keep working together to fight Kullos. I'm sorry, Daelen."

There were tears in his eyes, but he made an effort to smile. "It's OK, I understand. Kisses are off-limits. Are hugs still acceptable?"

Cat smiled and embraced him. "Always," she promised. Breaking the hug, she asked, "Do you want me to leave you alone for a while?"

"No," Daelen shook his head. "I still want to spend as much time with you as possible, even if it's just as friends. Shall we go and see what the others are up to?"

Cat agreed and took his arm. As they walked out of the medical wing, she suggested that later on, they could go for some lighter training in his new meadow; something a bit more magic-focused.

"There's something I'd like to try out. Something I've been working on in theory for a few years and I think I've figured out the practical side of actually doing it. This world has a better understanding of how energy works, and I've applied that same knowledge to magic."

"Alright, but first, how about dinner? Don't know about you, but I'm starving."

"Me, too," she affirmed. "I used a lot of energy, demolishing your training centre like that."

*****

A few moments later, they found Mandalee enjoying some friendly, three-way sparring with Jessica and Sara. Forgoing any fancy tricks or magic, they were each just armed with a pair of knives. Currently, they were sheathed for safety, but when Mandalee saw Cat and Daelen, she ran over to show them off.

The retractable blades were small, even cute, no more than an inch long, but Cat knew that in her friend's hands, they would be deadly. Mandalee now kept them strapped to her wrists. They were attached with a leather thong that would allow her to flick them into her hands so she could open them with the tiniest movement. The knives themselves were not made of metal, she explained. Instead, they were fashioned from grizzly souvenirs that Jessica had brought with her from their homeworld: dragon claws. According to the Chetsuans, their people had learned to their cost that they could cut through any armour.

"That's what you've been doing while we were talking?" Daelen wondered.

"Yeah," Cat agreed, with a mischievous smile. "I thought you'd be braiding each other's hair."

Mandalee matched the smile with one of her own. "We're doing that later. Didn't want to leave you out."

"Aww, thanks. You're the best."

"I know," the assassin nodded. "Anyway, finished with your little heart to heart?"

"Oh, I think we're good now, yes?" Catriona looked up at Daelen for confirmation.

From his weak smile and nod, she could tell he was still disappointed, which was understandable, but he was putting a brave face on it.

"We've mutually agreed that we're hungry," he told the others. "You guys want to join us?"

After sharing a look between the three of them, Sara spoke up. "OK, but after that stunt of yours this morning, Jess and I have decided we're having the rest of the day off."

"Which means we're not setting foot in your kitchen, dearie," Jessica added.

“Come on then, Daelen,” Mandalee grinned, sprinting away, “First one to your kitchen cooks dinner!”

“Don't you mean ‘last one’?” Daelen called out.

“No, believe me, you don't want her to cook,” Cat explained with a mischievous smile. “If you like your dinner edible, I suggest you get moving.”

Daelen took off instantly.

Chapter 26

After dinner, the two Chetsuans decided to go into the city, leaving Daelen alone with Catriona and Mandalee.

Having cleared everything away, they headed out to Catriona's Meadow where they relaxed for a while. As there was no danger of being overheard, now, Mandalee took the opportunity to broach a subject that had been on her mind since their initial conversation with their new friends from Phitonia.

"Why haven't you done more to protect the Chetsuans of Phitonia from the dragons?"

"Strange that you would ask me that," Daelen considered. "Not long ago, you thought I was just about the biggest threat to your world, despite how long I've been Tempestria's Protector. Now you want me to be Phitonia's Protector, too?"

Mandalee shook her head. "You don't get off the hook that easily. Despite what anybody thought, that didn't stop you from protecting us. Why should it matter what the Chetsuans might think?"

"Phitonia is just one world. If I help the Chetsuans of Phitonia, what about Lavos, the world where dragons are the endangered species? Should I go and help the dragons there? On another world, the people are just recovering from an invasion that could have destroyed their world. Should I have stopped that, too? As it turned out, a group of adventurers banded together and ended the threat in a far more ingenious way than my brute force approach – something you should appreciate, Cat. They achieved that victory all by themselves, should I have robbed them of that? What about all the troubles here on Earth? Should I swoop in and save the day like some kind of superhero? Put a stop to all their wars, resolve all their conflicts? I may be powerful, but I'm only one person. Am I never to have a life of my own? Am I always to be a slave to everyone in need?

"What if, while I'm on Phitonia, fighting the dragons, I get an alert that Kullos is attacking your world? Which world do I save?"

Mandalee turned away, face flushing. "You can't ask me to make that kind of choice," she objected quietly.

"Why not?" Daelen demanded. "You're asking me to. What if, instead of preparing to fight Kullos in your world, I go and conquer Phitonia, instead? Because that's what it would take. The dragons aren't going to stop hunting Chetsuans just because I ask nicely. And what if, while I'm there, Kullos gets all the pieces of his control device, decides he's tired of waiting for Michael and me to show up, and just uses Heaven's Surrender to destroy your world? Or what if the dragons figure out how to follow me back to Tempestria? Now we have to fight a war on two fronts. What if they decide humans and Faery look just as tasty as Chetsuans, and do to your civilisation what they did to Sara and Jessica's?"

Mandalee was deeply embarrassed. "I never thought about any of that. I'm sorry."

The shadow warrior put a reassuring arm around her. "Don't be sorry. I was having the same argument with myself centuries before you were born. I saved Sara and Jessica because not doing so would have meant genocide for their people. When I left you guys the other day, I was stopping something similar from happening on Lavos. Fortunately, I got to them much earlier in the process. Rescuing a pair of dragons and bringing them here to live with Jessica and Sara could have been a bit awkward."

"Just a bit," Catriona agreed.

Mandalee was still having a hard time processing all of this, and excused herself for a while, in hopes that a walk by herself would stop her moral compass from spinning wildly.

*****

"I put your world first," Daelen told Cat, after a moment, "because, as I've said before, I'm partially responsible for the danger you're facing. Even so, I generally only interfere when Kullos is involved, or in former times, my dark clone. Otherwise, you have to solve your own problems. When I first learned about wizards going missing on your world, I admit I wasn't particularly interested. Not because I didn't care, as my visitor suggested, but because it didn't seem like something that I should concern myself with until I knew Kullos was involved. People go missing on your world all the time. Am I supposed to start up a missing persons investigation every time? Where would you have me draw the line?"

More than ever, Catriona understood the enormity of the decisions the shadow warrior had been facing every day for who knew how long. She offered no debate, no judgement – how could she possibly be qualified? Instead, she simply held him tight.

"This is just a friend offering comfort to another friend," she whispered. For whose benefit, she wasn't sure, but it felt right to say it.

"I know," Daelen assured her, "and it's very much appreciated."

Still uncertain how long it was appropriate to hold him so close, on sudden impulse, she asked, "What's your favourite animal?"

"What?" Daelen asked, thrown by the random question.

"Suppose you were just an ordinary, lonely human boy with a love of nature, and your best friend was an animal – not a pet – a friend you could love and stroke and talk to. A friend you could confide in, in a way that was pure, simple, uncomplicated," she explained. "What animal would your friend be? What animal would you wish for? And don't say the obvious."

Daelen considered the question for a moment, then answered, "A rabbit. A little white rabbit with long floppy pink ears, cottontail and twitchy nose with whiskers. If I were that ordinary, lonely human boy, that's the animal I would have as my friend. The only one I could ever really talk to. That's what I would wish for."

"Then I think, after so long, it's time that lonely human boy's wish was granted," she decided.

With that, she stood and shifted into the form of a white rabbit, just as he had described. Picking up the rabbit and placing her gently on his lap, Daelen smiled and began to stroke her.

"Sharing your life and love is a beautiful and precious thing," he whispered, tenderly, "no matter what form it might take."

Their conversation from that point on was entirely private, gentle reader. As such, it has nothing to do with you or me, so I trust you will understand if I cut the scene here.

*****

After a while, Mandalee returned and took in the vista before her. Crouching down, she had a turn stroking the rabbit.

"Look at you!" she cried. "You're so cute, I could gobble you up!" She paused as a thought entered her head, and added, "Actually, don't let Shyleen see you in this form, or she'll *really* gobble you up."

The rabbit hopped down off Daelen's lap and shifted back to Catriona's natural form. "Good point!" she laughed. "I'll have to be careful of that one."

"Well, speaking of Shyleen, I've decided to leave the philosophy to her from now on and focus on doing what we're doing."

"Good policy," Daelen approved. "Now, Cat, didn't you say you had something you wanted to show us?"

"Yes, I did," Cat confirmed. The druidess explained that she believed she'd worked out how to counter an anti-magic field.

"You've sussed it?" Mandalee gasped, very proud of her friend. "This I have got to see. Dazzle us, Cat!"

"OK, practical demo first, then I'll explain.

The druidess stood and walked a few paces away. Then she asked Daelen to generate his most powerful anti-magic field around her, making sure it surrounded her like a bubble, not a dome that would leave her feet touching the ground.

Even Dreya had made that mistake the first time, she remembered.

The shadow warrior did as she asked, but to his amazement, after a moment's thought, Cat was able to put on a concert overture of her magical powers.

What made this even more spectacular was Daelen's impossible realisation, "The anti-magic field is intact. You haven't broken through it, and yet it's not stopping you. How is that possible?"

Cat sat down on a wooden stool that had just grown from a dead branch on the ground.

"OK, here's the theory part. For years, it has been in my mind that anti-magic fields are fundamentally flawed as a concept. 'Why?' I hear you ask. Well, tell me this: how do you power an anti-magic field?"

Mandalee knew the answer Catriona was looking for – she'd been to this lecture before. "With magic," she declared.

"Precisely – an anti-magic field is itself a form of magical energy, and in theory, any form of energy is useable, if you know how. So, all one has to do is adjust one's magic and adapt it to feed off the anti-magic field itself. The field detects magic being used, so it strengthens, which only provides more energy for me to tap into."

Mandalee applauded, while Cat stood and took a theatrical bow.

Daelen was wide-eyed, as he breathed, "All my years and I have never thought of that." Sweeping her up into a proud hug, he told her, "The way you create new magic by connecting half a dozen different ideas is like nothing I've ever seen before. You're a genius!"

When Daelen set her gently back down, a blushing Catriona explained, "Well, an anti-magic field is a standard defence against wizards, so I wouldn't be surprised if we faced one in the battles to come. It's best to be prepared."

"If they try it on you," Mandalee put in, "they're really in for a shock, and of course, you can use your druid magic to bind a wizard's hands, which will effectively neutralise them, but what about clerics? Suppose I went rogue and attacked you?"

"Well, you're a bit different because you have a unique connection with Shyleen. As for regular clerics, bring them on," she declared, confidently. "I'll give my Faithless spell a workout."

Mandalee put her hands on her hips in mock anger and huffed, "You always have to have an answer for everything, don't you?"

With a deadly serious look, her friend replied, "If I want to survive, yes I do."

Mandalee hugged her friend and told her, "Then don't you dare stop, cause I'm not going to lose you."

A concerned Catriona held her friend and asked, "Hey, what's this about, Mandalee? Who said anything about losing me?"

Pulling out of the embrace, the assassin replied, "It's nothing. Just after our conversation with Daelen, I'm beginning to realise how dangerous this quest of ours is. We've all been acting like it isn't – especially since coming to this world, but it is serious. It's deadly serious. I'm not stupid; I know I can be reckless at times, but

I know when it's time to be scared and now is definitely the right time."

"You're right," Catriona agreed, matching her tone, "I'm scared, too and," she dropped her voice to a whisper, "so is Daelen, though I don't expect him to admit it in so many words."

Daelen, who had been keeping a respectful distance, spoke up then.

"We are only part of the puzzle, Mandalee. Things are developing back on your world, and Michael is bringing others who will stand with us when the time is right. That moment is coming soon, but we still have some time, yet."

"In that case," Mandalee declared, composing herself once more, "we'd better not waste it."

*****

"So, are you still up for more training?" Daelen wondered.

Cat was pleased to have her opinion asked and decided to reinforce that behaviour with another hug.

Before she could speak, however, Mandalee asked, "Do I get a vote?"

"Of course," he replied, "I was throwing that question out to both of you."

"Yeah, Mandalee," Cat assured her, walking over to her friend and taking both her hands in hers, looking her straight in the eye. "When I was fighting for my right to be treated as an equal, I was fighting for you, too, you know? Sorry if I haven't been making that clear."

"Right then, I declare that the rest of today is officially Mandalee's Day," Daelen announced. "That means we'll do whatever you want to do. It's your choice."

Cat seconded the motion.

"OK," Mandalee smiled at her friends, "how about a mock battle – me and Cat against you?"

"That's a great idea," Catriona agreed, "that should be a pretty good workout. Combine everything we've learned together and see what works."

"Alright," Daelen agreed, "but I won't use my beam cannon or my higher planar powers. There's not much point to a training session if I just knock you both out in two seconds. Besides, I'd be worried about accidentally powering it up too much and hurting you seriously."

"Don't hold back too much," Cat warned, "or you might find yourself in trouble."

In a moment of pure tactlessness, Daelen laughed, "Come on, you don't seriously think you have the weapons to beat me, do you? This isn't just my ego talking. It's a fact that my power is far greater than yours."

Mandalee smiled dangerously, "You have no idea what a mistake you've just made. Cat, he's been trying to train us since we got here. Don't you think it's time we taught him a thing or two, in return?"

"Right there with you. Daelen, you are absolutely right…and yet you're also absolutely wrong. Your power is undeniably far greater, but you're wrong to assume that guarantees victory. Since we first met, I've been telling you that power isn't everything. It's time Mandalee and I showed you what that means."

Chapter 27

Without warning, as if on some pre-arranged signal that Daelen couldn't detect, Cat and Mandalee moved a few yards away and chorused, “Defend yourself, shadow warrior.”

Daelen flew into the sky, and immediately initiated his signature storm power, but anticipating such an opening move, Cat encouraged vines to grow around her ankles, anchoring her firmly to the spot. Meanwhile, Mandalee looked bored and stood in a bubble of perfectly calm air.

“Please, Daelen,” she taunted, “try not to be so predictable. The power of nature is more our domain than it is yours.”

“You want a storm? I'll give you one,” added Cat. A second storm blew in, then, hitting Daelen full in the chest and sending him tumbling through the air for a moment before he could adjust his flight to compensate. “How can you create a storm more powerful than mine?” he demanded. “It's just not possible!”

“I didn't create anything,” Cat answered, “the Mother of Nature did.”

“All Cat did was ask her nicely,” Mandalee added.

Lightning began to streak from the clouds then, startling Daelen, who was unaccustomed to being made to feel an intruder in the storms over which he was usually master. A highly localised rainstorm poured down, even as the sun shone on the broader area. Capitalising on his momentary distraction, Mandalee cast Starfire, igniting the air around her shadow warrior friend. She knew Daelen's power would act to protect him from serious harm, but by the gods, it would hurt. Plus, it would drain some of his energy. Daelen cried out and tried to fly higher to escape, only to find that a tree seemed to have reached out and grabbed him. Catriona’s handiwork, he guessed. He struck out with fireballs with one hand while he used his sword to cut through the branches with the other. The fireballs were little trouble to either of the young women; Mandalee using her lightning speed to sidestep the blast, while Cat created a waterfall shield out of the damp air.

That gave Daelen all the time he needed, however, to escape and go on the offensive, striking with acid arrows, magic missiles and more fireballs. For a moment, both Mandalee and Cat were kept on the run, unable to attempt any kind of fightback. But then Daelen spotted a double rainbow out of the corner of his eye, which distracted him. The wind had died down by now, which made flying more comfortable, but it also made him more vulnerable. A fact Daelen failed to realise until a pair of arrows stuck themselves in his back. They were tipped with a powerful herbal tranquilliser – he could feel their slowing effect on his body.

"My tranquilliser, Cat's arrows," Mandalee called out. "Of course, in a real battle, that would be poison in your veins."

In fact, Mandalee had always been reluctant to use poison in a real fight, but Daelen didn't need to know that.

"Distracted by rainbows – sunlight through moisture," Catriona giggled. "You do realise you basically just fell for the old 'look behind you' trick? Of course, this time, there really is something behind you."

Daelen whirled around just in time to see Mandalee sending out a Fire Arc towards him. She rarely used such direct magic, but she could do it if she wanted to. He tried to dodge and would have been successful if not for the other Fire Arc streaking towards his unguarded back from another Mandalee, side-by-side with another Catriona.

"Thanks for the Mirror Image, Cat," the assassin called out while Cat used her friend's fire magic to ignite flaming arrows that streaked towards Daelen. "I didn't know you could use it on other people besides yourself."

Cat laughed, "Neither did I, but it was worth a go."

"I think you should give him a chance and cancel our doubles," Mandalee suggested.

The Cat and Mandalee who had spoken vanished and Daelen suddenly realised they were the copies. He tried to turn to face the original pair, but he found he was paralysed from the prolonged effect of the tranquilliser. He expended energy purging it from his body, but the moment he broke free, he was dive-bombed by Catriona in her red-banded falcon form, scratching at the top of his head. Cat flew to the ground and changed back, before Daelen could catch her, and pointed out, "You realise that if this were a real battle, I would've gone for your eyes. Blinding you. How would you fight if you couldn't see?"

"Let's find out," Mandalee suggested, as she asked nature to create a dense fog around Daelen, effectively throwing him into darkness.

Once again, it was a simple enough matter for the shadow warrior to disperse the mist. Indeed, none of the magic the two bright young women had thrown at him had much chance of doing any real damage, but then they weren't trying to – it was only a mock battle after all. Plus, he had to concede they had kept him mostly on the defensive. They were also beginning to have a significant impact on his power levels. He hadn't had this good a workout for centuries.

The sight of a column of fire raging towards him from the South – conjured by Cat from a small pile of leaves that had ignited thanks to her keeping them bone dry despite the rain, plus Mandalee's previous fire attacks – snapped Daelen out of his introspection pretty quickly.

From the East, Catriona, from her vantage point atop some Windy Steps, fired blades of sharp ice, formed out of some water she had thrown into the air from a bottle she was carrying.

Mandalee, moving impossibly fast, North of where Daelen flew, inflicted multiple flesh wounds with a blade that returned unerringly to her hand. Simultaneously, she sent forth a volley of tranquilliser-tipped arrows. She had borrowed the arrows from her friend, but she didn't need the bow, using a simple clerical levitation spell, instead. She, too, was off the ground. Her friend had found a way to add moisture to her Windy Steps so that they split the light, creating a kind of Rainbow Road.

It also began to rain rocks on the shadow warrior's head. Daelen marvelled at how many spells Catriona could maintain at once without any noticeable magical energy drain. Recalling that it wasn't really her own personal power, but the power of nature, he began to suspect her magic was probably limited only by her ability to multitask. Rather than trying to counter all these things at once, Daelen chose to take the line of least resistance and fly in the one direction they hadn't covered: West. Except he flew straight into a wall of superdense air, hitting with an impact that almost knocked him from the sky. The column of fire hit his unprotected back before he could react, burning his flesh painfully.

"Ooh, I bet that smarts," Mandalee called out, giving her friend a high-five, as Jessica and Sara had shown them. "Don't worry, we promise to heal you later!"

Catriona was in hysterical tears. "Oh, Mandalee, I haven't had this much fun for ages. All I have to do is create a trap with an obvious escape route, and he takes it, not sensing he's just walking into a bigger trap."

Mandalee just giggled.

The mock battle continued for hours. Sometimes Daelen would gain the upper hand, forcing the others on the run by sheer power, but always, pretty soon, one of them would come up with some trick to turn the tables and give Daelen plenty to think about. He really couldn't understand how they could be matching him despite the vast power difference. True, he wasn't using his greatest power weapons, but then they weren't pulling out their best stuff, either. They were only breathing harder from laughter, not fatigue, and neither was showing signs of power drain. Everything he threw at them, they seemed to have an answer for. They anticipated his every move so well, he wondered if Cat was using telepathy, but no, she wasn't in his mind. Working together as a team, complementing each other's skills and helping each other out when necessary, they were formidable opponents. He was glad Cat hadn't chosen to assist her friend's assassination attempt a few weeks ago. Together, they might just have succeeded.

Daelen caught them in a kind of giant spider's web, thinking to keep them stuck tight in its hold, but it didn't hold them for long.

"Dust?" Mandalee remarked randomly to her friend.

"Mandalee, you read me like a book," Cat confirmed.

If this was a plan, Daelen had no idea what it was.

"Do you know the basic difference between a spider's web and a cobweb?" Cat asked him.

Daelen admitted he didn't.

Mandalee educated him. "Fresh spider's webs are practically invisible. That's why they're so effective at catching flies – if the insects could see them, they wouldn't blunder into them. But over time, because the webs are sticky, they gather dust. After a while, that makes them useless, so the spiders abandon them and make a new web somewhere else. The abandoned, dusty webs are what we call cobwebs."

"So, all we need," Cat continued, "to turn this sticky web of yours into a useless cobweb is..."

"Dust," Mandalee concluded. "Such as the dust Cat generated earlier when she reduced your training centre to rubble."

"You might want to close your eyes for a sec," Catriona advised her friend.

For a skilled druid, the small amount of dust that still clung to a few places in what was now Catriona's Meadow was all the raw material she needed to create more. Then a gust of wind covered the web in that dust, allowing them to pull free.

Mandalee used her super-speed to charge at Daelen, but she stopped in her tracks when she realised that she and Catriona were now fighting a copy. Concentrating, she felt something. Thanks to his training sessions, the assassin was able to sense Daelen even when he powered down into what he called 'stealth mode,' and knew that he was behind her. Sending Cat a sympathic warning, she sent out a Fear spell in his general direction. She couldn't imagine what the shadow warrior might be afraid of, but whatever it was, it made him cry out for a second before he realised it was an illusion. Time enough for them to narrow down his location. The disruption in his mind cancelled his copy, and Catriona quickly asked the plants to pin him in place. Mandalee called a Flame Hammer to her hand, throwing it at the shadow warrior and following it in, while drawing her Pureblade to switch to hand-to-hand combat.

Catriona prepared to back up her friend with magic, combining steel and spells to launch a new style of attack, but Daelen, breathing hard, called out, "I yield!" to put an end to the battle. Cat asked the garden to release him, and Mandalee sheathed her sword. "You make a great team, you two. In all my time in your mortal realm, I've never met anyone who fights the way you do. You always seem to have another trick up your sleeves. I get out of one trap and fall into another, despite all my experience."

"Thank you, Daelen," Catriona smiled, genuinely touched. She knew what that admission must have cost him in terms of pride. "That's almost the first time since I met you that I feel you've truly given us the credit we deserve."

"Yeah," Mandalee agreed, "maybe now you see why we insist upon you treating us as your equal partners."

“Do you understand the lesson we've been trying to teach you, Daelen? Power isn't everything. Agreed?” Cat prompted.

“Well, I see your point, but I wasn't using my beam cannon or anything like that. No matter what tricks you think up, you can't beat that. Not with the power I’ve gained since merging with my dark clone.”

“You think so?” Cat arched her eyebrows. “In that case, the lesson is incomplete.” She asked Mandalee to stand well back for safety, then told Daelen, “Shoot me.”

“What?”

“Use your beam cannon – shoot me.”

“You're not serious.”

“Deadly serious, if you'll pardon the expression.”

“Cat, be reasonable. You know what will happen if I do that – a direct blast from my beam cannon – you'll die. I've already killed you once by doing that, I don't want to do it again.”

“You killed me last time because I chose not to defend myself. I had to make you snap out of your dark clone's grip, and my death was the only thing I could think of that would be shocking enough. Therefore, I allowed you to kill me. This time I will not. If you're still worried, I'll cast a Mirror Image again, so you can just shoot my copy. If I fail, there’s no harm done, but if I succeed, my point will be proven.”

Daelen agreed because he could see nothing else would satisfy her. He walked a short distance away, Cat cast her Mirror Image, and the copy moved well away from the real Cat and Mandalee.

The shadow warrior fired his cannon straight at the copy and got the fright of his life. The duplicate produced a shield of polished glass in an instant – a mirror. The beam struck and reflected back, missing him by inches. The real Cat and Mandalee applauded as the copy took a theatrical bow and vanished.

“Now do you understand?” Mandalee asked. “Your cannon is basically just focused energy – harnessed, enhanced light. In a real battle, you can bet my friend wouldn't have missed.”

“But no-one's ever been able to defend against my cannon before!” Daelen gasped, unable to believe what he'd just seen.

Mandalee supported her friend, pointing out, “You've never fought a druid of Cat's skill before.”

"That's true," he admitted.

"It is my experience," the assassin continued, "that power breeds complacency."

"That's what I've been trying to tell him," Cat agreed.

"That can be fatal, especially in my profession," Mandalee concluded.

Cat continued the theme. "Your previous major battles have always been against other powerful beings who try to match your power with their own. I know your power is far greater than mine, so it would be futile to try to fight power with power. Therefore, I find other ways. I fight power with guile, cunning, finesse, style, and trickery. Why do you think I am taking druid magic to higher levels than ever before? Why do you think Mandalee chose Nature's power for her cleric magic?"

Daelen didn't know, so Mandalee told him, "Ultimately, everything comes down to nature. Even as powerful a weapon as your cannon must conform to natural laws like reflecting off shiny surfaces."

Catriona added to the lesson. "Take our initial storm battle. I don't create a major storm here in this spot the way you do. I can't. Storms like that don't just appear naturally; it's impossible. So, I do it nature's way: conjure a small disturbance far over the ocean and give it a push in this direction. By the time it reaches here – a process I can speed up – it's stronger than the storm you created yourself, and I don't need to expend much energy to do it."

Desperate to find a way out of admitting defeat again so soon, Daelen argued, "Ah, but going back to my cannon, your copy was able to deflect it because she knew it was coming. In a real battle, you wouldn't know."

"Yes, I would," Cat countered, choosing to conceal Dreya's lesson about the Temporal element she knew her magic to possess. "You always use your cannon. It's your most powerful weapon, and your instinct is to go for the quick kill. Therefore, you appear, fly, power up and fire. You're not exactly subtle, as I've told you before, so I'd have plenty of warning before you fired. More than enough to sprinkle a bit of sand from my vial and create a good enough mirror to reflect your cannon beam."

"Maybe I need to rethink my tactics, then, if I'm so predictable."

"He's learning," Mandalee remarked to Cat.

"Finally," she agreed, with a friendly smile.

"In that case, maybe I should open with something like this, instead," Daelen cried. Quick as a flash, he drew his sword…or at least, he would have done, had it not been stuck in his scabbard.

Trying not to smile, Mandalee explained she'd heated it with her Burning Blade spell, anticipating a hand-to-hand strike. The metal had naturally expanded and was now stuck tight.

"It's only temporary in this case," she assured him, "but I could melt it if I wanted to, then you'd never get it out again. You really must learn to be a little less predictable," she smirked. "Like this."

Mandalee stepped forward and kissed a stunned Daelen full on the lips. When she broke the kiss, she directed his vision to the knives in her hands. They were sheathed for safety, but in a real situation, she would have sprung them open in a split second and sliced open his neck.

"How did I not see those?" Daelen asked, incredulously.

"Jessica mentioned Sara had what she called 'tech skills.' I asked Sara about it, and together, we had an idea."

Mandalee was now sporting what appeared to be a ring on one finger of each hand, but they weren't merely pieces of jewellery; they each contained a tiny perception filter that concealed the knives.

"If you were my enemy," she flirted, gazing seductively into his eyes as though they were lovers, "my lips would be the last thing you ever felt. You wouldn't even feel my knives open your arteries. You might just have time to see your lifeblood fly from your body before you died."

Daelen grinned, "If that kiss was the last thing I ever felt, I could think of worse ways to go," he quipped.

Mandalee gave him a playful shove for his trouble, but she appreciated the compliment.

"Alright, you've convinced me," he admitted. "Now, I don't know about you two, but I think that's enough training for one—"

He didn't get to finish his sentence before the assassin, all smiles a moment ago, let out an agonising scream and shot off in a blur, towards the house.

"What happened?" Daelen asked. "I didn't hurt her, somehow, did I?"

Cat shook her head. "No, nothing like that." She turned to look at Daelen, her face ashen in shock. "I can feel it through our sympathic connection."

"Feel what?"

"Pain," she answered, tears welling in her eyes. "Not from Mandalee. From Shyleen. I think our enemies on Tempestria have found StormClaw and Shyleen's been injured – really badly. We have to get back there now!"

"I'll have to leave a quick note for Sara and Jessica."

"Do what you must," Cat growled, a look of fury and determination on her face, "but I'm not waiting around. Shyleen was hurt once before, and I wasn't there to help her and Mandalee. That is not happening again!"

Rather than waste time running back to the portal room, she simply widened the Prismatic Sphere micro-portal that had been allowing her access to her world and her magic while on Earth. She stepped through it to the other side. She didn't waste time closing it, deciding she might as well leave it open for Daelen, but she had no intention of going back.

Chapter 28

Mandalee tore through the StormClaw forest, with tears blinding her vision. She had to find Shyleen. Shyleen was more than she appeared. Shyleen was a part of her. She had given the leopard god half of her soul in return for the knowledge and power of nature. But more than that, Shyleen was, well, Shyleen. Her friend. Her only constant companion since she was a child. Even as Mandalee ran, she could feel half of her own self slipping away.

With a sob, she cried, "Shyleen, I'm coming!"

Moments later, she stumbled across a large clearing. The great leopard was lying there at the far end from her perspective, not moving and barely alive. Mandalee saw at once the vicious wound in her side and knew she had to heal her, quickly. But she also knew something else: this whole situation was screaming 'trap.' She forced the tears to stop as she got a grip on her emotions. Shyleen needed her to be in control. She had no choice but to spring the trap, but she could choose what happened when she did, and she decided at that moment that Shyleen was not dying today.

"I know you're out there!" Mandalee called out. "Waiting to strike. Please, just let me heal the leopard. She's my friend, though I suppose you know that." She stepped out of the treeline and made a show of stripping herself of her weapons. "Look," she encouraged them, "I'm unarmed now. Let me get to my friend, and I don't care what you do to me."

About a dozen people – warriors, wizards and clerics, along with half that many demons of various kinds – stepped out of the trees near Shyleen's prone form. Mandalee knew there were more, a lot more, and she wanted them where she could see them. She took a small step forward.

"Kill me, torture me, take me as a hostage to use against my other friends. Doesn't matter."

More enemies were emboldened to join their comrades. Still, Mandalee could hear the animals on the island communicating with each other. From them, she knew there were still more concealing themselves. If she let even one stay hidden, she would die and worse, so would Shyleen. That was not going to happen.

She took another step, slowly, carefully, making no sudden movements, keeping her enemies calm, allowing them to relax. The more relaxed they got, the slower their reaction time when she finally made her move.

Holding up her hands, she showed them that she was indeed carrying no weapons…at least, none that they could see. More enemies stepped into the light, taking the number well into the thirties. Still not all.

As she continued to step slowly forward, a mist began to roll in off the sea…surely a coincidence. Her enemies paid it no heed, whatsoever.

"I'm at your mercy." Mandalee allowed fear to creep into her quavering voice. "You can take your time with me."

She wasn't wearing her mask, and she recognised the looks on the faces of many there present. It was the same look she had seen many times before from people who couldn't accept her gender identity. It was the same look she had seen at that party in Walminster before she first met Daelen. The look that bartender gave her when he insisted on calling her 'sir.' She allowed the anger of that moment to fill her. She let all of her rage from all of those moments fill her. The rage she kept deep inside. The fury that slowly built every time she had to wear a mask to cover her face from small-minded people. It all built inside her, seeping into every muscle, every tendon. She was like a snake, coiled and ready to strike, but she needed to wait. The total was up to forty, but it still wasn't all. She needed them all.

"Think of all the things you could do to me, all the things you want to do to me. You don't want to miss out by holding back, do you?"

More stepped forward. Nearly all, but not quite. Mandalee was almost at Shyleen's side now. Just a few more steps. Just a breath or two longer. Some of them had started jeering at her now. Rude comments assailed her. Wolf-whistles came at her. Many began to describe the things they were going to do to her. The many ways they were going to enjoy themselves with her. How long they were going to make it last for her. And a couple of particularly imaginative souls simply went with, "Freak!"

"You can see the leopard's injuries," she implored them, ignoring the comments. "I know some of you are clerics like me.

You know how drained I'll be once I heal her." She could see some of them nodding. "So, let me do it. Please!" she begged. "I can do nothing to you. You can watch my every move, you can watch everything, but if you hold back too much, you won't be able to see. Think about what you'll be missing if you can't see."

Fifty-two. That was all of them and not one of those assembled now considered Mandalee a threat.

Their mistake.

The mist deepened instantly to dense fog, plunging the area into darkness. Mandalee's knives were in her hands in an instant, and before anyone could react, five demons and two humans died. Vital arteries were severed, tendons were cut, hamstrings were slit, bellies were sliced open, allowing intestines to drop out. Using her super-speed, she grabbed Shyleen and hid her out of harm's way. She didn't like moving her in her present condition, but she had no choice. If she left her in the clearing, she would be killed, whether by deliberate act or by stray weapon or magic would make no difference. Dead was dead.

Rushing back to the clearing, she ran up behind one of the two warriors she had seen carrying a crossbow. Reaching around him, she pulled the trigger, sending a bolt into the last remaining demon. She had so far avoided killing any wizards because she couldn't be sure which ones controlled which demons. The last thing she wanted was loose demons. Now, with them all gone, the wizards became primary targets. As a demon hunter-turned-assassin, she had learned that lesson years ago. Always kill the demon first while its powers are limited and under control of the wizard, then kill the wizard before he can summon another. Otherwise, she would spend the rest of her short life, slaying a never-ending supply of demons until just once – for once was all it took – a demon killed her instead.

Spells began to ignite around her, but she was too fast for them to target her accurately. Conversely, a flash of magic lit them up nicely for her in the darkness. Three wizards died before her next heartbeat. They switched to area-of-effect spells, trying to blanket the clearing, but Mandalee was unconcerned because she had a secret: her combat suit was magic-resistant. Sara had told her that detail when she'd first brought up the subject – Catriona wasn't the only one with a special gift for paying attention. She hadn't had a chance to check it out on Earth, there being no wizards there, but this was as good a time as any for a field test.

Ignoring the wizards who were using conventional magic, she listened out for the tell-tale chanting of summoning magic. She heard them – directly behind her. Before they uttered another syllable, she was by their side, slitting their throats. As they hit the ground, the two warriors on either side, whose job had been to protect the summoners, got their reward for a job well done when Mandalee's tiny, invisible knives severed an artery in their necks.

At last, one of the clerics decided to use her head and pray for sunlight to banish the fog. But Mandalee was a cleric, too. She felt the effect almost before it happened, and in response, she closed her eyes and prayed for even more sunlight. Her enemies cried out as one, as the bright light blinded them just as surely as the darkness had. Opening her eyes to mere slits was enough for the assassin to commit to memory the locations of her remaining enemies. She had cut them down by about half already.

The cleric who had cast the light spell died next, followed by the final sorceress – just in case she had any summoning powers – and three more warriors standing near her, before their eyes adjusted to the light. A trio of archers let arrows fly, but with a simple application of cleric levitation magic, she nudged their courses to kill three of their comrades instead. One of the archers, having not learned his lesson, nocked another arrow, but Mandalee slipped behind the still disorientated second crossbow wielder and helped the two kill each other. An Arc of Fire from the White Assassin's fingers burned out the eyes of the other two archers. A neighbouring cleric stepped over to heal them, but Mandalee taught her about the consequences of helping her would-be murderers by levitating a spent arrow through her heart. Swiftly following the path of the projectile, she killed the remaining archers.

Only a dozen warriors remained, but the assassin could feel herself tiring from using her super-speed for so long. She decided her best bet was to cancel it, now, and use the trees as cover for hit and run strikes. None of her enemies possessed any ranged weapons, now, which meant they would have to get up close and personal if they wanted to kill her. Which was precisely where she wanted them.

She feigned a trip, falling to the ground and the first two were upon her in a heartbeat, swords ready to strike. Fools. They clearly didn't realise that inside six feet, knives beat swords every time. She rolled underneath their guard and went for their wrists. The one on the left was too slow to react and cried out in horror as the knife opened all the blood vessels. He fell to the ground, desperately trying to staunch the blood flow. The one on the right had quicker reflexes, but Mandalee had still cut through the tendons, causing her to drop her sword, which Mandalee levitated to skewer the next nearest attacker. The first two ended their lives still clutching their wrists.

Down to nine, the remaining warriors were more cautious now. Mandalee was desperate to go and heal Shyleen, but she knew if she left even one of them alive, they would kill her. Then she would be no use to her feline friend.

Retreating into the trees, Mandalee switched to stealth mode, taking care where she stepped, never snapping a twig, never so much as disturbing a single leaf. The breeze made more noise than she did.

She circled the clearing, picking out her next target. One of the nine, perhaps sensing something, strayed a little too close to the treeline and died, silently. None of the others even noticed Mandalee hide the body in the undergrowth. She thought about how Shyleen would approach this if she were here hunting her prey. She would stalk her prey. She would not rush out until the odds were stacked in her favour. So, Mandalee observed her targets and waited until she had a clear plan. Less than two minutes later, and all eight were already dead in her mind. She could see it as clearly as the trees in front of her now. Her enemies had no chance. None. They could not stop her. They were too late. They were already dead. They just didn't realise it yet. One more breath and it would all be over for them. One more breath was all they had left. They were all looking away from her position. The time was now. They had each taken their last breath.

The assassin burst from cover, silent as a shadow. Two hands, two knives. Vital arteries in two necks were severed. The remaining six started to turn. Too late for two more as their kidneys were punctured. Wasting no time on those who were incapacitated, the assassin dropped to one knee and sliced open two more bellies.

They threw down their weapons, futilely trying to stop their insides falling to the ground. The last pair leaned down to grab Mandalee. She could see the look in their eyes. The look she had seen before. Both men thought they had her. They weren't even going for the kill. They didn't care about the fifty who had fallen. Their thoughts had already turned to the 'fun' they were going to have with the 'Freak.'

Mandalee allowed herself a smile at the cosmos that had allowed this. She hadn't planned on making these two the last to fall to her blades, but she was grateful for the providence that made them so. Even as that word formed on their tongues, a knife split them in two and cut open their throats. Taking no risks on leaving an enemy behind her, even if they seemed to be bleeding out, she put them all out of their misery.

Maybe 'White Assassin' wasn't such a terrible title, after all, she reconsidered. This was why she had become an assassin in the first place. She didn't revel in killing. It wasn't fun. It wasn't sport. She just wanted to defend innocent people, protect her friends and be free to live her life as herself. The people who came to this island today had thought they could take that life from her. With that decision, they had forfeited the right to their own lives, and now they would harm no-one ever again.

Wasting no more time on them, Mandalee ran to where she had hidden Shyleen. She was still clinging to life, but she didn't have long.

Mandalee lifted the leopard's head and whispered, "It's OK now, I'm here."

Mandalee's magic came from Shyleen, but being so severely injured, she could give no more, so Mandalee immediately set to transferring every drop of energy she had left inside her, giving it up so that Shyleen could live. The Cleric of Nature was already exhausted, so she didn't have as much to give as she would have liked, but it would just have to be enough because Mandalee had already decided: Shyleen was not going to die today.

A short time later, Mandalee collapsed, unconscious, but just before her world faded, she saw the leopard stand. Her friend, the other half of her soul, she was going to be alright.

Shyleen, fully recovered and knowing what her friend had done, carefully picked Mandalee up by the neck of her body armour, being mindful of where she was putting her teeth, and carried her away, melting into the forest.

Chapter 29

Elsewhere on the island, Daelen caught up with Catriona, who was studying the ground, intently. She had her staff out, and her bow and arrows on her back, prepared to deal with any trouble in the most expedient way possible.

"Have you found her yet?" he asked.

Fear for her friend brought out her sarcastic streak, as she replied, "Yes, Daelen, of course I've found her. That's why I'm standing here, staring at the ground."

Daelen let that go in favour of trying to offer helpful suggestions. "What about your sympathic connection?"

"It isn't a tracker," Cat sighed, regretfully, "or even a direction finder. While Mandalee's so distressed, it's hard to get any clear readings from her anyway. Now she's shut me out."

"Why would she do that?"

"The last thing I sensed was her gearing up for a fight. She couldn't afford to have me in her head, distracting her. She needed to focus. It's not like she could give me a location, anyway. I mean, what's she supposed to send – an image of a tree? That'd narrow it down! That's why I'm staring at the ground: I'm trying to track her the old-fashioned way."

"Maybe you could scout around from the air as a falcon," Daelen suggested.

Cat shook her head. "Given that most of this island is a forest, her position is likely to be hidden from the sky."

"What about following her scent as a wolf?"

Again, Cat shook her head. "Mandalee can move fast when she has to, and at that speed, her scent will scatter on the wind. No, I've run through every magical power I know, but nothing helps. This isn't a magic situation. We're going to have to track her the old-fashioned way. Just stay behind me, so you don't crowd me or destroy any vital clues. I'll ask the animals hereabouts to help us, too. I can't communicate with them as well as Mandalee can, but every little helps. Don't worry, we'll find her."

With that, they set off, slowly and carefully at first, moving more quickly once a clear direction had been established. The animals of the forest helped a lot. Sympathic communication was limited, but it was enough to confirm that Mandalee had indeed passed this way in a hurry. After what seemed like hours, they reached the clearing where Mandalee had killed the force that had come to StormClaw.

"She did all this by herself?" Daelen breathed in wonder.

"To save Shyleen?" Cat returned. "You bet she did."

"She's been holding back in our training sessions."

A patch of dried blood was evidence of a vicious attack on the leopard. A bit more tracking and Cat found the merest trace of footprints leading to another, smaller patch. Daelen took her word for it on the tracks – he could see nothing at all.

"No, you wouldn't," Cat agreed, nodding as she crouched down to examine the site more closely. "She's a Cleric of Nature – she knows how to conceal…her…movements." She trailed off as another thought struck her. "Oh, Mandalee," she gasped, "you are so smart!"

"Why? What has she done?"

Cat stood and faced Daelen. "She's a Cleric of Nature – she knows how to conceal her movements," she reiterated, "even from me if she wants to," she added. "But I can see them."

"So?"

"So, she got down to some serious fighting here," she continued.

"Obviously," Daelen agreed, still not quite seeing what she was getting at.

"But I couldn't see a single trace of her movements anywhere in that clearing. They must have felt like they were fighting a ghost."

At last, the shadow warrior caught on. "And yet she left just enough evidence for you to follow her tracks here."

Cat nodded. "This is where she moved Shyleen out of harm's way. That way, even if she died in the battle, her feline friend would have remained concealed from anyone but me. Then even if I was too late to help Mandalee, I could still save Shyleen."

"So, what happened?"

"Well," Cat considered, thinking it through. "If Shyleen had died, Mandalee would have buried her, and she would have either returned to us or stayed here, relying on my ability to track her. If Mandalee had simply healed Shyleen and everything was fine, again she would have returned to us or waited here. Therefore, the only reasonable conclusion is that healing an animal who was so severely injured took every drop of energy she had left and so Shyleen returned her love by taking Mandalee away to another hiding place."

"Why wouldn't Shyleen have stayed here?"

"Probably because Mandalee didn't have time to tell Shyleen the plan, but if we're lucky," she continued, searching all around, "Shyleen didn't bother to cover her tracks. There," Cat pointed out paw prints heading away from the area.

"If you say so," Daelen accepted, entirely out of his element with this and sensibly deferring to one who knew nature so well. "Where do we go from here?"

"Now we can use one of your original ideas. Shyleen won't risk moving very fast or very far with Mandalee so hurt and drained, so if I change to my wolf form, I should be able to pick up a dual scent of leopard and human. That should lead me to them. Daelen, I need you to fly discreetly overhead."

"Why? Wouldn't it be better to stay with you?"

The druidess shook her head. "Shyleen is likely to be spooked enough with a wolf suddenly appearing on the scene without you blundering in, adding to the problems. I will make no effort to conceal myself so you can keep track of where I'm going. Shyleen will be able to sense me coming a mile off and hopefully won't attack me as a potential threat. If she *does* attack me, though, let me handle it. I can get myself out of trouble without harming her; you might kill her with your power if you get agitated. Any questions? No? Good. Now go away."

Daelen wasted no time arguing, and simply took to the sky.

In her wolf form, the combined scent of leopard and human was sharp, so following the trail was no problem. Cat glanced up occasionally to make sure Daelen was following in the air. After a few minutes, the scent grew even stronger, telling her that she was very close to Shyleen's hiding place. She slowed her pace to a level that would appear non-threatening and wouldn't seem like stalking. A moment later, the trail ended in a shady spot beneath an overhanging cliff. A pair of eyes glowed in the soft light, and they moved closer to reveal a great leopard, hackles raised and growling softly. This was the bit that needed to be handled carefully. Cat came to a halt a few feet away from Shyleen and adopted a submissive, non-threatening pose while sending out sympathic impressions of '*peace, healing, concern, friendship.*'

Shyleen cocked her head, relaxing slightly and returned '*questioning, puzzlement, patience.*' Clearly, she had never before met a wolf that could or wanted to communicate in such a way.

Trying to explain, Cat sent, '*wolf camouflage. Human of nature concealed.*' Now was not the time to quibble over being half-Faery.

Shyleen relaxed further and offered, '*invitation, reveal human.*' Cat shifted to her human form. She expected Shyleen to recognise her, but the leopard seemed even more agitated than before. She sent, '*weapons, questioning.*'

Cat was also getting waves of pain, and she understood. The part of Shyleen that was from a higher plane couldn't think clearly because of how much Mandalee was hurting. The part that was actually a leopard was running on little more than instinct.

Cat continued to explain, sympathically, '*defence, protection, like claws.*'

Shyleen accepted this, but insisted, '*retract claws*' – an order for Cat to disarm, which the druidess complied with fully, laying bow, arrows, staff and all spell components on the ground. In return, Shyleen retracted her own claws and sat down, though she still guarded the path to Mandalee.

Reverting to human speech, Cat urged, "Shyleen, it's me, Catriona – Cat. I'm your friend. I'm Mandalee's friend. Please let me past you so I can heal her. Please, Shyleen. I know you hurt terribly, but you must fight through it and recognise me."

Shyleen brightened at that, getting up and walking over to rub her flank against the druid. After a good sniff, Shyleen sent a new sympathic message. '*Mandalee scent on Cat. Friendship confirmation/acceptance.*'

Catriona smiled at the sudden warmth from the big cat and asked, "Will you let me see Mandalee now? I will try to heal her."

Shyleen nudged Catriona towards the spot where Mandalee lay quiet, pale and still. She was alive but drained of all energy. Shyleen sent '*trust, protection*' and resumed her guard duty. As far as she was concerned, she now had two humans to defend.

Catriona's examination revealed something off in her friend's system. It didn't seem like poison. Rather, her magic seemed to indicate an infection that Mandalee had absorbed from Shyleen. Cat took out her water skin and poured out a little into a carefully cupped hand, so she could begin sprinkling droplets on the assassin's body, thinking to use the healing properties of water to draw out the infection. She didn't dare bring it into herself as she would if it were poison. What if her Faery side was more susceptible to whatever it was? She would be no use to Mandalee if she got sick and died. She would have to use water. It was less efficient, but it was the better option under the circumstances.

Clearly, though, this wasn't going to be so easy, as her first attempt had no effect. Thinking it through for a moment, Catriona hit on an idea and sent out a message to Shyleen, '*staff*.' The leopard understood and obediently went to fetch it. Cat could have just willed it to her hand, but she was worried about scaring Shyleen. Using the staff would aid her focus. To heal Mandalee without draining herself as severely as her friend, she was going to need every bit of help she could get. Taking the staff from Shyleen, she used her druid magic to shape the ground a little. Next, she poured some of her drinking water into the newly shaped area and multiplied that small amount into a human-sized shallow pool.

Cat then stripped Mandalee of her clothes, saying, "Don't worry, my friend, I'm not just fulfilling some secret fantasy about seeing you naked again. I need to bathe you in nature's healing water, and I can't do that while you're wearing clothes made from stupid magically resistant synthetic super-fabric."

Catriona asked the leopard to help her move Mandalee carefully into the water. Shyleen wasn't too keen on water, but she could see it was barely more than paw-deep at the edge and she didn't mind a bit of wet fur if it would help Mandalee. Once in the water, Catriona set about bathing her friend, enhancing the healing properties of the pool, and asking the surrounding soil to absorb the tainted water at the same rate as she replenished it with fresh, clean, pure water. She also sprinkled a little into Mandalee's mouth and induced the swallow reflex to ensure it would not go the wrong way and enter her lungs. There was no point clearing Mandalee's infection, only to drown her instead. Once the trickle of water was in the right place inside her, she could carefully multiply that, too, so it could begin the healing from the inside out as well as the outside in.

Cat knew she had to take her time, healing gradually to avoid draining her own strength or taxing the healing reserves of Mandalee's body, but she could afford to relax a bit, now. Mandalee was no longer in any immediate danger. It was just a matter of time.

Chapter 30

It was into the night, and the temperature had begun to drop before Mandalee came around.

Sensing her friend was with her, she croaked, "Cat? Why am I freezing cold and wet?" Opening her eyes, she then saw that she was devoid of clothing. "And also naked?" she added.

Cat smiled at her friend and joked, softly, "Well, I told you this pool was too cold and shallow for skinny dipping, but would you listen?"

Mandalee tried to laugh, but it hurt too much, so she stopped and just asked, "Is Shyleen OK?"

The leopard came over and nuzzled her friend, '*I am right here, do not worry. Please thank Cat for me – communicating her way is difficult*.'

Mandalee relayed the message, then asked, "Cat, where's Daelen?"

"Still flying around out there, I expect. I was waiting until you recovered so you could reassure Shyleen. She was a bit wary of me at first; she was hurting so much. I didn't dare risk Daelen dropping out of the sky and scaring her, so I told him to go away."

Mandalee raised a quizzical eyebrow. "You've certainly got him well trained, now."

Catriona's eyes twinkled as she replied, "That's the general idea."

It was what she'd been trying to achieve on Earth. She allowed Daelen to believe he was training her while she got on with the real task of training him to pay attention to her. Heaven's Surrender was a terrible weapon and when the moment came, it was imperative that it should be under Daelen's control. Cat agreed wholeheartedly with that, but the way she saw it, Daelen himself was a powerful weapon, and his power also needed to be under control. Specifically, hers. She would have liked a few more days to work on him, but circumstances had dictated otherwise. Hopefully, it would be enough.

After a quick telepathic exchange in the language of leopards, Mandalee told her friend, "Shyleen says he is welcome to join us, so you can call him."

"OK," Cat agreed, "and while I'm doing that, I think you should dry off and get dressed."

"Well, only if you're sure you've seen enough of my body, Cat."

"Yeah, I've seen enough," she laughed, "and don't think I've forgotten my promise to, shall we say, tweak it a bit here and there? Still can't do it, yet, but I swear I'm close."

With that, she left her friend while she called for Daelen to come down.

*****

While he had been flying, Daelen had found no evidence of any other intruders on the island. Sadly, though, he did find casualties: the invading force had torn the *StormChaser* apart where she was anchored in the harbour, and her crew were all dead. He wept for them – they had deserved better – but there was nothing he could do for them now, except whip up a storm to push the ship away from the harbour, into the bay, and allow it to sink, giving them all a sailor's burial at sea.

As he did so, however, he realised Catriona's original travel plans had been vindicated, because nobody had even noticed the unremarkable *Dolphin* patrolling the waters. His elegant ship had drawn focus, while the very nondescript nature of the other vessel had spared it from harm. As difficult as it was for his ego to accept, he knew he was going to have to start listening to her more in future. His power, he dared to believe, allied with Catriona's intelligent mind and Mandalee's extraordinary battle prowess and fierce loyalty to her friend, might just be enough to turn the tide in the coming conflict.

As soon as his three companions were sufficiently recovered to travel, before leaving the island, he felt it was important to check his base for any signs of intrusion. As they searched the building, Mandalee took the opportunity to thank Daelen on behalf of Shyleen as well as herself.

"Without your training, at least one of us would have died today."

The shadow warrior shook his head. "That was all you. I may have helped you sharpen your edge a bit, but that's all."

'In the contest between predator and prey,' Shyleen insisted in Mandalee's mind, *'a sharp edge can be the difference between life and death.'*

Mandalee was mid-translation when they reached the door to the portal room and Cat yelled, "Stop!" and slapped Daelen's hand away from the handle.

"What's wrong?" Daelen asked.

There was a lot of higher planar energy behind the door, which was to be expected – it was powering the permanent portals – but something was different. Wrong. There were two different signatures. One was Daelen's. The other was the same as what she had sensed outside Justaria's house. "Don't you sense it?" she asked.

Without her warning, he knew he wouldn't have noticed, but thanks to her special ability of paying attention, he could now clearly see the word 'trap' laid out before him.

In case whatever-it-was, was monitoring the door, somehow, Cat decided to take an alternative route. Shapeshifting into a mouse, she used woodshaper magic to make herself a rodent-sized hole in the skirting board, which she extended into a tunnel into the portal room. Overhead, she felt rather than saw a strange kind of light travelling in a thin focussed beam across the face of all the portals. She didn't know what to make of it, so she tried to project a sympathic image to Daelen.

'Don't shift back,' he warned her. *'If you interrupt that beam, you could die.'*

Now that he knew there were no sensors on the door, he opened it, trusting that it was safe.

"What's wrong?" Mandalee asked.

Peering into the portal room, without crossing the threshold, Daelen pointed to a small metal box to the left of the portals. Mandalee had no idea what it was, beyond a thing of technology. All she knew was that it hadn't been there before.

The shadow warrior identified it as a bomb. "An explosive device, triggered to explode the instant anyone steps through one of my portals and interrupts the beam of invisible light it's emitting."

He employed a similar tripwire system himself on his Earth base, to ward against intruders, though his version was non-lethal.

Mandalee, however, shook her head and insisted his theory didn't make sense. "Why didn't I set it off?"

Daelen admitted the Cleric of Nature was right.

Shifting back well away from that invisible light beam, Cat asked, "Could this technology be designed to detect you, specifically?"

"Yes," Daelen agreed. "Of course, Kullos couldn't have known that I'd taught you to make your own portals. If I hadn't, I would have naturally come back to StormClaw this way and set off the bomb. He wouldn't have wanted either of you to trigger it."

"That's nice of him," Mandalee remarked, acidly, knowing full well it wasn't an act of kindness.

Daelen confirmed it. "He just wanted to make sure I took the full force of it."

"How bad would it have been?" Mandalee wondered.

"Difficult to say without setting it off."

"OK, never mind. It's fine," she assured him. "I can quite happily live the rest of my life without ever knowing."

Seeing that Cat, ever curious, had wandered over to inspect the device, he stepped forward to warn her against getting too close.

Rather than reply, she let out a gasp and frantically surrounded the device with thick walls of rock. No sooner was the device fully encased than it exploded. She desperately fought to keep her walls from shattering, trying to reinforce them with compressed air but within seconds, she was fighting a losing battle, until a shimmering bubble of higher planar energy surrounded it.

"It's OK," Daelen told her, striding forward and laying a reassuring hand on her arm. "You can stop now."

By now, the rock had been completely obliterated by the raging inferno. The energy barrier had expanded to block all access to the portals, but now it was holding firm, keeping the continuing explosion contained within.

"My containment field will hold it back until it burns itself out, and then dissipate," he explained. "But I think we'd better go before anything else happens."

The others nodded. With *StormClaw* compromised, it was clearly too dangerous to stay. They would be better off back on the *Dolphin* in open water.

*****

"What actually happened in there?" Mandalee asked, as they quickly made their way to the coast.

Cat explained that she'd seen the display on the device flare up, presumably in response to Daelen's presence in the room.

"A proximity sensor," he realised. "A backup system in case I managed to avoid the primary tripwire."

What he didn't know was how Catriona, who was unused to technology, could have recognised the danger so quickly.

"I'm not sure," she admitted. Perhaps it was thanks to her exposure to technology on Earth, or maybe it was just her instincts at work. Either way, when the light on the box changed colour, she knew she didn't like what she was seeing and acted, although clearly, she had underestimated the power of higher planar energy and her shield of rock and air was not enough.

"No," Daelen admitted, "not by itself. But your quick thinking gave me time to save five precious lives."

"Five?" Mandalee wondered.

Daelen nodded and explained that in addition to two mortals and one leopard in that room, the blast would have travelled through the portal to Earth and ripped through his base, killing Sara and Jessica.

"Even I wouldn't have escaped unscathed," he told them.

The blast wouldn't have killed him, but it would have led to a serious injury. Between that and the fifty-strong force, he would have expended a great deal of energy, and the loss of the *StormChaser* would have forced him to use his powers to cross the Ocean. Kullos could then have tracked him there and forced a confrontation before Michael and his forces could join him. All of which would have tipped the balance of power massively in Kullos' favour.

"Kullos could have won the war today," he concluded, "but he underestimated what the four of us can do now that we're a team."

Cat pounced on that. "Oh, so we're a team now, are we? Not just pesky mortals who desperately need to be trained because our power could never match up to yours?"

"Your powers *don't* match up to mine," he insisted, indignantly. Then he smiled and added, "Fortunately, power isn't everything."

"Finally!" Cat cried in victory, rewarding him with a hug. "Although, I admit power does have its place."

"In the end, I'd say we all trained each other," Mandalee decided.

'*Like Daelen says,*' Shyleen put in. '*A team.*'

Having seen the power of one small bomb powered by higher planar energy, Cat could scarcely imagine what Heaven's Surrender would be capable of. But if Daelen StormTiger was listening to her at last, maybe there was hope for the world yet.

*****

Under cover of darkness, the *Dolphin* launched a small wooden lifeboat to quietly pick them all up and bring them aboard. They all immediately went below decks. The vessel then drifted away, slowly at first, then faster as Cat encouraged a perfectly natural breeze to pick up and accelerate them discreetly away, joining the regular shipping routes between the two continents and blending in with all the other vessels going about their ordinary business.

"Will they be OK?" Mandalee asked, after a while. "Sara and Jessica, I mean. With StormClaw compromised, what if something gets through the portal to Earth?"

"They'll be fine," Daelen assured her. "With us gone, there's no further value in attacking this island. Any invaders intent on attacking my base on Earth would have to find the right portal – remember there are six of them. I've also left a message to warn the Chetsuans to arm themselves, just in case. You've sparred with them both, so you know they're quite capable of taking care of just about anything or anyone that might come through."

"A powerful wizard—" Mandalee began.

"—Would have a bit of a shock when his powers failed against those magically resistant bodysuits," he reminded her.

The assassin nodded. She had first-hand experience of how well that worked.

"Plus, if they did find themselves in more trouble than they could handle, I've enhanced the perception filter surrounding the place, so it now works as a containment field, preventing anything from crossing, except authorised people."

Mandalee nodded her understanding, "So, Sara and Jessica could escape your grounds and your enemies couldn't follow. You're right. I'm worrying over nothing. I'm just sorry I had to leave them without saying goodbye."

Daelen shook his head. "It's not goodbye. You'll see them again." He hoped. "Now, try not to worry any more. That goes for you, too, Cat," he added, although she had so far voiced no opinion on the subject. "Get some rest."

Mandalee left for her cabin with Shyleen.

To Daelen, Catriona seemed far away, mind on other things as she gave him a distant smile and left for her own cabin.

Alone at last, aside from Pyrah, Catriona was stretching out her sympathic senses, receiving an update from far across Tempestria, before sending out a message of her own.

'*Back home. Island all clear. Third portal from left. Caution: Earth defended. Good hunting.*'

*****

As my mother and her companions head for a new continent, gentle reader, where Kullos' army awaits, this seems like an opportune moment for me to take a break. Just before I do, however, I find it curious that the argument I made to the modern-day Black and Red Guardians was much the same as what my mother said to my father a thousand years ago. We can't afford to go on, like it's business as usual. Things have changed and we must adapt to those changes. The events I have been relaying are some of the most pivotal in Tempestrian history. They are, as Aunt Mandalee put it, events that ought not to be tampered with any more than they already have been. Unfortunately, the void-creature has been busy tampering with these events, tampering with Time, which means we need to tamper some more. But not in the surgical way my Aunt tried here. It's not enough to simply get the Timeline 'back on track' anymore. We need to win. And to do that, in my opinion, we need to change the rules.

To further demonstrate that point, in my next instalment, I will show how, if the Original Guardians hadn't completely disregarded the rules, none of us would be here today.

A sneak preview of the sequel to
Gathering Storm

Shadows Fall

The Salvation of Tempestria
Book 3

Gary Stringer

Available December 2021

Chapter 1

Sara and Jessica were on full alert. There was an intruder in the portal room, and they had tripped a silent alarm.

The black-robed figure of Dreya the Dark stepped out into the long corridor, unconcerned, unhurried. She sensed them before she saw them, hiding at the far end. She had taken no more than two steps when two purple catlike alien girls stepped out from where they thought they were concealed, each pointing a weapon at the woman in black, who continued to walk slowly forwards, regardless.

"Sorry, love," Jessica spoke up, "but I don't think you're meant to be here."

Still, the intruder's steady pace continued.

"In the interests of fair play," Sara advised her, "in case you're unfamiliar with guns, these things can kill from a distance."

"In the interests of fair play," Dreya countered, still not stopping, "in case you're unfamiliar with wizards, so can I."

"Oh well," Jessica accepted with a shrug, "can't say we didn't warn you, dear."

With a shared glance, they both fired at once. To their astonishment, however, the beams seemed to hit some kind of invisible shield surrounding the intruder, which filtered the energy, allowing some to penetrate, while keeping the rest out.

"Thanks for the energy top-up," called out the sorceress, who finally did stop walking. "Just what I needed after a long journey. Now, I believe it must be my turn."

Bolts of electricity shot out of both hands, striking the two defenders, but they were equally unharmed.

"Magically resistant body armour," Sara explained, "which means you can't do anything to us."

The two Chetsuans drew swords and rushed down the corridor, but with a flick of her shoulder-length hair, Dreya caused the weapons to fly from their grasp. Undaunted, they switched to the knives they had strapped to their wrists and closed the gap, but all they struck was a shadow.

They scarcely had time to recover from that shock, before a large linen cupboard flew across the corridor to slam Jessica painfully against the wall. Sara cried out her sister's name, but her breath was knocked from her lungs as the grandfather clock flew out, catching her full in the face and pinning her against the wall on the opposite side. Struggle though they might, they could not break free. The swords they had dropped floated in the air, threatening their owners.

"Lesson learned, I trust?" Dreya remarked, materialising before their eyes. "Magic resistance only stops direct magic. I still have a thousand ways to kill you with indirect magic."

The Chetsuans weren't ready to concede defeat yet, however. They didn't get much chance to use their telepathy. Earth humans couldn't do it, and they knew each other so well, they really didn't need special powers to know what their sister was thinking. But the mental abilities of two Chetsuans together, especially twins who were naturally in harmony with each other, were considerable.

Staring intently at Dreya, from where they were pinned, their eyes glowed with amber light, as they chanted, "You don't want to harm us…You don't want to harm us…You don't want to harm us…"

Dreya felt the assault on her mind and raised her eyebrows, intrigued. She hadn't experienced such a ferocious mental attack in a long time.

"You two are powerful," she acknowledged, "and I don't often say that. If any other wizard from my world came through that portal, they would find you a serious threat, but your telepathy won't work on me for two reasons.

"First, in addition to my own mental discipline, I am protected by a sympathic link."

Upon hearing that word, the girls stopped chanting.

"Wait, sympathic link?" Sara wondered, a puzzled look on her face. "I've only ever heard that once before."

"From a certain half-Faery druidess called Catriona Redfletching, no doubt."

"You know Cat?" Jessica asked.

"Better than most, or so I like to flatter myself. Which brings me to the second reason your mental attack was always going to fail: I really *don't* want to harm you."

"You don't?" Sara checked, tentatively.

Dreya shook her head as the swords clattered to the floor. "I never had any such intention. I'm not a tyrant, despite what some on my world might think. I didn't come here to kill you. If I had, we wouldn't be having this conversation. As I said, I have a thousand ways to kill you, yet I haven't used any of them. You attacked me, and I don't generally react well to that, but you were defending your home, and I respect that, so I'm willing to give you both a pass this once." She raised a warning finger. "But only this once, is that clear?"

They both nodded.

"Excellent. Now, I'm going to release you both. When I do, I suggest we put this misunderstanding behind us and start again. Agreed?"

"Agreed," they chorused.

True to her word, Dreya cancelled her magic and allowed both Chetsuans to free themselves. They immediately sheathed their weapons.

Stepping forward in a non-threatening way, Dreya offered her hand and introduced herself.

"So, are you, like, Cat's friend or something?" Sara asked.

"A friend, yes," Dreya confirmed, "and more besides."

"More besides?" Sara wondered.

"Of course!" Jessica cried. "Don't you see, Sara? That's why she wouldn't get into a relationship with Daelen – she was already in a relationship with Dreya, here."

"Jess!" her sister hissed in warning, worried that Dreya might not take kindly to the news that her girlfriend had feelings for someone else and she might take it out on them.

Guessing her fears, Dreya smiled, reassuringly. "Don't worry, I know all about that. It's not a problem."

"Then why wouldn't she just tell him she was with you?" Sara wondered.

"An unintended side-effect," the Faery woman explained, regretfully. "Keeping me a secret via a magically backed promise was a strategy. It was never supposed to cause her emotional distress. Believe me, I would never do that, and I would have met up with her to remove the block any time she asked. She chose to keep it because she still believed the strategy was sound. And just to be clear," she added, "the magic never stopped her from doing whatever she wanted. It didn't force her to choose me, it only prevented her from telling anyone that she had."

"So, you're linked with her at all times?" Sara asked.

"To a greater or lesser extent. The link has a privacy mode, like closing a door, but in an emergency, that door could be flung open at any time."

"Then you could swoop in and save her if you needed to?" Jessica wondered.

"Or stand and fight with her. Whatever the situation demands." She shrugged. "I love her. It's as simple as that."

"Wow, that's actually proper romantic!" Jessica grinned.

"If it's true," Sara pointed out, who was less willing to take Dreya's word than was her sister.

"Sara!" Jessica scowled, hands on hips. "Don't be a misery just because you're missing your elf boy. You can't go around asking people to prove they're in a relationship. How's she supposed to do that, anyway?"

"Actually," Dreya ventured, pulling something out of a pocket, blushing as she did so. She didn't usually do things like this. "If it helps, I do have these."

She produced a pair of photographs, taken in the studio in Gaggleswick the last time they were out together, a few days before Catriona went out to investigate Justaria's disappearance and began her adventure with Daelen. They were small and in black and white, hardly up to Earth photography standards of the time, but it was clear what they showed. One was just a portrait shot of Catriona alone. The other was Cat and Dreya together mid-kiss. She'd never shown them to anyone else before. Even the photographer, like everyone else in that town, took it as read that they needed to be the soul of discretion in anything relating to Dreya the Dark. As for Dreya herself, the kinds of feelings she had for Catriona were still new to her, and she hadn't yet worked out how to show them to the world while maintaining her image. With these two, for the first time, she didn't need to worry about that.

"Aww!" Jessica gushed. "Look, sis! Satisfied now? Oh, my gods, Dreya, you two are so cute together!"

Sara's scepticism evaporated. "I'm sorry for doubting you, Dreya," she apologised, holding out a hand.

Dreya shook it. “No apology necessary.”

Jessica could barely tear herself away from the photos, but she reluctantly handed them back.

“That’s it,” she told Dreya, “you two are totally my new top celeb couple.”

“Er, Jess,” Sara put in. “I just realised.”

“Realised what?”

“We tried to kill Catriona’s girlfriend.”

Her sister’s jaw dropped. “So we did,” she agreed.

“I won’t tell if you don’t,” Dreya promised.

Jessica flashed a smile and agreed, “Good plan. Well, dearie, what do you say we all have a nice cup of tea and a chat somewhere a bit nicer than this draughty old corridor, eh?”

“That would be lovely, thank you,” Dreya acknowledged. “Might I suggest the library? There’s something I’d like to show you.”

“Show *us*?” Sara frowned in puzzlement. “In *our* library?”

“Oh, yes, I fully intend my visit to be mutually beneficial.”

“Well,” Jessica declared, “you can colour me intrigued.”